a *Random* EXCHANGE

a *Random* EXCHANGE

Dale K. Ingersoll

a novel

Tate Publishing & Enterprises

Published by Tate Publishing & Enterprises, LLC
127 E. Trade Center Terrace | Mustang, Oklahoma 73064 USA
1.888.361.9473 | www.tatepublishing.com

Tate Publishing is committed to excellence in the publishing industry. The company reflects the philosophy established by the founders, based on Psalm 68:11,
"The Lord gave the word and great was the company of those who published it."

Book design copyright © 2009 by Tate Publishing, LLC. All rights reserved.
Cover design by Amber Gulilat
Interior design by Jeff Fisher

Published in the United States of America

ISBN: 978-1-61566-130-5
1. Fiction, Christian, General
09.09.15

Dedication

To Paula—I'm in awe of your special gift as a wife, mother, grandmother, and servant of the Lord.

Acknowledgements

Thanks to co-workers Barbara Barber and Louise McGuinness for giving the manuscript the first coat of paint. Joanna Greene applied the final coat. Dr. T. Terry Miller applied the polish to the text. His years serving as professor of English and Literature at Indian River State College were of great benefit to resolving my grammar impairment. Finally, thanks to fellow author, Bette Crosby, for reading the final edit. Terry Miller would often quote an old saying to me: "A work of art is never finished, it is just abandoned."

I have squeezed all the good-will from my faithful friends. It is time to abandon this work. Thanks to all!

What lies behind us and what lies before us are tiny matters compared to what lies within us.

—Emerson

Chapter One

Sarah sat looking out the window. She was stunned. A wave of nausea launched from her stomach to her throat. The doctors sat silently as she continued to stare out the window, looking down at the cars moving so predictably through the parking lot. The moment was incomprehensible. It was unimaginable, but it was real. Gerald, her only son, was dying. Her retarded son was fading under the assault of cancer, and the finality crushed her soul. Gerald was everything to her life, and now the future appeared blurred and dismal without him.

"Is there anything that can be done?" Sarah whispered. Her upper lip quivered uncontrollably.

The doctors were uncomfortable, and no one desired to speak first. Sarah Bretherick was among the wealthiest in the country, and the hospital often reaped the benefits of her generosity. Her husband, Ben, lived on the fifth floor, in a suite donated by the Bretherick Corporation for Alzheimer's patients. Sarah represented millions in prospective gifts to the hospital, and the medical staff knew that a poorly chosen reply could prove costly.

"Gentlemen, I am aware of your regard for who I am. I want to assure you, I'm not looking for a sacrifice. I want to know options. Please, I need a physician, not a politician." Her head throbbed from the stress. Sarah determined to remain silent until one of the physicians responded.

Dr. Game, the youngest of the doctors around the table, spoke first. The glare from the hospital administrator in his direction was designed to insure his silence, but the young physician continued, "Sarah, there are clinical trials in stem cell research ongoing at this moment. Obviously, the results aren't in yet, but—"

Standing to his feet, Dr. Presley cut off the young physician immediately, "Dr. Game, I can't possibly believe you are telling my patient this pie-in-the-sky drivel without first discussing it with me. Sarah, I'm sorry this happened to your son, but these procedures are nowhere near ready to be tried on him. Your son is terminally ill, and I believe we shouldn't expose him to unnecessary and ineffective risks. Especially someone like Gerald, who wouldn't comprehend anything we would be doing!"

She felt the sting of the inference to Gerald's mental acuity. Sarah was calm as she spoke, "Dr. Presley, the stem cell research going on, are they trying it out on other women's sons?" Dr. Presley shifted in his seat uncomfortably, and acknowledged yes with a blink of his eyes.

Sarah was searching for answers and desired the doctors' input. She asked, "Of all the patients involved in these trials, how many of them comprehend what is done to them?" Even at the age of seventy-eight, she sounded like the dynamic attorney she had been for years. The room remained silent until Sarah spoke again. "Then I could assume that even though Gerald is retarded, his level of understanding regarding the treatment process would be no less than anyone else undergoing the same treatment." Again, the room was silent. She continued, "The real question that needs to be answered is this: is the life of a fifty-four-year-old retarded man significant enough to undergo the rigors and risks of this research?"

Dr. Presley spoke immediately, "Mrs. Bretherick, I can assure you that isn't the issue of anything stated here this morning. Simply stated, Gerald is terminally ill, and it's in his best interests, medically speaking, to give him simple palliative care from this point forward. I think that best sums up what we are trying to express. I'm very sorry, but this is the reality we are working with."

Sarah refused to belabor her opposition. "Dr. Presley, you are a good doctor and a good man. You have done your best for Gerald, and I want you to know I appreciate it. By your own admission, you've done all you can for Gerald, short of the palliative care you offer. Therefore, I thank you for what you've done. I understand your perspective; however, I will place Gerald under another physician's care. I will seek more options, and I desire a physician with the same passion and focus as myself. Now, if you gentlemen will excuse us, I would like to speak with Dr. Game and the hospital administrator."

Sarah returned her gaze to the window as she looked across the horizon, viewing the buildings donated to the hospital by the Bretherick Corporation. The buildings that bore their family name stood strong and majestic, untarnished by the years, yet each family member bearing the same name was frail. Ben suffered with Alzheimer's, Gerald was dying, and she was feeling all of her seventy-eight years.

When the door closed, Sarah again spoke to Dr. Game and the administrator. "I will have a check to the hospital for the amount of ten million dollars designated for the purpose of initiating stem cell clinical trials. Dr. Game, you will be Gerald's primary physician. I expect two things from both of you. The first is communication. I expect to be made fully aware of anything and everything pertaining to Gerald's treatment. The second is honesty. Under no circumstance are you to lie, omit, or cover up anything. I mean anything!"

Sarah looked hard into their faces as they nodded their heads in agreement. She noted the questioning expression on Dr. Game's face. "Dr. Game, there is something that you want to say. I can see you're stifling it, so let's begin with communication. I just advised you that I want communication."

Dr. Game was bold but not foolish, so he searched carefully for the words. "Mrs. Bretherick, why are you so adamant about going into these clinical trials with Gerald? I know I was the first to mention them, but my interests are scientific, and to be honest with you, I am arrogant, and I don't like to quit on anything. I know why I want to press ahead, but I'm not so sure about your motives. Is this what you want, simply because financially, you can? Dr. Presley was correct in his assessment of Gerald's condition. I hope our new policy of honesty is not too brash for you."

Sarah watched the hospital administrator cower within his flesh. She marveled at the reckless abandon of the physician.

Sarah smiled at the young physician. "No, Dr. Game, to both of your questions. Your honesty is not offensive; on the contrary, it is refreshing for me to hear a direct, uncensored response. And no, this is not an exercise in fertilizing the world with Bretherick cash. It is something much more meaningful. It's about years of shame and guilt."

Sarah noticed the discomfort the administrator was experiencing and requested a few minutes alone with Dr. Game.

As the door closed, Sarah leaned forward. "Dr. Game, I am accustomed to wealth. I was born into wealth, and I have lived every day of my life getting wealthier. Impressing people isn't something I've had to do. In fact, I am indifferent to most people and much prefer my own quiet places. Gerald is part of my quiet place. He is the most unselfish and loving person in my life. He has loved me unconditionally, when in fact, I'm the person he should hate the most."

Even the bold Dr. Game thought this self-critique too harsh under the circumstances, and spoke, "Surely, you don't blame yourself for Gerald's condition?"

Sarah allowed a tear to fall from her face. "It was my fault. I know exactly what I did." Sarah gasped for breath, and gazed out the window at the donated Bretherick buildings as she described Gerald's birth fifty-four years ago.

"Every time I look at Gerald, I experience emotions of shame and guilt. Gerald loves everyone. He gets up every Sunday morning and makes our driver take him to church. Before he leaves the house, he makes me write down the names of friends and people who are hurting or have special needs. He gives that list to the pastors so they can pray for them. I have watched Gerald on the coldest, windiest, snow-filled days battle his way to church so the ministers could pray for the people on his list. Never once in all the years that we made the list did I ever hear him request a prayer for himself. Gerald loves people, and once people get past Gerald's awkward ways, they love him, too."

Dr. Game couldn't help himself, "Did you go to church with Gerald?" As a physician, he wouldn't believe in anything that couldn't be explained rationally, and now he wondered how this successful and brilliant woman could possibly be religious.

"No, Gerald befriended a child in the special needs school he attended years ago. The father of the child was a pastor at this church, and he invited Gerald to attend a special class with his son at their church on Sundays. The minister and child moved away years ago, but the church and the people had become the high point of his week; so, for many years, Gerald has been a faithful member of Resurrection Baptist Church. I allow Gerald to go because of what the church means to him. I was raised a Jew, but my feelings for a loving God faded the night Gerald was born."

Game could see the hurt on her face and leaned forward to ask, "Then why the guilt?"

Sarah searched Game's face to extract some proof that the man could be trusted. "I've never shared this story. Ben and I lived with this guilt all these years without ever discussing it between ourselves, and certainly with no one else, but today the secret is too much to bear."

Sarah hesitated a moment, "Ben and I met at Cornell University while I was in my second year of law school, and Ben in his last year of graduate school in engineering. We were both brilliant. How's that for arrogance? We both came from families that spoiled us. It was the springtime. We had the world by the tail. And we were madly in love with each other. We were like butterflies on first flight. We were everywhere together, experiencing everything we could experience."

"Nothing in the world is more beautiful than upstate New York in the spring. Ben and I would rent a boat and spend the day drinking wine from local wineries and racing the boat all over Seneca Lake. We spent afternoons after school, sitting at an outdoor bakery in downtown Ithaca, eating donuts and drinking the most divine coffee. We were the ultimate hedonists. Unfortunately, doctor, the bill comes due some day, and our bill came due three days before Ben received his graduate degree. I found out I was pregnant with Gerald."

"When I told Ben, he handled the news without any negative emotion. He wanted to marry me. He was overwhelmingly excited. I didn't accept his proposal quickly. I loved Ben so much, and I didn't want him to marry me under the stress of an unexpected pregnancy. He ultimately convinced me to marry him with the most dramatic marriage proposal a woman could experience. I petitioned Cornell for a one-year withdrawal for health purposes, and we married in one of the grandest weddings. Oh God, it was gaudy!"

Dr. Game was impatient and wanted to move ahead, "Sarah, I know fifty-four years ago people were more hypocritical and puritanical concerning premarital sex, but for God's sake, certainly by now you're enlightened to the fact that a pregnant bride is far from unusual."

Sarah laughed, "Oh, doctor, you're bored with my story so soon! You came to the wrong conclusion. Be patient. I'm neither naive nor puritanical, but there were things that happened that stir my conscience even now."

"Let me continue. Ben wanted me to finish law school at Cornell, so he took a job with a small engineering firm in Ithaca, developing new products in conjunction with grants given to Cornell. He loved the work, and together we enjoyed a few months of bliss before Gerald came."

Sarah breathed deep and her face started to wrinkle, "Ben and I partied hard during my pregnancy. I was going to my obstetrician, and he told me everything was fine. He told me the usual, 'Don't gain so much weight. Stop drinking alcohol. Stop smoking.' You know doctors, the usual 'deny-yourself-completely' speech. In the end, my self-indulgence would be the genesis of Gerald's fate; I wouldn't deny myself anything." Again, Sarah struggled to keep her lips from quivering.

"I was due the last week of January. I knew it, but what the heck? My life was about having fun and doing whatever I desired. Ben bought a Jeep from army surplus, and he loved to drive it. It was a gray Sunday afternoon, and Ben suggested we break out some wine and take the Jeep for a drive. I waddled outside, rolled myself in, and off to Watkins Glen we went. We sipped wine and sang as we drove from hilltop to valley on the way to the Glen. When we arrived, the snow was falling fast and furious, but we were well on our way to being joyfully drunk. Ben started playing games on the slick streets with the Jeep, going in tight circles, and honestly, in my state of mind, it was fun. I asked Ben if I could drive the Jeep, which was standard shift, and in his drunkenness, he overlooked my inability to shift and said, 'Oh, yeah.' I remember doing several donuts, that's what Ben called going in tight circles in the snow, and that's all I can remember."

The next thing I recall is a middle-aged nurse standing over me, telling me that Ben was seriously injured, but the doctor believed he would live. She said that I would be fine, but there had been some complications with the birth."

Sarah started to sob. Dr. Game spoke softly, "What happened to Gerald? What did the nurse tell you about Gerald?"

"She said the trauma from the accident thrust Gerald into the birth canal; the umbilical cord wrapped around his neck in the process, starving his brain of oxygen."

Dr. Game looked perplexed, "Sarah, I don't understand. If you were in trauma, and they performed a caesarean section, why would the cord be an issue in this birth?"

Sarah was angry, "How would I know? I was drunk. I hurt my husband and child, and when I became coherent, both Ben's parents and mine bought off every cop and official in town. I was told to go home, never discuss it again, and take care of my retarded child."

Sarah clasped her hands together. "That, doctor, is the

undaunted truth. Gerald could have been as normal as you and me, if I had been more of a mother and less of a selfish, fun-seeking child ..."

Sarah was ashamed and turned her eyes to gaze again upon Memorial's parking lots. "So there you have it, doctor. The story that causes me shame every time I look at Gerald, and the guilt that haunts me in the middle of the night."

Chapter Two

The snowflakes mesmerized Sarah as she watched the familiar sights of Cleveland pass by the window of the limousine. Cleveland was the joy of her life. She loved the years that she and Ben had spent on Sunday afternoons at the Cleveland Browns Stadium, screaming and hollering, eating stadium hotdogs, and fighting off the bitter winds coming off Lake Erie. She loved the celebrations at the New York Spaghetti House and the Top of the Town. Sarah loved the professional theaters, shopping downtown with Ben at Macy's, and eating lunch at the Terminal Tower. Everything she saw through the window brought forth lovely thoughts, and simultaneously, a sinking sense of desperation. Ben would never share her life again, and Gerald was on the verge of dying. She gazed upon her aged hands and stared intently at the marks and wrinkles, wondering what would motivate her to want to continue. She had it all, but all of the magic and purpose was slipping away. The corporations and the billions of dollars at her disposal could never fill the gap.

The limousine pulled up to the entrance of Memorial Hospital, and as usual, a member of the hospital administration whisked Sarah past the guest registration, taking her immediately to Dr. Game's office for the promised consultation concerning Gerald's experimental treatment. He greeted her as she walked through the door of his office. She surmised that he was warned of her arrival the minute her car pulled up to the entrance. She liked this doctor. He was confident of his abilities and he was not about to suck up to her or anybody else. Sarah trusted him.

True to form, Sarah took control of the meeting, dispatching the normal greetings and small talk, addressing the matter with a force honed by years in the courtroom.

"Dr. Game, I have done much reading on the subject of stem cell research, and I want to address these concerns." Sarah produced a legal pad with what appeared to be numerous sentences of highlighted portions. Dr. Game was aware of her legal prowess from watching her decimate opponents on television. He hoped his scientific knowledge was adequate to withstand the intellectual gymnastics that Sarah was about to put him through.

Sarah looked at her notes and began the interrogation. "Doctor, I have read that the stem cell delivery system to tumors has not been perfected as well as it should be. The treatment is known to cause significant toxic side effects and the benefits are short term. Further, I would like—"

Dr. Game interrupted, "Sarah, no doubt by now you are an expert on the subject of stem cell research; however, let me discuss with you what we will do with Gerald specifically, so perhaps we don't spend the day discussing stem cell treatment generally."

Sarah normally would have ignored the interruption and charged ahead, continuing with the interrogation, but this was not a legal case, and this doctor was not the opponent. This time she realized it was about the life of her son, and this doctor was her only hope. She laid the legal pad down, folded her hands together, and focused her attention upon the young doctor. She relinquished control.

Dr. Game noted the change in attitude and decided he would try to be especially compassionate—but still thorough with her.

He began, "For the past two weeks, we have established many benchmarks and collected numerous test data which will be critical to Gerald's treatment. We began with a gnomic study, which involves a complete work-up, studying and identifying your son's genetics. We have performed DNA studies and numerous other tests. We feel at this time we are ready to begin treatment."

The physician took out his legal pad and began to diagram what they would do. "Yes, in earlier stem cell trials, the problems you mentioned were major issues, toxicity, and relatively short-lived benefits. However, we will be using a known anti-cancer therapy called 'interferon beta,' which undisputedly kills cancer cells. We will manipulate certain types of stem cells to encode the interferon beta gene." He looked at Sarah to note any confusion over the medical terms and technology. Indeed, she was cognizant of everything he had said.

He continued, "These manipulated stem cells will then target the tumor, as if we had shot it directly with a gun. The targeted stem cell will produce high concentrations of therapeutic proteins within the tumor. We believe this delivery system will minimize the toxicity effects and maximize the longevity of the treatment, because the treatment goes directly into the tumor, therefore avoiding any healthy tissue."

Sarah took advantage of the pause to ask "Where will you obtain these stem cells?"

Dr. Game pointed to a chart, "The cells are called mesenchymal stem cells, and they come from bone marrow."

Sarah stopped him immediately. "Ben and I will be checked for the potential of being the donors."

"We will use stem cells we remove from Gerald. However, since this is a research project, if you and Ben are willing, I would like to take samples of your blood to investigate generational genetics. It's not necessary, but it would help give us a more complete database in understanding cancer and generational probabilities."

"We will give you whatever you like." Sarah would hold nothing back in this battle with cancer.

"Sarah, as Ben's guardian, you will need to sign for your husband's participation in this study. Do you want me to schedule your work-ups together?"

Sarah hesitated for a moment at the thought of putting Ben through these tests. His Alzheimer's made him fearful of every little change, but this was more important than anything in their lives. She dismissed the thought without guilt.

"Doctor, I will sign the release at once, and if possible, I would like the samples drawn while I'm here."

"Of course, I'll get everything moving right now." Game wondered the last time someone said no to this woman.

Dr. Game's phone call surprised Sarah. He was apprehensive and unwilling to discuss his concerns over the phone. Sarah was uneasy as she told Carol Thatcher, her assistant, and the security detail that Dr. Game was coming to the house this evening. She thought it odd for a Memorial physician to make a house call, despite her status in the community. His voice denoted a sense of urgency, or perhaps her lawyer instincts were looking for something to give her an advantage. "Why couldn't he tell her what he wanted on the phone?" She pondered. Could the doctor be coming to pander for more funds? But no, it would not be Game that would come on such a mercenary task; he was too independent and arrogant to play the role of a fundraiser. Sarah reworked every scenario and probability until she was weary of thinking, so she settled for sipping tea and listening to the Cleveland Orchestra on the radio, while appreciating the shadows of day fading in the glistening snow of her backyard.

Carol Thatcher walked into the room to announce the doctor had arrived at the main gate. Sarah watched Carol as she left the room, and tried to remember how long Carol had worked for her. She admired the woman. Carol loved the Lord, speaking often about God's will and the power of prayer. Sarah wished she could possess Carol's simple faith, and her ability to enjoy whatever the day brought her. Carol might be the most content person she knew. Sarah wondered to herself if Carol's faith was like Novocain, numbing the sensibilities and dulling reality. She could never picture herself accepting the thought of an all-knowing and all-powerful God. There were too many things in her life that made her believe that individual knowledge and the power of money constituted the real gods of this earth. She would never believe.

Game lacked his usual power strut as he entered the room. He settled next to Sarah on the couch and leaned into the cushions as if he were going to bed. He looked at the glass of wine in Sarah's hand and asked if he might have one himself. It was plain to see the physician was unsettled, and this unsettled Sarah. Sarah poured the wine. She needed the moment to prepare herself for the worst news of her life. She knew Gerald was either gone or would be soon.

The doctor swallowed the whole glass of wine. "Do you remember the day you made me promise to be completely honest and willing to communicate everything pertinent to Gerald?"

This was an odd introduction, Sarah thought. "Yes, I remember." She wasn't comfortable not being in control of the conversation.

"Last week, you and Ben underwent many tests and specifically some genetics and DNA studies. Do you remember them?"

This was starting to feel like a deposition and Sarah didn't like the pace of questioning, "Yes, doctor. I may be old, but I can remember last week, and I am fully aware of both what those tests were and exactly why we took them. Now, what is the point? Obviously you're not here to discuss Gerald's condition, which I know is bad, but you're here to tell me something indicated on those tests concerning Ben or myself. Doctor, for all intents and purposes, Ben left this earth months ago. He doesn't recognize me, and for myself, I'm old and fully expect bad news any day. Now will you get to the point?"

"Sarah, based on the test results, it is absolutely impossible that Gerald is the biological son of either you or Ben."

Sarah locked eyes with the physician, looking for a sign of indecision or deception, and she sensed none. He was resolute and uncompromising. Her fingers became immediately cold and her brain began calculating rapidly, but all the computations became garbled. She heard a cry, "Oh, God. Oh, God. Oh, God." It was her own voice. She slumped to the floor, and for the first time, she lay limp on the floor, sobbing uncontrollably. Game knelt down beside her and allowed her to pour out fifty-four years of shame and guilt. These expressions and emotions were foreign to both of them. Sarah was noted for possessing granite emotions, and Game had never scored points for his bedside manner.

Chapter Three

Sarah felt the emotional overload of the revelation. Tonight, even the wine refused to numb her thoughts. In reality, nothing had changed. She still loved Gerald, and she would care for him as much tomorrow and the next day, as she had his entire life. Fifty-four years of sharing in his life could not be removed from her simply because some medical tests declared he was not their child. Sarah lay in the bed, feeling herself sink into the mattress, focusing her eyes in the darkness upon the blinking smoke alarm, erratically changing from blips of green to red. She focused on these phenomena, trying to determine a pattern to the color changes. Sleep would be elusive tonight.

Ben would never know the truth, and Gerald could never comprehend the concept of being someone else's child. Even her brilliant mind struggled to make sense of it all. There was no other family to share this hurt. Sarah breathed deeply, and the thought of having no other family suddenly rocked her consciousness. Without a doubt, she knew there was more to her family than she thought possible. In her confusion, she still grasped a few significant facts. Fifty-four years ago, she was totally faithful to Ben, and she was absolutely impregnated by him. She had delivered a child. Even if that child wasn't Gerald, there was a child born to them. Now she wondered, was it a boy or girl? What happened to that child? Where was that child? Now Sarah knew she could not survive the rest of her life without knowing the answers to these questions. Resolve must come, good or bad. These questions had to be answered. The clock read two thirty a.m. as she reached for her telephone; and she knew exactly what tomorrow would bring.

"Carol, Carol, I'm so sorry for waking you, but I need you to help me this moment. I need you to start packing for a trip to Ithaca, New York. Pack for about four days. Would you also get Sean on the phone as soon as possible? I want him to have the Gulfstream ready to fly within the next five hours. I know I'm making no sense, but I need you to support me, and help me with a thousand details. I will tell you what is going on when we are on the plane. I need you, Carol, now more than any other time you've been with me."

Seconds later, Sean McCurdy was on the phone, sounding groggy but still trying to act as if he had been up all night and fully alert. Sean had worked faithfully with Ben for more than thirty years. He was second in command only to Sarah in the Bretherick Corporation. Sean made frequent overtures to Sarah concerning retirement, but she knew Sean could never live the retired life. He worked because he loved the work. It certainly was not for the money; he was extremely rich. She knew Sean would be supportive and aggressive once he knew the facts. However, he could be extremely cantankerous, and she suspected waking him up in the middle of the night would bring out the cantankerous Sean.

"Sarah, are you okay?"

Sarah was relieved. It was concern she heard in his voice, not the growl.

"No, Sean, I'm not okay. I'm not okay at all."

Sean knew at once Sarah was stressed. She was as tough as anyone he knew in business. He also knew she wouldn't call him in the middle of the night unless the need was earthshaking.

"I will explain briefly. I know you will want to ask a lot

of questions, but please resist the urge, as I don't have all the answers and I'm not even sure of the right questions."

Sarah was silent for a moment as she sought the exact words to tell an old friend that a major portion of her whole life was an accident. This would be the first time she would tell this saga. It felt unreal. She felt like a traitor to Gerald, but despite these feelings, she would find the words. The feared litigator calculated the weight of each word to minimize the painful discussion.

"Sean, a few hours ago I was informed by a physician at Cleveland Memorial that Gerald isn't the biological son of either Ben or me."

She said it. The words came directly out of her mouth. Gerald was not her biological son, but still her heart exploded within her, "Yes he is!"

Sean struggled for words. He had known the Bretherick family as well as his own. Perhaps he was dreaming and needed to wake up.

"Sean, Sean? Are you still there?"

"Yes, Sarah, I don't know what to say. I'm at a loss for words. What do you want me to do? I'll do whatever you ask."

"Sean, I'm laying here thinking there is only one way Gerald is not ours; a switch of Gerald and another child must have occurred. That is the only possibility. We didn't steal Gerald, and I know I delivered a baby in Watkins Glen, New York, on January 28, 1951. Sean, I'm confident our biological child was switched."

Sean knew Sarah would move heaven and hell to get to the bottom of this mystery.

"I think I'm starting to understand the reason for Carol's call to get the Gulfstream ready to fly this morning. You're going to find your kid, aren't you, Sarah?"

Sarah winced at hearing Sean refer to this child as 'your kid,' almost making a contrast that Gerald wasn't hers. She knew she would be sensitive to this concept. She decided it was time to put her feelings in check until she could manage these new realities. Another thought came to her. This "kid" was no kid at all. He or she would be fifty-four years old, perhaps with fully-grown kids. Grandkids! Oh God, grandchildren! A new concept to her; not unwelcome, but startling.

Sarah began her list of instructions.

"Sean, I would like a team of attorneys and investigators to meet me in Ithaca; tomorrow sometime. I want the best you can find. I want this puzzle solved and solved quickly. I want stones turned over tomorrow. I need the truth now."

"Sarah, I would like to go with you tomorrow, if I may."

Sarah had known few helpless moments in her life, and while she had just experienced one of them, she knew she had a plan. Everything would be fine.

"Thank you, Sean, but that won't be necessary. Carol will be accompanying me, and if you can pull off everything I am requesting for tomorrow, you will have done everything you can for me."

"Sarah, everything you've asked will be done. The attorneys and investigators will be there. The plane will be ready when you are. Sarah, we will use every tool in our arsenal to help you. I love you and Ben, and I promise we will find this kid together."

~

True to his word, the Gulfstream Five was sitting on the tarmac with the jet engines purring. Sarah could see the scurrying of attendants as they came down the steps to greet her. The pilot came down last.

"Mrs. Bretherick," the pilot spoke first, "it has been a while since you have flown with us. It is good to see you again."

It seemed odd at this moment of personal crisis to engage in meaningless banter. Her mind was muddled, thinking of a million details. Sarah smiled. She thought sharply to herself, *First of all, I am not flying with you, you are flying for me! This is my plane, and my payroll; therefore, I'm not some disgruntled passenger with a discounted ticket going on vacation.* But it occurred to her that she was arrogant, and unappreciative of an attempt to be friendly. She decided humility and courtesy would be the garment of the day.

"Why, thank you, Captain." She couldn't remember his name, and she couldn't make out what it said on his identification. Her eyes were dry, blurred by the darkness of early morning.

"Captain, will you be sure to attach a stenographer with me this morning? We will be extremely busy when we land in Ithaca; please arrange for some fruit, croissants, and coffee for both Carol and me." Sarah turned to Carol, "Will this suffice for you this morning?" Sarah knew the breakfast order was fine with Carol. She had fruit and coffee every morning of her life. Carol simply nodded her head.

"Mrs. Bretherick, Sean called just before your arrival and informed me that the legal staff you requested will be waiting for you in the terminal at Ithaca. He arranged a private room for your meeting. Sean said he thought it best they hear the task directly from you." The captain was dying to know what the task was, as Sean never called him personally. "Is there anything else we can arrange for you during or after the flight?"

Now the captain was starting to sound like an employee. "Thank you, Captain. I appreciate the excellent service." Even at this old age, perhaps it's not too late to learn diplomacy, she thought.

Within seconds, the lights in the cabin of the Gulfstream were dimmed and ground crews signaled to the flight crew. No matter how many times she had taken off in a plane, she considered these moments to be magical. This morning, it was even more surreal. She felt like the pregnant wife running off to the hospital to give birth. She anticipated the pain of the experience, but she was anticipating with great joy the moment of viewing this child for the first time. She desired to know whether it was a girl or boy. She wanted to hold it, to share herself with it, and to love it with everything that was within her. Yes, this was how giving birth should have felt, no remorse for an act of stupidity, no tears for a child that could never experience all that she and

Ben could have given him. No, this time it was different. Today was a second chance.

The Gulfstream turned the corner hard into the runway, and the engines went wide open. The vibration of the wheels and engines pulsed through her body as she plummeted down the runway and lunged into the sky. Sarah's spirit was just as energized as she looked down at the waves of Lake Erie, breaking into the stone barriers around Cleveland. To Sarah, Cleveland was a grand place to live. Cold, but wonderfully grand.

Sarah turned to Carol, "I haven't shared with you yet why we're off to New York in such a hurry. I'm going to have the stenographer take down some notes to pass out to a group of attorneys and investigators that will be meeting us when we arrive. Carol, I want you to listen at the same time I am dictating these notes to her. I wasn't aware of my predicament until last night, so please forgive me for not sharing this with you before."

Sarah wondered why it was important to her that Carol should know and understand her situation. Carol sat upright in her seat with her Bible and the mechanical pencil that was always present when she studied Scripture resting on her knees. Carol didn't just read the Bible; she diagramed, highlighted, meditated, and wrote in the margins. She devoted time every day to sitting and reading the "Word" as she called it. Carol placed the mechanical pencil into the leather cover of the Bible and closed it. She reached over to Sarah's hand and squeezed it with a grimace on her own face.

"Sarah, I feel something is very wrong right now, but no matter what it is, know that I'm here for you. And know that God has a plan."

Never before had Sarah so appreciated Carol's friendship. She felt compelled to ask, "Carol, how long have you been with us?"

"Oh, I can never remember birthdays or years of employment, but probably about twenty-five years. My husband died five years ago, and you and Ben were kind enough to give us a cruise as a gift for twenty years of employment. My husband passed away two months after the cruise; that was five years ago, so I'm guessing twenty-five. I'm not much for keeping up with dates and details."

It dawned on Sarah. "Why, you must be around sixty-five! I never thought about you retiring. I'm sorry, Carol. I will arrange for an extravagant retirement income at once. Forgive my thoughtlessness."

Carol laughed. "Sarah, you don't have to arrange anything for me. I'm already very rich. Mr. Ben gave me stock in the Bretherick Corporation for every year I worked for you. That stock has increased more than a hundredfold. No, don't give me another nickel. I can't decide what to do with everything I have already, let alone add some more. I'm like you; I haven't anyone to leave my wealth to after I'm gone." Carol immediately regretted the thoughtlessness of the statement. She loved Gerald too.

Sarah was shocked again. Truly, revelations of all sorts were occurring to her from out of nowhere. "Why in the world are you still working, when you could be taking it easy and enjoying your life?"

Carol knew Sarah would not comprehend. "Sarah, what I do with you and for you is my life. I'm not looking for easy. Simply put, I cannot think of one thing I would rather do tomorrow than what I'm doing today."

This time, Sarah reached across the seat and gripped her hand. She felt a tear going down her cheek, crying a second time in less than twenty-four hours. She had never comprehended the depth of their friendship until this moment.

Sarah called the stenographer to sit with her. "I want you to take these notes and prepare them to distribute to the legal staff when we arrive on the ground."

Sarah began with the details of her life, starting as a student at Cornell. She filled in all the details leading up to January 28, 1951. She didn't omit a single sordid fact. The story involved the inebriation, the car wreck, the cover-up, and the birth of a retarded son. The stenographer stopped typing at the point of hearing the results of the genetics and DNA studies. Sarah gave her a moment to recover before she continued.

The stenographer read back the notes and summary details

pertinent to solving this case. Sarah leaned back into the seat and listened with an attorney's attentive ear. She sat and pondered. Yes, the what, where, and when details were all there to distribute. It was the why, how, and who questions she could not fill in.

Sarah dismissed the stenographer and looked at Carol. She sat with her hands folded over her Bible. Tears streaming through closed eyes. Her breathing was labored, but unlike Sarah, she was not sobbing after hearing the revelation. Sarah knew Carol was praying.

Gazing out the window of the Gulfstream, Sarah could see four of the five Finger Lakes stretched out over the upstate New York horizon, each glistening in the morning sun.

Chapter Four

Six men grouped in a semicircle greeted Sarah in the airport terminal. Each had a Styrofoam cup with coffee in his hands. Surely, she thought, they must be totally off guard this morning. The only thing they must be sure of this morning were their hourly fees, which she knew would be the highest rate. She had spent an entire lifetime struggling to extract every dollar possible from the world, and today, she was willing to give it all back for the right information. Her purse was wide open. She could care less about their fees.

She had struggled with her emotions all night. Determined not to cry or allow her lips to quiver, Sarah took the initiative to speak as she charged through the door. "Good morning gentlemen; my name is Sarah Bretherick. I was informed earlier this morning that a room was available here at the airport where we could discuss some matters."

A middle-aged, clean-cut looking man reached out his hand, "I'm David Birmingham, and I will show you the way. We have coffee and Danish there for you also."

As they walked toward the room, each of the gentlemen introduced himself and stated his position on this quickly assembled team. Sarah counted two private investigators and four attorneys in the group.

Carol reached for the coffee, pouring a cup for herself and Sarah. It occurred to Sarah that she had never really noted the regularity with which she and Carol had coffee each morning. She took for granted the special blends and flavors. Sarah made a mental note: from now on, she would surprise Carol and prepare coffee for her in the mornings. Certainly, the days ahead would require new perspective and some needed changes.

Sarah sipped the coffee, made eye contact with each of the men around the table, and looked at her watch, "Mr. Birmingham, I have nine ten a.m. on my watch. What time do you have?"

Birmingham looked at his watch. "I have the same time."

"I will be in town for four days. If I have all the information back to me that I am requesting within forty-eight hours, in addition to your normal fees I will give each of you a bonus of fifty thousand dollars. Therefore, at nine ten a. m., forty-eight hours from now, this bonus offer will expire." She had their attention. Sarah turned to the stenographer and took the folder that contained the fact sheets describing the circumstances involved in the delivery of her child in 1951. Always the careful attorney, Sarah passed out confidentiality documents, which would bring significant financial penalties upon the violator. Sarah wanted assurance no one in this room would dare violate confidentiality in her lifetime, or that of her child. After carefully reading the signatures of each man in the room, Sarah had the stenographer and Carol witness and sign the documents. She then passed out the fact sheets and allowed the men to read the purpose of their services, as well as the facts that Sarah thought pertinent in helping them discover the information.

David Birmingham was first to speak. "Mrs. Bretherick, I don't understand. You want us to discover the identity of your child along with several other pieces of documentation, without filing a lawsuit, issuing subpoenas, or taking a deposition? Obviously, we will be performing in an arena without the tools with which we normally work."

"Mr. Birmingham, I do not want this case in the newspapers. Can you gentlemen imagine what the publishers would do with this story? My goal is to discover my child, quietly, without turning this child into a headline. Further, what good would a lawsuit do for me or this child? I'm seventy-eight years old, and one of the richest people in this country. I need time, not the money. This child will be magnificently wealthy once I can identify him or her. No, gentlemen, lawsuits take time. I haven't the luxury of revenge, nor the advantage of time. Let me be clear: No lawsuits, subpoenas, nor depositions. I'm employing you because you know the systems of records and court documents. You know how to use your legal status in getting people's attention. And you have the abilities to penetrate the cloud of lies that appear when great liability is evident."

Birmingham looked down at the summary sheets. "The clock is running and the task is clear. Jonathan, I want you to check every newspaper article that was printed concerning births in a four-county area on January 28, 1951. Remember that Watkins Glen is in Schuyler County. Gene, I want you to go to the Schuyler County Clerk of Courts office and write down every recorded birth for that week. Dennis, I want you to go to the historical society and make a list of all the physicians that practiced in Watkins Glen in 1951. Also, look for any pictures or information regarding that hospital. Specifically, names of administrators, nurses in the news. I want to know if that hospital had plumbing problems in 1951. We're looking for names of individuals that worked in the hospital that night, someone who could possibly help us fill in the blanks. I will go personally to the hospital. I believe they will be very guarded once they get a hint of what is going on. I want both of the investigators to go back to the office and wait for the information we will be calling back to you. I will expect you to take these leads and begin interviews and research on the internet with any of the information that we give you. I expect charts, timetables, and names to be maintained."

Birmingham turned his attention back to Sarah, "Can you think of anything else before we leave?"

Sarah held up her cell phone for everyone to see, "I want to know the minute you have something substantial to report. Mr. Birmingham, I would like an update from you every four hours. My cell number is on the fact sheet. I don't care what time it is, call!"

As the men exited the room, Carol asked Sarah, "May I get you another cup of coffee?"

Sarah smiled. "No, Carol, I'm going to get us the coffee."

"Carol, I'm going to show you a good time." Sarah tried to remember the streets connecting to the house she and Ben lived in when they were first married. It felt good to be back again. She was filled with nostalgia, thinking of herself and Ben walking the near vertical brick streets to the Cornell campus, the football games, and the evening strolls. Tears welled in her eyes as she thought of Ben back in Cleveland, lying in bed in the Alzheimer's unit. Why hadn't she insisted on coming back for visits? There were so many missed opportunities in their marriage.

Finally, she found the house. Sarah got out of the car and stared. She envisioned the day they brought Gerald home. In her mind's eye, she saw her family sitting around the table. Ben was young, skinny, and full of energy. Except for a color change, the home looked exactly as it had back in 1951. The house was in infinitely better shape than any member of the family that once resided there. She fought the urge to knock on the door. Perhaps going into this old house would stir even more emotions than she was prepared to deal with today.

Carol never pictured Sarah and Ben living in anything as simple as this little house. The moment had taken her by surprise. She never knew a time that anything was simple in the life of Sarah Bretherick.

"Carol, if I can make my way back to the campus, would you like to see our old stomping grounds?"

Carol nodded and smiled. Sarah launched into the Cornell alma mater. "High above Cayuga's waters—"

"Oh, Sarah, stop! Obviously you didn't major in music while you were here. "

Slowly they went uphill and downhill through the expansive campus. They observed the college students weighted down with backpacks, treading the hills effortlessly. Occasionally there was a young couple holding hands, looking intensely interested in what the other was saying. Everyone looked so young. Sarah pointed out old buildings and shared stories about her first dorm, a roommate, a foolish act, but mostly she related her beginnings with Ben on this old campus.

Sarah pulled the car off the narrow road and came to a stop just before crossing a bridge that stood high above a ravine. The tears started streaming down her face again. Adrenaline rushed through Sarah's body as she thrust the car door open and began walking toward the bridge. Carol struggled to keep up with her as they walked to the middle of the bridge on the pedestrian walk.

Sarah stood silently for several minutes as she looked down at the depths below the bridge. Together they stood and observed the little stream, and listened to the babble of water as it flowed over the rocks. The winter weather stripped the heavily wooded ravine of all the foliage, but the beauty was still evident. Every breath they took launched out into the cold air, disappearing within a moment. The sights, sounds, and emotions compounded with each second for Sarah.

Sarah began laughing. "When we were students here, this was called Suicide Bridge. It was not uncommon for one of Cornell's brightest and finest to receive the first bad grade in life, and in miserable desperation, come to this bridge and jump."

Breathing deeply, Sarah grasped the rail of the bridge, "One night more than fifty-four years ago, Ben Bretherick stood up on that rail. I was mortified. Carol, can you imagine Ben Bretherick standing on this rail? Can you imagine anyone?"

No, Carol could not imagine the serious, focused Ben Bretherick doing something so outrageous. She looked down filled with horror at the thought of falling that great distance.

Sarah continued, "Well, there he was, standing on this rail

with a small box in his hand. He yelled for the whole world to hear, 'Sarah, if you don't accept this ring and marry me, I'm going to jump."

"Of course, he was just being dramatic, wasn't he?" Carol asked.

"I'm not sure. I remember saying to him, 'Ben Bretherick, you are a fool.' And he said to me, 'Yes, I am, and I'm doing nothing to hide the fact. Sarah, I'm crazy in love with you, and if you say no, then this is it.'"

Sarah looked down at her hand and twisted the wedding band on her finger, the same ring she had received from Ben that very night. Sarah looked over the edge of the bridge and whispered into the cold air, "I love you, Ben Bretherick. I have always loved you." She took one more glance at the campus horizon before returning to the car. She determined in her heart that after taking care of the details of her personal traumas, she would return and donate the money to Cornell to build a building in honor of Ben Bretherick.

The news from Memorial Hospital was not good. Gerald was not responding to the stem cell treatment. He was in isolation, and the drug-induced coma meant that Gerald was unaware of Sarah's absence from him. Dr. Game insisted to Sarah during their discussion that her days would be best spent looking for her other child, as her sense of helplessness might be greater standing outside Gerald's room, looking through the glass, unable to do anything. She appreciated the doctor's phrase, "her other child." She felt more at ease with the concept of having two children, versus gaining a child and losing a child. Game assured Sarah that Ben was having a good day. Ben had lost contact with the world of reality several months ago. Sadly, she knew he wasn't missing her today, or any day.

Deterred by sentiment momentarily, Sarah checked her watch and refocused. "Carol, do you have Mr. Birmingham's cell number available? He committed to call me every four hours. I'm going to shake his tree just a little."

Sarah opened the cell phone to begin dialing and discovered the phone was shut off. Pressing the power button, it flickered for just a moment, but just long enough to indicate the battery required charging. She had neglected to take notice of the battery charge after talking with Dr. Game. "I hate these phones. Why can't they design a battery that lasts a year or two? I forgot to bring a charger with me." Undeterred, Sarah read the directions on the phone in the hotel room to place a local call. Determined, she placed a call to Birmingham's cell phone.

"Mr. Birmingham, this is Sarah Bretherick. Is there anything you can share with me so far?"

"Mrs. Bretherick, I'm beginning to know how the three wise men felt in search of the Messiah. There seems to be a shining star guiding us to your son."

"A son." Sarah fought the strain in her voice, not wanting anyone to witness her emotions. The tears continued to flow down her face, and Carol came with a tissue to wipe them.

"Yes, we know for sure you had a son. Watkins Glen is a small town. Therefore, the search for your child hasn't been all that confusing. We know from the local newspaper archives that only two children were born in Watkins Glen during the week you gave birth. Gerald Bretherick and Brett Walker, both delivered by the same doctor and on the same day, according to the records at the county court house. We are busy researching the location of Brett and the parents who raised him. We should have a good handle on both of these details by late tonight. We also checked the hospital's historical records. There were only four doctors in Watkins Glen in 1951. All of them have passed away, but by chance, I met with a lady at the hospital who stated that her grandmother was an emergency room aide at that time, and she gave me a phone number to contact her."

"Mr. Birmingham, bear with me, I'm still trying to absorb this information. You say my son's name is Brett Walker. Do you by any chance know his middle name?" Sarah's emotions betrayed her. In high-pitched voice, she asked questions like a new mother discovering details of the coming baby. Sarah no longer cared about her image as the seasoned attorney. She felt again like an expectant mother.

"Yes, from the clerk's record, his full name is Brett James Walker."

Sarah wrote the name on the hotel stationery and focused upon each name. Oddly, she would stroke the paper with her left hand as she continued to talk. Carol peeked over her shoulder and shook her head affirmatively, in agreement with Sarah in the magic of this moment.

"Mr. Birmingham, please give me the phone number of this aide? I would like to be the one that speaks with her."

"Are you sure, Sarah? I thought you wanted to keep this investigation off the radar screen of public attention."

"I have no intention of coming onto this lady like the Fifth Cavalry. She must be somewhere about my same age. Remember that I have spent many years digging truths from professional liars. I have no intention of ruining your excellent investigation."

Reluctantly, Birmingham gave her the phone number of Willa Mae Summers, a resident of an assisted living center in Odessa, New York.

Sarah hung up the phone. She picked it up again to call the number Birmingham had given her. Sarah waited patiently as the attendant went to get Mrs. Summers to take the call.

"Hello. This is Willa Mae."

"Mrs. Summers, my name is Sarah Bretherick. You don't know me, but I have some questions about something in the past that perhaps you could assist me with." There was a long silence on the other end of the phone. Sarah looked at Carol and shrugged her shoulders in bewilderment. Perhaps the old woman was hard of hearing or somewhat senile.

The silence was finally broken, "I know who you are, Sarah. I've been expecting a call from you most of my life. I was hoping to die without ever talking with you." She paused again, "Will you be coming with police? Are you going to sue?"

It was Sarah's turn to collect her thoughts. "No, no, I have no intention of contacting anyone. I certainly have no intention

of suing. I beg you; please don't tell anyone why I'm com
Money is not the issue at all. I only desire to know the truth.

"Sarah, I haven't told a soul about what happened to you
back then. I have no intention of telling anyone. But, now, if you
will allow me that privilege, I would like to tell you the truth.
It has been a burden and curse to me every day since your son
was born."

Sarah was numb. It had never occurred to her that the switch
of her child was known to anyone. She assumed the switch was
an unwitting accident, yet this woman knew who she was, and
was burdened and felt cursed by some truth of which Sarah was
unaware.

"Yes, I would like to meet you at ten a.m., and I will need
directions."

"Ten a.m. will be fine. I will put an attendant on the phone
to give you directions. Would you mind if we went outside to
talk when you arrive? These walls have ears."

"That would be my preference too." Sarah hung up the
phone and looked at Carol, "It doesn't appear the boys were
accidentally switched. This lady knows exactly what happened."

Sarah looked at her watch and reflected upon the last
twenty-four hours. In this span of time, she had discovered she
was the mother of another child. She now knew the identity
of the child, and hoped to pin down the truth of what happened to these two kids. She was surprised by her own serenity.
There wasn't a small iota of desire for revenge. She wanted to
be rejoined with her son as quickly as possible. This would be
the second night in a row of sleeplessness in the anticipation of
what tomorrow would bring. She placed a call to Birmingham,
leaving him the message that she was taking a sleeping pill in
hopes of getting some sleep, and he could fill her in on the
rest of the details tomorrow. She decided not to advise him of
her conversation with Willa Mae Summers. She couldn't mentally bear discussing and rehashing the conversation tonight.
Sarah swallowed the pill and lay fully clothed on top of the bed,
focusing her attention out the window, observing from the sixth
floor the sparkling lights of Ithaca. They gleamed like diamonds
against black velvet. She missed Ben.

Chapter Five

"Beautiful, isn't it? Breathtaking, the splendor of these majestic hills." Carol had never traveled this area before, and the sight of the herds of deer and the occasional turkey turned her into an ecstatic child. "Look at all those cows ... look at that charming farm house ... oh, look at that big red barn."

Sarah saw the awe and pleasure in Carol's face, and appreciated her all the more. Even Sarah was enjoying the drive to Odessa on the old Ithaca road. She wondered if she would remember or even recognize Alpine Junction when she came to it. Ben had taken her to a little country restaurant in Alpine Junction for breakfast many times on weekends when they lived in Ithaca. She was tempted to share with Carol a multitude of memories that occurred as they drove along, but she resisted. The appointment with Willa Mae weighed on her. Carol appeared to be quite content just taking in the scenery without commentary. It occurred to Sarah when they came to Alpine Junction and turned right toward Odessa that this was the same road she and Ben had traveled the day this child was born.

Sarah had always said that buildings tell stories about those who work and live in them. The assisted living center Willa Mae lived in told the story that this woman had limited means. She was just getting by, and this was all she could afford. The building indicated to Sarah that Willa Mae had known some hard times.

Sarah looked in the mirror to check her makeup. She decided not to carry her purse. At this moment, a thief could steal it, but she could care less. A thousand times, she had appeared in courtrooms, but she could not remember a time her stomach was so tied in knots. Perhaps she should have let Birmingham interview this lady. Looking at Carol, she asked, "Are we ready?"

Carol stared straight ahead without looking at Sarah, "No, we are not ready. Sarah, for twenty-five years I have worked for you, and I've never pushed my faith. I know you let me think and do whatever I want when it comes to my faith. Sarah, I desperately want to cross that line of silence this morning. I want to pray for you before you talk to this lady. It would make me feel so much better, and I am confident if we ask the Lord, he will be a participant in this conversation."

Sarah was taken aback, but somehow comforted by the faith of her friend. Prayer was an alien act to her, but if it would help her friend to pray, surely she could be gracious. "Of course, you can pray."

Carol took Sarah's hand, closed her eyes, and bowed her head. Sarah continued to watch Carol as she began to pray. It seemed surreal to observe her close friend speak to deity on such a personal and impassioned way.

"Dear Lord, be with Sarah. Be present in the conversation that is about to take place. Comfort Willa Mae as she bares her soul in confession before my friend whom she has hurt. Give Sarah strength to hear the unbearable, and the compassion to forgive that which is humanly unforgivable. Let us walk in your love and grace, that your glory will be present. My friend is great in will and skilled in wit; make her this day even greater in wisdom and stronger in resolve, that your plan and purpose for her life and those she loves will be made manifest. Amen."

Sarah almost said "Amen," but for some reason resisted. The butterflies and anxiety passed after the prayer. She felt peace.

The attendant brought Willa Mae through the narrow corridor into the living room. Willa Mae glanced at Carol and Sarah, but could not make eye contact with either of them. She looked toward the backdoor leading to the porch, "Would you like to visit outside?"

Carol took the cue and grabbed the handles of the wheelchair, pushing Willa Mae toward the back porch. "Yes, we would enjoy that very much. I noticed the pond and the ducks when we drove up. It would be pleasant to watch them."

Carol situated her wheelchair along the side of the porch rail, and while she adjusted Willa Mae's blanket, she noticed her amputated legs.

Willa Mae saw Carol's realization. "I lost them to diabetes. The doctors are cutting me up, throwing me away inch by inch."

Sarah nodded. She decided to let this woman go at her own pace. The truth had been veiled for fifty-four years. A few moments more wouldn't change a thing. "Have you got it all under control now? Has the diabetes done all the damage it can do?"

Willa Mae shook her head. "No, I'm losing my eyesight, and I have wounds under this blanket that will not heal. The diabetes has taken everything I have: my body, my home, my finances, everything but my reputation. I suppose I'll lose that this morning when we finish this conversation."

Sarah looked at the woman and found it hard to believe they were about the same age. "I can assure you, Mrs. Summers, I'm not here to destroy or take a thing from you. All I ask for is the truth."

Willa Mae's face wrinkled tightly, and her hands covered her face as she began to sob. "I remember the night you and your husband arrived in the emergency room. He was in bad shape and you were unconscious. The snow was falling heavily and drifting badly. I was scheduled to get off at three in the afternoon, but the snow kept the second shift nurse's aide from coming in. Lord, you have no idea how many times I wished that aid had shown up for work. I wished I'd never been there."

Sarah braced herself to hear whatever would follow. She empathized with Willa Mae. For fifty-four years, she experienced guilt for Gerald's retardation. She knew the dread of living under self-condemnation.

Willa Mae continued, "Dr. Fisher was drunk as usual. He'd been denied privileges for drunkenness at a hospital in Pennsylvania, but our little town needed doctors so badly ... nobody cared. In everyone's consideration, he was better than nothing. That night he was in the doctor's lounge ... drunk beyond belief.

"I was on duty with the head nurse, Victoria, and we had a sixteen-year-old girl in labor who just happened to be her daughter-in-law. Victoria hated this girl. Her son came home from the Marine Corps and got this girl pregnant. The girl came from a poor farm family, and Victoria despised her. Victoria saw the young girl as nothin' but white trash."

"The girl was in labor about twenty-four hours. She was a small girl with narrow hips. The baby was big, like his father, and we had problems with the cord wrapped around the baby's neck. The doctor was passed out, so Victoria and I delivered the baby. We did our best, but we could tell by the baby's color when it was delivered that oxygen had been deprived to his brain. Victoria said the child would have difficulties all of his life. Her son worked for a minimum wage in a factory, and she worried what would happen to them when they had to take care of this brain-damaged child. I've often wondered if Dr. Fisher had been sober, how different our lives would have been."

Sarah sat stunned. The brain-damaged child she was talking about was Gerald. This damaged child gave her a lifetime of love, laughter, and companionship. How could anybody think of him as simply "brain-damaged"? She would never comprehend why anyone would consider Gerald a burden. Sarah's mind lingered for a moment, thinking of Gerald back in Cleveland, lying in isolation, receiving stem cells to fight off death.

"Just after delivering this baby, you and your husband arrived in the ambulance. Your husband had broken several bones and had a few lacerations, which I attended to. Victoria attended to you. You were unconscious and bruised, but otherwise, with a few days to recuperate, I think you would have been fine. I believe the fact that you and your husband were drunk might have saved your lives.

"When I finished with your husband, Victoria had you in the operating room administering anesthesia to you. It sounds strange to tell you a nurse was doing that, but in the Glen, with just four doctors, we learned to do it all and we were expected to do everything. The doctors always signed the orders, but then again, they always received the fees. We all just covered for one another.

I asked Victoria what she was doing, and she said, 'Delivering a baby. We're going to do a caesarean section on this girl.' I didn't question her. Nobody dared question Victoria. Her wrath and power in the hospital were without equal, so I quietly went along.

When the baby was delivered, she banded the child "Baby Walker," and tagged her grandchild "Baby Bretherick." She filled out the paperwork for Dr. Fisher to sign in the morning. He never laid eyes on either of the mothers or the babies. I was the only witness to the whole matter. You would take home the Walker's baby, and they took yours. Neither of you would ever know the difference. Victoria assured me repeatedly that I would forget about the births in a few weeks. She was wrong. I've been haunted by that night every day of my life. I believe my whole family has lived under a curse for my sins."

Sarah knew Willa Mae was sharing her heartfelt belief. The woman actually believed that she and her family were cursed because of this evil deed. She couldn't help herself, "Why did you go along? Why didn't you say something years later?"

Willa Mae looked Sarah straight in the eye. "I would have, if that was the only evil thing I had done." Willa Mae looked down at her lap blanket, and her fingers traced the pattern in the material as she spoke, "My husband was in Korea when I was living in Watkins Glen and working at the hospital. We had two kids. His military pay was pitiful, and I had all I could do to keep the kids clothed and fed. The only job I could find that I was qualified to perform was that nurse's aid job.

Just after I began working there, I bought a car and took out a credit line. For the first time in our marriage, the kids and I were enjoying more than the basics; we got some of the things we wanted. I spent more than I should have and got into some serious financial problems. One night at the hospital, I spoke with Dr. Fisher and unintentionally shared with him my financial problems. With that information, he came on to me. He let me know that if I didn't let him have his way, I would be out of a job. I resisted him, but in the end, he raped me. I never said anything. He promised he would never touch me again. I needed the job to pay the bills. I thought it was over.

Three months later, I'm pregnant, I knew for sure who the father was, and it is not my husband. I shared this situation with Victoria, and she told me not to worry about a thing. She would take care of it. She performed an abortion on me in the middle of the night. Later I learned that she told Dr. Fisher what she had done for him.

After my husband came back, Dr. Fisher came on to me again while he was drunk. When I rebuked him, he told me I shouldn't worry. The back room would always be open to me…to take care of any mistakes. I knew then that Victoria had told him. I'm not surprised. She was evil."

Sarah had to know, "What happened to your family?"

"My oldest son graduated from high school and joined the Marine Corps. I was so proud of him when he became a sergeant. Shortly after making sergeant, he was sent to Vietnam and died two months after arriving. He was killed in a firefight at Khe Sanh. I thought of you when I saw his body lying in a casket, all decked out in his uniform. His death was my curse for what happened to your son. My daughter got pregnant while still in high school and married a man that made her life hell on earth. I believe her life has been cursed because of my illegitimate birth. My husband had a stroke at forty-three. He lived in a wheelchair for two years without the ability to say a word.

Now I am wasting away inch by inch and body part by body part.

I lacked the courage to admit to my husband that another man had taken me. I never wanted the world to know I had an abortion. I could never tell anyone about the switching of those two kids, because to tell of Victoria's insurrection and sin, I would have to confess my own, and I could not bear it."

Sarah was numb and, oddly, felt as if she too had been cursed. Strangely, Sarah felt compassion for this lady. Despite the evil done to her, she desired to find resolution. "Willa Mae, listen to me. I don't know anything about curses, but I do know this. I regret my biological child was taken from me. It makes me feel incomplete and empty, to be sure. However, not less than two days ago, I had no regrets about anything. The child I took home from that hospital is mine. I love him with my whole heart. There is not a day in my life I have regretted being his mother. He has lived with Ben and me these fifty-four years, and I would think it unbearable if he were taken from me."

Willa Mae continued, "I sort of kept up with both families over the years. Your son tore up local football teams while he was in high school. I went to see him a few times. He won every award a high school player could win. He was something to watch. I noticed once in the newspaper under military news that he was in the Marine Corps too. I know he grew up on a farm around Horseheads. A sports writer once referred to him as a "strong farm boy." From time to time, I would see your name in the newspaper too, under national news. What a success you are. I often thought to myself, 'Of all the girls this could have happened to, why one of the most powerful women in the world?'" Willa Mae breathed heavily. "You're not the overpowering woman I had envisioned all these years."

Sarah thought about all Willa Mae had said. He was a football star, and a Marine! She was starved to know all about him, but it appeared this was the extent of the information Willa Mae knew, and it was enough. She would have Birmingham find every newspaper article ever written about Brett Walker. She desired to read about every game. Somewhere there had to be some high school yearbooks, and somewhere there must be a picture of her Marine in his dress blues.

Willa Mae waited in silence as Sarah seemed to be far removed in thought. She took advantage of the silence and continued, "Did you know that Victoria died in a house fire."

Sarah winced to think of the horror of her death; however, the news of Victoria's unseemly death was not all that disturbing and was somewhat satisfying. "What happened?"

Willa Mae shrugged her shoulders in a look of bewilderment. She glanced nervously at the door to see if anyone else was around, "I guess it's just a case of 'what goes around, comes around.'"

Sarah sensed that Willa Mae was struggling with the intensity of the past and decided to set her free from reliving it. "Willa Mae, you haven't heard the last of me. I would like to hear every detail you can remember, but you have filled in the blanks for me today. We will meet again on another day." Sarah wasn't sure she meant what she had just said.

Willa Mae grabbed Sarah's hand. "You're an angel. I can't believe this is the meeting I have dreaded every day of my life."

Sarah hugged her, and Carol started pushing the wheelchair back into the home.

Sarah walked to the car slowly. She conjured mental images of helpless infants switched from their mothers by evil hands. She hesitated for a moment, waiting for Carol to catch up. Looking at Carol over the top of the car, she asked, "So, what do you think?"

Without hesitating, Carol spoke, "I think God works in mysterious ways."

Chapter Six

Sarah's mind was blank. She tried to put thoughts together, but the past hour spent with Willa Mae derailed her ability to focus. She sat in the parking lot of the assisted living center with the key to the car in her hand, with no idea where to go next. She could not discern whether it was her age that was affecting her ability to think, or the magnitude of realizing her child had been unknowingly missing for fifty-four years. Her mind looped over and over with thoughts: Brett Bretherick, where are you? What are you like? Will you love me? Will you accept me? Is there any way we can possibly make up for all these lost years? Sarah resolved to know these answers, but sitting in the parking lot of the assisted living center in Odessa, New York, it seemed a remote beginning to such a specific task.

Carol observed, wonderingly, this rare moment of Sarah's indecision. She, too, wondered what was to follow. "Perhaps, Sarah, you should call David Birmingham. I know we gave him your cell phone number on the fact sheets, but your cell phone battery was dead last night, and without the charger, he has no way to contact us. I'll bet he's tried to call us; your instructions yesterday and last night were very specific."

Sarah was grateful Carol was there. "Yes, of course. I should have called him earlier this morning. Let's go find a payphone." Now she was back on a plan of action. Find a phone. Get updated on the details from Birmingham.

How odd, Carol thought as she watched Sarah standing outside a gas station, talking on a payphone. Carol had never had a child, but as she watched Sarah's grey hair blowing in the wind, dressed in clothes costing over five thousand dollars, making her own phone call on an outside payphone, she began to understand. This wasn't the mega-rich, brilliant, well-organized woman she had known all these years; this was a mom in search of a child, and all the externals would be sacrificed in the task of finding him. Carol was saddened, watching her torn by the cold wind.

Sarah stuffed her hands into her overcoat pockets to keep warm. The air temperature was dropping, and she felt her fingers going numb from the cold. She reached into her pocket, removed the key and a small notebook. She immediately turned on the car and turned the heat to full. "I'd forgotten how cold it gets in these hills."

Sarah looked down at her notebook. "Mr. Birmingham wants us to meet him for lunch in Watkins Glen, at the Glen Lodge on the Lake. He said he has a lot of information, both old and current, about Brett."

Carol looked at her watch, "How long will it take us to get there?"

Sarah now had her focus as she looked in both side mirrors and the rearview mirror. Then she looked straight ahead and slammed the pedal of the car to the floor. With tires squealing, Sarah yelled, "We are about to find out!"

Sarah braked the car down to forty-five miles per hour as she crested the top of the hill and Seneca Lake came into view. A wave of nausea passed through her body, caused by the memory of coming over that same hill fifty-four years ago and viewing the lake during its late-January freeze. How foolish she had been those many years ago, racing with Ben down that steep hill into Montour Falls, intoxicated, in a rickety old Jeep. The majesty of the twenty-two mile lake and the farmhouses on distant hills should have been the intoxication. They could have had a life free of guilt if only they had exercised some common sense. Yet, even now, after all the years spent mentally rehashing the foolishness of that fated day, she found herself racing over the hill at a ridiculous speed! "Truly," she thought, "fools are fools to the end!"

Sarah contemplated every sight they passed. "I believe, Carol, that cranes used to be produced at that old plant. That property obviously hasn't been occupied in many years." Passing a waterfall, she pulled the car over to stare for a minute. "I remember this waterfall. It seems like Ben and I were posing in front of it just yesterday, with a stranger taking our picture."

Entering Watkins Glen, Sarah spoke almost to herself. "I'd forgotten how much I loved this little town." She told of the time she and Ben stood along the street as sleek-looking race cars ran through the village, something known internationally as the Grand Prix. Sarah recounted the stories of their special days, climbing the steep Glen, passing several times under the misty fall, and coming out on a flat plain at the pinnacle of the steep hill. She told stories of the excursion boat located at the marina that gave tours of Seneca Lake. She pointed out spots significant to the history of the Seneca Indians. The salt mines were still there, even after the passage of all these years. She wondered how many tons of salt had been removed over these past fifty-four years. Sarah tried to remember the home Ben took her to with a real estate agent. Ben loved the little village with its gigantic old houses perched on the hillside, overlooking the beautiful waters of the majestic lake. She had forgotten Watkins Glen was their special place once upon a time, before their drunken folly that January day. After leaving the hospital fifty-four years ago with Gerald in her arms, neither of them mentioned again returning to the Glen. The surroundings filled her with bittersweet emotion.

Birmingham stood under the awning as Sarah swung the car into the Glen Lodge. He struggled to maintain an even expression, but he was mentally amused at the sight of these two old ladies wheeling around town.

"Mrs. Bretherick, Carol, it is good to see you. I hope the meeting with Mrs. Summers went well this morning."

Sarah assessed Birmingham as he opened the door of the car to let her out. She noted the large stack of documents in his left hand. She knew that within his grasp, many of the questions concerning Brett would be answered. She wondered how much hardship would be discussed in the next few minutes. Sarah glanced at Carol and instinctively knew Carol was aware of the stack of papers.

"I have much to share with you, Sarah. The internet is an amazing tool of our day. Our team has compiled a mountain of information concerning the life and location of your son. I'm having copies made for your own use. They should be brought to us before we start to eat. The sheets I possess are handwritten drafts, internet copies, and information we should not have been allowed access—legally. Sean prevailed upon a source he calls Bean Pole to gather a lot of information we could never legally access. He said you would know the source by the code name. Frankly, I'm very uncomfortable with the classified information Sean obtained. I would prefer not to know the source, in the event there are any legal ramifications for obtaining them. I will also count on your discretion not to reveal any of the sources I share with you. We have tried to scrub your copies of all references and notations which would reveal any sources we have utilized."

Sarah laughed. "I can't believe Sean got Bean Pole involved. I can't believe that guy! Oh, don't worry, David . . . you have nothing to worry about. This source is untouchable, but someday it's going to cost me! Big time!"

Eating food seemed a waste of precious time at this moment, but Sarah understood the venue. They needed a place to talk and have time to absorb information. Eating was an acceptable part of the format. She would be patient once more. She ordered soup and a sandwich, but knew she would eat very little of it.

Birmingham lifted the cover from the thick volume of documents. He looked at Sarah. She looked straight into his eyes. She couldn't help seeing the fatigue on his face. "How much sleep have you had in the last two days, David?"

"Mrs. Birmingham, I'll bet if we added the total sleep of our whole team investigating the details of Brett, we wouldn't have eight hours."

"David, I'm sorry this has taken such a toll on you. Tell your team everyone has earned the fifty-thousand-dollar bonuses I promised."

Birmingham was surprised. "Don't you want to hear the information we have before you pay us a bonus?"

"David, I'm a very good judge of character. I know you and your team will deliver exactly what I've requested, as quickly as you are able."

Birmingham looked down at the table of contents and asked, "Do you want a *Reader's Digest* version, or do you want the whole volume?"

Without hesitation, Sarah responded, "The whole volume…no, I can read a lot of the little details later…perhaps the *Reader's Digest* version…just the big stuff."

Carol wanted to hear all the details. She hoped Sarah would share a copy of Birmingham's report with her. Knowing and finding Brett Walker was now a desire of her own.

Birmingham scanned the table of contents one more time.

"Let's start from the beginning. The parents that raised Brett were called Charles and Susan Walker. Susan died of breast cancer while Brett was in the seventh grade, we estimate. Charles died in a farm accident while Brett was serving in Vietnam…June 1970. We have copies of the orders for him to come home from Vietnam for the funeral."

Sarah's eyes welled immediately. Taking her napkin from her lap, she dabbed at the stream of tears on her face. "This is going to be hard," she whispered.

"The best information we have today, Brett has one living

relative, a brother. His name is Richard. They appear to be very close. The phone records indicate they call each other several times a week."

Sarah grabbed Birmingham's arm to stop him from speaking. "No David! You might want to make a note in your file, Brett has three living relatives. His mother and father are still very much alive!"

Birmingham smiled. "Your son was a good student. It appears he not only excelled in academics, but he also set records athletically and socially. You will enjoy reading some of the teachers' comments."

Sarah couldn't resist, "Oh, read just a few."

"Well, we have twelve years' worth, so I'll just read a few."

"'Brett learns quickly but has the ability to stir rebellion in the class room.' That was first grade, and here is one from fourth grade: 'Brett is not performing at the level of achievement he is capable of. He appears to be daydreaming the better part of the school day.' In the seventh grade, a teacher wrote, 'Brett likes a good fight.'

I'll just skip to his senior year. This is the notation from his guidance counselor: 'Brett is one of the most intelligent students to have passed through the halls of this high school. Subject material comes easy to him. He possesses an IQ of 162. His SAT scores would meet the standards of any college in the United States. In spite of his native capabilities, Brett has indicated he will not attend college, and has signed an agreement to enter the Marine Corps upon graduation. His mother passed away while he was in junior high. His father hasn't the financial ability to send him to college. While Brett established numerous school records both on the football and track teams, because of his size, the only schools interested in recruiting him were division three, which do not give scholarships. The United States Marines recruited the best of a few good men!'"

Sarah traced the pattern of the tablecloth with her finger as she absorbed Birmingham's report. She would have demanded her son accomplish everything he was capable of. She had the money to send her son anywhere. With Gerald, she had no choice but to accept whatever society would allow him to participate in, but with Brett, she could have helped him attain whatever dream he sought.

"As you already know, Brett went to Vietnam. A few months after returning from his father's funeral, specifically September, Brett was badly wounded in a gun battle. Almost the entire platoon was killed. One GI was taken as a prisoner of war, and one is still listed as missing in action today. Brett was wounded in the neck and right shoulder area. He was shipped back to the United States, and listen to this, he was sent to the Veteran's Hospital in Cleveland, Ohio, for numerous surgeries and rehabilitation."

Carol looked at Sarah, "Sarah, do you know what this means?" Without waiting for Sarah to reply, Carol said, "Brett is familiar with our town. He already has some insight into your life."

"He might be more familiar with Cleveland than you think. He fell for a nurse that worked at the Veteran's Hospital and married her. Her name is Fay Rennick. Upon discharge from the Marine Corps, Brett attended Case Western University in Cleveland and earned a Bachelor of Science degree in civil engineering."

Sarah interjected, "His father graduated from Cornell with an engineering degree. It doesn't seem like the apple fell far from the tree."

"Brett spent the next few years working for a firm in a little town in Ohio, called Ashtabula. Ashtabula was Fay's hometown. It appears from many of these documents that Fay is a deeply religious lady. You will see when you read the whole file. In Ashtabula, Fay and Brett had two boys. The oldest, Aaron, is thirty years old now. The youngest, Adam is twenty-eight. I guess you can tell by their names the biblical influence of Fay in naming them."

Sarah could not contain herself. "Is there anything you can tell me about the grandchildren?" She rubbed her arms to try to warm the bumps that covered her entire body.

Birmingham pulled the table of contents page out, moved

his finger down the page to the section called "genealogy." Turning to the section, he stared at the page for a second. "You will have to excuse me, Mrs. Bretherick. I was never good at charts and mathematics. That's why I needed to go into something as imprecise as law."

He paused and began again, "Okay, if I start with the youngest, I can trace my way back. Adam is a special agent for the United States Customs in Seattle, Washington. He's been there four years. He is a graduate of Florida State University. He's been married for six years to Michelle, an attorney. Adam has a Master's degree from the University of Central Florida in criminology and, according to this, no children yet."

Birmingham breathed deep again and exhaled as he traced the diagram on the page, "Your oldest grandson, Aaron, is an assistant pastor at a church in Fort Pierce, Florida."

Carol let out an audible "praise the Lord" upon hearing this news. She gripped the table with both hands and squeezed it in a muted gesture of celebration. She turned to Sarah, "It cannot get better than this. I would be the proudest grandmother in the world if my grandson were to become a pastor. It just doesn't get better than this." Sarah remained mute, overwhelmed in the odd twists of mortality. Sarah never considered going to church, let alone consider that a descendant of hers would serve as a pastor in a church.

"Well, Carol, from your perspective, there is even better news. You might be more pleased to know whom he is an assistant to in Fort Pierce for these past ten years."

"Is he serving with some famous preacher?" exclaimed Carol.

"I don't know how famous the pastor is, but I do know the pastor is also his father!"

With that news, Carol closed her eyes, tears streamed down her face as she grabbed Sarah's arm and squeezed it. "That is wonderful news, Sarah. Trust me, Sarah; I now know everything is going to be better than great!"

A peace came over Carol's face. Sarah knew of Carol's strong faith in her Lord. Now she was witnessing this faith in action.

Carol started eating as if she had not eaten in two days … which, in this case, would be exactly right.

Sarah looked confused. "I thought you said Brett graduated as a civil engineer and went to work in Ashtabula, Ohio."

"That's the problem with giving *Reader's Digest* reports; I skipped a lot of years and incidents. We skipped the years of selling his own firm, taking his family to seminary with him for schooling, and a lot of history as they took a small church in Fort Pierce and raised the boys. Sarah, I'm giving you a lot of facts. Someday you will have to ask Brett yourself what motivated a very successful businessman and an engineer to give it all up to become a minister."

Carol looked up immediately. "Mr. Birmingham, that is certainly a question of perspective. I don't believe Brett gave up a thing! I believe he gained! No, not only gained, but he was elevated to a position no businessman, or engineer, or even an attorney could attain."

Sarah had never witnessed Carol respond so sharply to anyone before. A startled look went around the table. Carol looked sheepish after realizing that the tone of her voice was sharp.

Carol apologized quickly to Birmingham. She felt the awkwardness of the moment needed repairing. "Mr. Birmingham, may I tell you a joke?" Sarah had never heard Carol tell a joke. Everything about the lunch conversation was momentous.

Birmingham nodded in agreement.

"Okay, what is the difference between God and an attorney?" Birmingham acquiesced.

"God doesn't think he's an attorney."

For the first time during the lunch, there was levity among them.

Sarah was the first to get the conversation back on track. "David, you didn't finish telling us about Aaron." Sarah caught herself in mid-thought to say "us." Finding Brett and the grandchildren was now intensely personal for Carol.

"Aaron also graduated from Florida State University. He too married his college sweetheart," Birmingham perused the sheet for details, "a Lynne Oaks." They have been married for ten years. They have two kids. A boy, Seth. And a girl, Ava."

Sarah squeezed Carol's hand this time. "Did you hear that? I'm a great-grandmother too!"

A gentleman approached the table with two briefcases. Sarah recognized him from the meeting at the airport as member of the investigating team. Birmingham told the gentleman to leave the briefcases with him, dismissing him with a simple, "Thanks."

"Mrs. Bretherick, these briefcases contain more information concerning your son and family. I know you have many more questions. Your son is living in Fort Pierce, Florida. He is the pastor of an extremely large church. All the current information concerning him is here on this cover sheet. There is a lot of information about him on the internet. When you have time, you should listen to one of his sermons on the internet. He is a captivating speaker."

Sarah was stroking the cover sheet with her fingertips as she read. Carol reached over and grabbed her hand. "Sarah, in just a little while, you will be touching his face."

Birmingham spoke, "I can't emphasize enough that these documents can never be discussed or shared with anyone else. Your friend and partner, Sean McCurdy has worked diligently with us to accomplish this herculean task in just a few hours. He called in every political favor that is owed him. Based on your name and his, there are not only confidential school records in those cases, but Brett's federal income statements, tax returns, credit reports, military records, college transcripts, phone records, and on and on and on. You are a very important woman to those in high political positions. They have gone out of their way to assist you. Leaking of any of this information would damage the careers of many, including mine, yours, and your friend, Sean. A lot of legalities were overlooked to obtain this information."

Sarah nodded in agreement. "Mr. Birmingham, I would be the last person on earth to disclose what we have been given, and I know you can count on Carol's integrity."

Birmingham opened the briefcase and searched the pockets, finally pulling a cell phone out. "Mr. McCurdy had us obtain a cell phone for you. We have written the area code and phone number on the back of the phone. The phone comes with two chargers, one for the car, and one for your hotel room. He wanted to be sure he could contact you when he desired."

Sarah placed the phone and chargers in her purse. "What a good friend Sean has been to our family over the years. He never misses a detail."

Sarah looked at Birmingham, "I have one more task for you, before you abandon me.

Sarah continued, "You mentioned Brett had a brother, Richard. You didn't say where he lives."

Birmingham flipped the file open again and dragged his finger down the table of contents. He opened the file containing the information regarding Richard. He studied the file momentarily. "Richard lives about thirty minutes from here. He lives and works the farm where Brett was raised."

Sarah stood to look over his shoulder at the information. "Have someone copy this page for me right now, and on the back of the page, write out clear and concise directions to get to this farm."

Birmingham looked baffled, "Why are you interested in this man, in view of all the people and facts we have given you? He seems a minor character in the sum of this story."

"You forget that I raised this minor character's brother as my own son. This minor character was raised as my son's blood brother. This man is entitled to know one of his brothers is very sick. And time is of the essence. Based upon the man and his character, I will have to determine whether to share this dilemma with him or not."

Birmingham removed the sheet from the file and motioned for the gentleman in the hallway to come over. He stood, gave instructions about the page, and returned to the table.

"Mrs. Bretherick, while we are waiting, may I sound like an attorney and give another attorney some legal advice?"

"Of course, you may."

"You are a very rich woman. There are enough screw-ups and deceptions already in your life. I am 99 percent sure Brett Walker is your biological son. We have a ton of objective evidence. However, if something ever happens to you, or if our information is even slightly amiss, you know every loony in the world will sue to claim all or part of your estate. You know we can set this issue aside and be 100 percent sure of Brett's lineage with a DNA test. That would solve any questions either personally—or legally."

He was right. Sarah knew he was right, but her instincts overruled. "I would like to get to know my son first without getting into estates and financial issues. He has no idea how wealthy he is at this moment. I would like him to love me first…for me. His mother."

Birmingham hugged her. "I have a feeling he will love you, with or without money. However, I have a plan. I called Brett early this morning…"

"You did what?"

"Hold on! I called him to inquire if he would participate in an analysis of medical premiums for church personnel concerning medical risk. I stated we were investigating the hypothesis that church personnel should pay less for medical insurance because church employees neither drink nor smoke and live healthier lifestyles. I informed him that all he and his staff had to do was answer a questionnaire and allow a nurse to perform a cursory physical of the professional staff. I offered his church a stipend of five thousand dollars if they would participate in the study. Brett said, 'Why not?'"

Sarah didn't care for the deception, but the finality and the legal issues concerning his future would be settled forever.

The gentleman handed the copy with instructions on the back to Birmingham. Birmingham turned the paper over to Sarah. "What do you want me to do, Mrs. Bretherick? I have a nurse and a questionnaire ready to visit your son."

"You're very thorough, David. No wonder Sean chose you. Thank you for a job well done. Send the nurse."

Carol grabbed Sarah's arm as they departed the restaurant. "We're going to visit Richard, aren't we?"

Sarah winked at her. "Not yet. We have a major purchase to make first."

"What in the world are you going to buy?" Carol couldn't imagine anything major Sarah would need.

"We are going to buy some real estate that overlooks the lake. This time, I want to make sure we come back to the Glen."

Chapter Seven

Sarah slowed to twenty miles per hour as she drove past the mailboxes on Ithaca Road. Ithaca Road was listed on the directions given by Birmingham as a rural road. In one sense, it met the criteria of a rural road. There were only farms, fields, and Holsteins grazing everywhere, but the traffic was zinging by her at seventy-five miles per hour. Whenever there was a curve or solid double yellow lines, the traffic would build up, impatiently honking and tailgating them. Her stomach was in a knot, as much from the traffic congesting behind their vehicle as in anticipation of meeting Richard Walker face to face. She decided not to call ahead. Sarah couldn't think of what she would say to him over the phone.

On the other side of the road, Carol spotted a silo and pointed with her finger for Sarah to see.

Sarah ran her fingers through her hair. "Oh Lord, I sure hope that's the place. This is exhausting."

As they approached the farm, the mailbox was leaning sideways, so Carol got out of the car to read the numbers. She turned to face the car and raised both arms in the sky, signaling to Sarah the quest was over. They had arrived.

Carol tenderly entered the car and fastened her seatbelt. Sarah was in no hurry to pull into the driveway on the other side of the road. Carol sensed the anxiety Sarah was experiencing. "What are you thinking?"

"That's the problem, Carol. I'm not thinking anything, and that's a big problem. I haven't got a foggy idea what to do now that we are here. Got any ideas?"

"I'm afraid my thoughts and approach wouldn't feel comfortable to you."

"And just what exactly would make me feel any more uncomfortable?"

"You would simply pull in that driveway and trust the Lord for the words to say and the opportunity to say them."

"Believe it or not, Carol; at this moment, your way sounds very appealing."

Sarah put the car into gear and crossed the highway to enter Richard Walker's driveway.

Rutted and stony, the driveway threatened the undercarriage of the car. The center of the driveway was mounded from years of farm equipment and heavy rains washing the gravel downhill to form two parallel ruts. Carol white knuckled the door handle as the driveway challenged her ability to sit with any degree of stability. Out of nowhere, three large dogs surrounded the car, barking madly as they bounced along toward the house and barn. Carol screamed, "Sarah, there is a dog looking down on me. His nose is up against the window. He's big and I'm sure he's a wolf. Oh Lord, he's got a whole wolf pack with him, too."

Sarah wasn't to be deterred. The mission was to see Richard, and no pack of dogs or a miserable driveway would stop her. The driveway turned hard to the left, opening the view of the small, square, white lopsided farmhouse. The block milk house stood only a few feet from the very simple home. A huge silo stood next to the barn. The family name appeared in large red block letters on the top of the silo, Walker Family Farms. Cats stalked everywhere. Most of them little kittens.

Sarah soaked in as much of the panorama as she could. She envisioned her son growing up on this farm. Unsure of how long she could sustain a conversation with Richard, she wanted to take advantage of this special moment to absorb some insight into the life of her son, which she had yet to meet. Carol remained cowering in her seat. Sarah gazed again at the farm equipment parked around the open area. A little red Farmall tractor, a green John Deere combine, an orange Case tractor with tricycle tires in the front, a huge John Deere Tractor standing tall, with two huge tires surrounding the driver, and two large tires in the front all shared space around the barn. Sarah thought to herself, "What a paradise of toys for a little boy!"

Carol pointed her finger at the door on the first floor of the barn. Since both doors were open at both ends of the building, the figure of a large man could be seen walking within the dimly lit barn in the direction of their car. As he stepped outside, the sunlight allowed Sarah to discern his features. He was a big man in every way, vertically and horizontally. Carol put her head down and exhaled as she whispered, "Oh Lord, give Goliath a tender spirit." Sarah rolled the window down about two-thirds of the way.

The big man walked up to the car and yelled at the dogs to quiet down. He bent over and asked, "Is there something I can do for you, ladies?"

Sarah yelled out, trying diligently to be heard over the barking dogs, "I'd like to speak to Richard Walker."

"You're talking to him."

"I'm here because of Brett Walker, your brother."

"In that case, you better get out of the car. Let me guess, you're one of his church members, or you listen to him on the internet, or you read one of his books, and you wanted to see for yourself this farm he is always telling stories about."

Sarah wouldn't be lying about hearing Brett refer to the farm. She and Carol listened to Brett's latest sermon on the internet in the hotel manager's office last night. He was, without a doubt, one of the best orators she had ever listened to.

"Why, yes. Just last night he was referring to a line, something to the effect of "The righteous shall live by his faith.""

"I listened to that same sermon myself two nights ago. My big brother's good, isn't he?"

Sarah nodded in agreement and was thinking, so is your biological brother. "Last night, Brett said that when he was just a little boy, he was afraid to walk the three-foot runway between the wall of the barn and where the cows' heads stuck through. Their big heads with protruding horns and big eyes scared Brett as they swung their heads powerfully, resisting the restraint of the metal bars. He said he conquered his fear by following his father down the small runway for several days. Brett compared that lesson learned on this farm to lessons of life. You know, those times when something scares us so intensely, our personal faith is too weak to move on, so the only way we can continue is by living in God's faith."

Carol heard what Sarah had just said, but after all these years of attempting to reach out to her about her faith in God, she was now standing in a barnyard, listening to Sarah illustrate a biblical lesson to someone else. The Lord indeed worked in strange ways.

"I don't believe I got your names."

"My name is Sarah Bretherick."

Carol waited a moment to see if Richard had any reaction to Sarah's name. Noting that his reaction did not change, she said, "I'm Carol Thatcher."

"Call me Rich, please. Well, ladies, it just so happens I'm done with chores, so let me give you a tour of Brett's most used illustration, this farm. How about a tour of the property? I've given this tour to others that have shown up, and they seemed to like it."

Rich took them to a large metal building, took a key off the wall, and opened the door to a Jeep Cherokee. Sarah gazed around the building filled with all kinds of motors, chains, and tools. The vehicle in the corner covered in canvas caught her attention.

"I doubt you'll ever hear Brett mention her in a sermon."

"What is it?"

"His first love affair. A GTO convertible."

"Why wouldn't he ever mention it?"

"Probably, the things he did with it are not fitting for a preacher to tell in a pulpit. Then too, I believe there are some things that Brett has buried deep, and that car is one of them."

Sarah was drawn to the car like a magnet. "Tell me some stories … please."

In all the visits of those coming to the farm, Rich always guarded Brett's secrets, but today, he could sense this old lady wasn't seeking juicy inside stories, she desired to know from some need of her own.

"Brett is only twenty-five months older than me. When we were teenagers, he would take me with him to drag race on the streets. One night, Brett was lecturing me that drag racing was more than engines and shifting. It had a lot to do with a driver's disposition. So he had me practice the poker face. Now, the poker face required a lit cigarette dangling loosely from your lips and staring blankly at the driver of the car next to you before you gun the engine. Now, I need to take a minute to tell you that when we were teenagers, our dress slacks were made of polyester. Brett never left the farm without being dressed up, unlike me.

Anyway, we were down on Westinghouse Road with this car, Brett telling me all about the poker face, both of us smoking away on those cigarettes, and up comes this hot Chevelle at the light to challenge us. Brett said to me, 'Watch this. Watch how to do the poker face.' So Brett gunned the engine, looked over at that Chevelle a couple of times with the poker face, cigarette dangling, smoke curling. The light turned green and Brett popped the clutch. Now, when he popped that clutch, the lurch was so strong the cigarette popped out of his mouth and onto his polyester pants. That cigarette about melted the whole crotch out of those pants before Brett could grab hold of it. He had burns between his legs. What a sight! We spent the rest of the night shopping for slacks, just like the ones he ruined, so Dad wouldn't find out."

Sarah could see the obvious delight in Rich's face as he remembered the story. "Did your dad ever catch Brett in any of those shenanigans?"

"Oh, once in a while. Brett's best friend, Ronnie, was with him most of the time. He was as wild as Brett. They were what you would call in poker, a pair. There wasn't anything either one of them wouldn't try. One night, both of them went hunting coons way back in the hills on Johnson Road. Ronnie's dad couldn't afford insurance, and he hadn't saved any money; so Ronnie couldn't get a driver's license, but that didn't matter to Brett. Once they left the main drive, he let Ronnie drive the GTO. So this night, they had one beer too many, and Ronnie was driving them back on that twisty dirt road. He went too fast on a gravel corner, and the GTO went off the road. It was off the road so far those guys had to walk home in the dark and call a wrecker. Dad drove them back to meet the wrecker. Just as the wrecker was lifting this baby up on the hook, Dad asked if they'd been drinking. Ronnie responded, 'Oh, no sir,' and at that precise moment, the beer cans started rolling and clanking backward as the front of the car was being lifted. Those guys always had something going."

Sarah smiled. "Those boys were lucky they made it to adulthood."

Rich looked stunned. "Actually they didn't. Our little valley is well represented on that wall in Washington, D C. Ronnie lost his life in Vietnam, and Brett came close to losing his there too."

Sarah stared at the car and lifted the canvas to see the interior. "In that case, I rejoice for every wild moment they enjoyed. Why didn't Brett ever drive it again?"

"I suppose the memories and the lack of money to restore it. Dad died tragically here on the farm while Brett was serving in Vietnam. When he came back, he was pretty messed up physically. The war, numerous surgeries, and months of rehabilitation ... they changed Brett. When Brett bought this car, he and Dad spent days out here, working on it. With the loss of Ronnie and Dad, Brett could never bring himself to restore the car, yet he never would allow anyone to get rid of it. The title and keys are in an envelope in the house. If I had the know-how or the money, I'd fix this thing up like new and make him drive it. When he comes home, he always comes out here to pull up a chair and sit for a while."

Those familiar tears were welling up again in Sarah's eyes. She rubbed the tears from her eyes with her coat sleeves. "This car will be restored again. I promise you."

Rich fought back his own tears, "C'mon, I'm going to show you some things and tell you some things that you will enjoy. Rosalie went into town to buy groceries and will be back in a while." They all climbed in the Jeep Cherokee.

"Rosalie gets on me about four times a week to fix this driveway. Someday she'll take a bat to my head and I'll get it done." Rich stopped the Jeep before pulling onto Ithaca Road.

"You ladies see that mound of dirt right there?" The mound of dirt was about thirty feet off the highway.

Carol spotted the mound first. "Yes."

"Now can you see those three beehives, one up close to the road, and the other two beehives up closer to that mound of dirt?"

This time, both Sarah and Carol said yes.

"That mound of dirt used to be where a large maple tree grew. Dad put a swing in the tree when Brett and I were kids. In the summer of Brett's senior year, Dad decreed on Saturday morning we weren't to make any plans because we were supposed to help him cut down that tree and chop it up. He had even gone out and bought a new chainsaw to do the job. There was only one problem. My brother already made plans for Saturday morning, and he knew the consequences of skipping out on Dad, so Brett came up with another plan.

On Wednesday mornings, Dad always went into town to pick up feed. He always went by himself, so Brett told Ronnie to be at the farm first thing Wednesday morning. Brett put together the chainsaw, mixed the fuel, and started it. He had all the ropes we needed laid out. Dad even complimented Brett for taking the initiative to get everything ready for Saturday morning.

As soon as Dad gassed the truck onto that highway, ole Brett came around the corner of the barn with that orange Case tractor up there. Brett put Ronnie on the tractor, tied a big rope to the hitch bar, climbed the tree, and tied the other end of the rope to the tree almost to the top. He let down another rope to me. I tied the chainsaw on the end of the rope, and he pulled it up into the tree.

Brett yelled out to Ronnie, 'Take up the slack!' and from that moment, all I can remember is pandemonium. I was looking at Ronnie with the taut rope and heard the chainsaw start up. In the blink of an eye the top of that tree came crashing down, but not where Brett had calculated. It headed straight for the beehives. I took off like a bullet to the house. I glanced back at the maple tree. The bees were forming a dark cloud in that area, and I could see Dad's brand new chainsaw flying out of that tree. I watched the rest of the show from the picture window there in the house.

Ronnie abandoned the tractor, and it continued on a path that eventually destroyed the chicken house. Ronnie ran to the water hole where the cattle drank; all you could see of him was his nose poking out of the water. The dogs came by the picture window, dragging their butts on the ground, howling in pain.

Back in the sixties, very few cars had air conditioning, and this day it was hot.

The car windows were down. About the time a car would get even with our driveway, they would be slamming on their brakes. Those bees were tearing those innocent passersby up!"

Sarah and Carol gave way to tumultuous laughter. The laughter felt so good.

Carol, possessing an extremely compliant nature, put her hand over her mouth. "What in the world did your dad do?"

"It was a man's world here on the farm after Mom passed away. Dad was not into warm fuzzies, saying I love you or anything like that. But Brett and I knew we were loved. He never said a word. He was more concerned about Brett's and Ronnie's bee stings. Dad's mother, Victoria, would rant, rave, and punish. Dad determined not to raise us like that, so we pretty much got off easy on a lot of things that other kids would've been punished for. I'll tell you one thing though, I think Brett and I feared letting Dad down more than any punishment he could give us."

Sarah could not let it go. "You mentioned Victoria. What about her?"

Rich was startled again. "You know about Victoria? Brett wouldn't speak of her in a million years. Besides, it's not good for a preacher to speak evil of anyone."

"I know Victoria by reputation. It's a long story, which I'm sure I will share with you later."

"Well, this woman gave my father fits. Even worse, she and Brett went at it every time they saw each other. For some reason, she never liked Brett, and believe me, the feeling was mutual."

"When did she die?"

"Physically, she died in a house fire in 1971. To me, she died right after Brett's notification came that he was hurt in Vietnam. Dad was gone, so when the notification came, it came to me. Rosalie called Victoria to tell her about Brett. I wouldn't have called her, but that's another story. Anyway, Victoria came up to the house and said something ugly like 'this was bound to happen to him anyway, because he was a fool.' Then she went on to say that the farm couldn't support two families, so it was just as well. I was hurting and feeling hopeless already, and I let out all my rage on Victoria. I told her I never wanted to see her again. Dad was dead, so there was no reason for her to ever come back to the farm again."

"You never saw her again?"

"No. And I didn't want to either. After her death, I took care of her affairs and felt no regrets."

"Brett never wanted to come back to the farm?"

"I believe Brett has always known that God gave him life for a purpose that far exceeded the limitations the farm would have placed on him. In fact, I'll share something with you. After Dad's funeral, we went to the attorney's office. Both of us were emotionally drained. We listened to the attorney read Dad's will and last wishes. He left the farm to both of us, and if one didn't want it, the other could buy out the brother's share based on an appraisal.

I was engaged to Rosalie and barely had the money to buy her a ring. I was just out of high school and didn't know anything but farming, so I couldn't buy out Brett. Brett said he had other plans, maybe going to college, and didn't have any inclination to be a farmer."

"So you bought Brett out."

"No, Brett and I shared the farm in joint ownership. He let me run it and keep the profits from it. When he was able to get out of rehabilitation, he came home to be my best man for our wedding. His wedding present to Rosalie and I was contained in an envelope. He gave us his half of the farm. He made only one stipulation."

Carol was caught up, "What was that?"

"We would let him build a log cabin someday at the meditation place."

Now Sarah couldn't stand the suspense. "Where is the meditation place? Did he do it?"

"Shoot no, preachers are like farmers. They do it because they love it, not because there is money in it. Brett is comfortable, but he couldn't afford to build the log cabin Fay picked out. She has a plan tucked away."

"Would you like them to build up here near you?" Sarah quizzed.

"Absolutely! Rosalie and I were unable to have kids. Aaron and Adam are like sons to us. They spent the majority of their summers here. This farm goes to them when we die. Even though Brett and I live so far apart, we talk to each other several times a week. Unlike our father, we never hang up the phone without telling each other, "I love you, big brother." He's older than me, and I'm much bigger than him, that's why we call each other big brother." Rich turned the Jeep hard to the left, "I'll show you Brett's meditation place."

The meandering path through the woods opened into a grassy flat area, surrounded by magnificent trees with a babbling creek to the side.

"I can see why it is called the meditation place. It is so peaceful and serene." Carol could picture herself spending hours in this place.

"When Brett was discharged from the Marines and rehabilitation, he would take a tractor and come and spend the day here, reading and thinking. He also brought Fay here to propose to her."

Rich looked at his watch. "Ladies, Rosalie will be home anytime now. I didn't leave a note telling her what I'm up too, so we better head back."

Sarah couldn't help herself, "My husband calls that 'keeping a tight leash.'"

"I think that sometimes too, but after Dad had an accident up here with a tractor, we agreed to communicate where I'd be. Dad bled to death. We had no idea where he'd gone. Normally, I carry a radio with me, but I left without it."

Sarah teased Rich again, "Is Rosalie going to be jealous if she finds you driving two women around the farm?"

Rich laughed. "Hardly! First of all, she doesn't have a jealous bone in her body. More important, she knows me too well. She says there isn't another woman in the world that would put up with me."

"I don't know about that one, Rich. I haven't known you for long, but I'm a good judge of character. I think she is a fortunate woman." Sarah was sincere.

Chapter Eight

Rosalie came out of the house when the Jeep pulled up. Petite and smiling, Sarah could tell from the look on her face that Rich was her delight. Rosalie came over to help Sarah out of the Jeep. "Rich, what in the world were you thinking, bouncing these ladies all over this farm in that rickety old Jeep?"

Rich hugged her tiny frame in his massive arms. "Rosalie, I'd like to introduce you to two friends of Brett's, Sarah and Carol."

Rosalie immediately hugged them. "Any friend of Brett that is here during lunch must stay for lunch. I'm so glad you're here."

Sarah could feel the strength of the bond of this family. She knew Brett had known some hard times, but this family was built to share them.

Rosalie grabbed Sarah and Carol by the arms and led them toward the house. Sarah's cell phone chimed. Taking the cell phone out of her purse, Sarah noted the calling number was Sean's.

"Hello, Sean."

"Hey, Sarah." There was silence on the phone.

"Sarah, where are you right now?"

"Carol and I are visiting with Brett's brother, Richard, and his wife."

"Sarah, can you find a place where I can speak with you, without peering eyes watching you?"

"Yes, as a matter of fact, I'm standing alone outside Rich's home."

"Okay. I spoke with Dr. Game a few minutes ago. Gerald has taken a turn for the worst. The doctor doesn't believe Gerald has long to live. It may be just a few hours."

"Oh God, this cannot be happening." She dropped the cell phone to the ground and struggled to breathe.

Rich was the first to hear Sarah. He blasted through the door and scooped her into his arms like a feather. Carol picked up the cell phone. "Hello."

"Carol," Sean recognized her voice. "Gerald may not live through the next twenty-four hours. The soonest the Gulf-stream can land in Ithaca is ten p.m. tonight. Can you have her ready and there?"

"Yes."

Sean inquired further, "How does it stand with Brett's brother? Have you told him everything?"

"No."

"Do you want me to fly in tonight and talk to him?"

"No, if Sarah doesn't. I'll talk to him."

"Sure."

"He's a kind man. I'm confident he will listen to us."

⌒

Sarah sat down at the kitchen table, rested her elbows on the table, and placed her face in her hands. Carol stood behind her, rubbing her shoulders, and valiantly trying to fight back the tears. She had a fond affection for Gerald.

Carol glanced at Rich and Rosalie as they awkwardly watched the pair of them sniffle in their kitchen. Carol weakly smiled and cleared her throat to speak, "We owe you both an explanation."

Sarah spoke up, "It's okay, Carol. I'll tell them."

Rosalie reached for Rich's hand. Sarah hesitated. She struggled for a reasonable beginning to the story, an understandable transition from the reality everyone in the room thought they knew to a reality that would seem totally impossible to good and reasonable people. "Rich, Rosalie, this is extremely difficult to share, but what I will tell you will probably be as hard on you as it has been for us."

"Rich, just a few minutes ago I told you I would share with you my knowledge of Victoria. I never knew her personally, but the evil this woman was capable of far surpassed the evil you have already experienced in your knowledge of her."

Sarah looked directly into Rich's face. "On January 28, 1951, your mother and I delivered babies at the hospital in Watkins Glen. Victoria, the head nurse at the time, delivered both babies. One baby suffered from a lack of oxygen in the process of the delivery. Victoria knew the child would have significant brain damage. That was the child she sent home with me. That is the child I have raised and loved...and loved...and loved...and now he is about to die."

Rosalie's face hardened, and her voice inflection rose, "You're not implying Brett is not Richard's real brother." Rosalie looked fixed and coldly at the pair of them. She felt threatened by their presence.

Sarah understood. "I know what you're feeling. I'm still reeling from the moment when I discovered Gerald wasn't my biological son, but let me warn you, that doesn't change my love for him one iota. I would use every resource at my disposal to keep anyone from taking him or his love away from me. In my heart, Gerald is my son. By the same token, the man I raised has a biological brother that he never knew he had. I just thought you might be as interested in him as I am in Brett. I have no interest in competing for family ties. My desire is only to complete our family."

Sarah saw the broken look on their faces. She knew their hearts were now in control. Her judgment was right; they were good and kind people.

Rich shifted his weight. "How do you know Brett is your real son?"

"Let's be clear. Listen to me. I'm not looking to make a trade. Gerald is my real son too."

Sarah regretted taking such sharp exception to Rich's question. "I'm sorry. Normally I'm more controlled."

She pulled a tissue from the holder and dabbed her eyes. "Gerald is dying of cancer. I engaged an experimental stem cell treatment for him as a last-ditch attempt to cure him. In the process of preparing Gerald for the treatment, some of his DNA, my husband's, and my own DNA were examined. Because of the experimental nature of this stem cell research, the DNA was compared among the three of us. During the comparison, the researcher discovered that Gerald couldn't possibly be the biological son of my husband or myself."

Richard remained in a fixed position with both hands folded across his chest.

"I've spent more money than you can imagine to find that answer. At first, it was the probability there were only two births on January 28, 1951, in that little hospital. However, yesterday, Carol and I talked firsthand with a worker who witnessed the switch take place."

Rosalie sat down. "Are you 100 percent sure of all of this?"

Sarah looked directly into Rosalie's brown eyes. "I am 99 percent sure, but even as we speak, the 1 percent question is being addressed." While she was looking into Rosalie's eyes, Sarah felt her pain. Rosalie had no children of her own. Rich had already shared their affection for Brett's kids. She could see the hurt setting into Rosalie's face.

Sarah got up from the table, walked around, and placed her arms around Rosalie. "Rosalie, I'm seventy-eight years old. My husband is in an Alzheimer's ward for the rest of his life. The son I have raised has only a few hours to live. Believe me. I'm not here to hurt this family at all. In fact, if you have it in your heart, I would very much appreciate it if you would help me become a part of this family. I already know how special the both of you are. Please help me recover what little is left of my existence."

There was silence in the room. Sarah could hear the cars rushing past the farm on the road in front of the house. Sarah felt compelled to initiate the conversation again.

"I have made no attempt as of yet to contact Brett. I understand it will take some time for you to think about and talk about what I have told you. However, Gerald is now in critical condition, and we must return home to Cleveland." Sarah hesitated and looked at Richard, "Would you like to come with us to meet your other brother?"

Richard unfurled his arms and grabbed the counter with his hands, leaning his whole weight upon them, looking intently at Sarah.

"Yes, I would."

Rosalie spoke up, "Rich, I think you should. I'll stay here and take care of the farm. You know I can do it. Please go."

"Rosalie, I need you to go with me too. Your brother is out of work. He knows exactly what to do for the short time we would be gone. Can I ask him, please?"

Rosalie nodded, "Yes, they need the money anyway. Let me call him, while you work out the details with Sarah."

Carol blurted, "You both can fly out tonight with us at ten p.m. from the Ithaca airport. We can take care of everything."

Sarah interjected, "You can stay at my home, and I will supply you with a vehicle."

Richard grinned. "First of all ladies, I'm a farmer, and that means there is no way I could pay for two plane tickets leaving tonight. Secondly, I wouldn't think of imposing on your graciousness by utilizing your personal vehicle and having you house and feed us."

Sarah stood up and grabbed Rich. "Listen to me. Each of us has a lot to learn about each other, so I'm going to ask you to do something beyond what a stranger can ever ask another stranger. I'm going to ask you to trust me! Trust me! Trust me like you would your very own mother. Remember, I'm the mother to the only two men on earth that you can call brother. From this point on, I'm covering every one of your expenses and all travel arrangements."

Rosalie walked into the room with a portable phone to her ear. "Jeff says he will be glad to take care of the farm. He wants to know if you want to borrow his car to make the trip."

Richard looked at Sarah again undecidedly, breathing in an anxious breath. Sarah squeezed his arm tightly and whispered, "Trust me."

Without turning his sight away from Sarah, Rich answered, "Naw, everything is taken care of."

Rosalie covered the receiver with her hand, "Rich, are you sure? Our truck is not that reliable to be so far from home."

"Yeah, I'm sure, besides we're not driving. We're flying, according to Sarah."

Sarah smiled and hugged him.

Rosalie returned to the kitchen, looking at Rich with an expression that clearly denoted she thought he had lost his mind.

Sarah turned to Rosalie, "I pleaded with Rich to trust me while you were speaking to your brother. From this moment, I don't want you to worry about anything. I will make sure your every need is taken care of, and it will cost you nothing."

"Sarah, I didn't mean to sound sharp. I'm still spinning, and I'm certain you are just as off balance." Rosalie turned to Rich. "C'mon Rich, we've got some packing to do. Sarah, do you want to wait on us, or do you want us to meet you at the airport?"

"If you don't mind indulging us, I would love to wait and leave with you."

Sarah rode with Rosalie in the truck, and Rich was glad to accommodate the request to drive the rental car back to Ithaca. Sean had already arranged for the car rental to pick up the vehicle at the airport. Rich struggled, allowing Sarah to pay for the elegant dinner the four of them enjoyed at the Box Car Inn. Sean interrupted dinner twice with phone calls to Sarah. The last call announced the Gulfstream would arrive earlier than predicted, eight thirty p.m. Sarah could tell from Sean's intensity that they were in a race against time. She never imagined that Gerald's condition could have deteriorated so quickly.

Rich paced the length of the windows inside the terminal area. Rosalie nervously watched every movement, both inside the terminal and outside.

"Neither one of us has ever flown before. How big is this plane? What airline is it?"

Carol was surprised. Neither Rosalie nor Rich was aware of the magnificent wealth of Sarah Bretherick. They actually thought they were going to fly on an airline.

"Rosalie, we will be flying on one of the finest private jets made in the world. We aren't flying a commercial airline. I own the jet."

"You own a jet?" Rosalie's face fully communicated that she thought Sarah was mentally disturbed. "Rich, you need to come over here."

Carol took over. "Rosalie, she really does own the jet. In fact, that jet is almost insignificant in comparison to the other things she owns. Have you ever heard of the Bretherick Corporation?"

"You don't mean to tell me…oh God…Sarah Bretherick…you're the same Bretherick as in Bretherick Corporation?"

Sarah took Rosalie's hands into her own. "For better or worse…that's me."

Rich came up to them mystified, as to why both were smiling so mystically. "Yes, honey? What is it?"

Rosalie winked at Sarah. "Oh, nothing Rich. It was really nothing."

The door opened to the tarmac, and an official of the airport came through it. "Mrs. Bretherick, I wanted to meet you before you left tonight. The tower radioed that your plane is just about to land. We are proud to have had you use our airport for your travel. Can we be of any personal assistance to you?"

Sarah shook her head. "Thank you so much for your kindness. This has been a very productive trip. We have everything we need tonight, but thank you for asking. Perhaps you can walk us to our plane." Sarah waved for all of them to start walking toward the door, fully expecting the airport manager to catch up with them and guide them.

The turbines of the Gulfstream roared loudly as it smoothly touched down on the runway. Rich watched intently at the magnificent jet shimmering in the lights of the airport. It turned at the midpoint of the runway toward the terminal. The emergency lights blinked and interior lights dimmed, and the sight of the Gulfstream appeared to increase the farm boy's testosterone by the second. He turned to the ladies. "Wouldn't you guys love to fly on that baby tonight?"

Rosalie shook her head no to Carol and Sarah to silence them. She wanted Rich to be surprised and enjoy himself fully. The hours to come would contain more than enough sorrow for all of them. A little joy along the way would make it a bit more bearable.

The Gulfstream parked directly in front of their group. The stairs of the Gulfstream lowered to the ground. Crew members came down the stairs and approached Sarah. Rich walked to the side of the jet and read the name printed across the fuselage, "Bretherick Corporation."

He ran immediately to Rosalie, "I've got something to tell you."

"I already know."

"Oh, no, you don't! Do you know who Sarah really is?"

"Yes! She is Mrs. Bretherick Corporation."

―――――

Fatigue, sorrow, and old age had taken their toll on Sarah. She could barely keep her eyes open. Her ability to communicate had long passed. Carol sensed Sarah's deteriorated physical and mental condition and appointed herself as Rich and Rosalie's caretaker. They were more than a little overwhelmed with the Gulfstream and the whole situation.

Rich turned around in his seat and saw Sarah stretching out on the couch. He felt sorry for her. She looked so tired, frail, and vulnerable lying there. He felt moved to go to her, taking a blanket off the rack and tenderly covering her. He whispered to her, "I'm sorry."

She lifted her hand to his face. "I can't thank you enough for trusting me and coming home with us." She laid her head down as Rich went back to his seat. She felt the acceleration of the engines and the vibration of motion as airport lights blipped through the windows as they rolled along to the main runway. She looked at Carol, Bible on her lap, reading light focused, and mechanical pencil in hand. Sarah made a mental note to purchase a Bible of her own. She determined not to be ignorant about the very book her son and grandson lived to teach to others. Sarah looked down the aisle and noticed Rich and Rosalie, talking with their heads close together. They were obviously very much in love and were comfortable sharing with each other. They made Sarah jealous. She missed Ben.

Chapter Nine

"Sarah, wake up. Sarah!" Carol alternated between rubbing her arm and caressing her grey hair. Cold air entered the compartment as the crew of the Gulfstream lowered the stairs to the ground.

Sarah squinted her eyes to focus on Carol's face. She raised her head slightly and looked around the cabin. She could hear the sound of airport service vehicles moving around the plane. Rich was engaged in a conversation with the pilot. Emotionally, she wanted to pull the blanket over her head and take refuge from the pain of dealing with Gerald's imminent death. Realizing that her desire to see him was greater than her dread of losing him, she threw the blanket on the floor and groped for her purse. "I'm ready. Let's go."

The crew said nothing to Sarah as she fumbled to the exit. They simply touched her shoulder as she passed by. She saw compassion in their faces. Sarah had flown with this crew many times. It saddened her that she had never inquired if any one of them had children. The expressions on their faces gave evidence that they too were parents. At once, she felt like Ebenezer Scrooge experiencing the ghost of Christmas present. She was startled into awareness of a life composed of too much business and far too little caring about others. Sarah stopped at the door. "Thank you for making this unscheduled trip tonight. I appreciate it."

The captain met Sarah at the bottom of the stairway. Sarah reached her hand out to him. "Do you have children, Captain?"

"Yes ma'am. I have two kids…two boys."

"How old?"

"Nine and eleven."

Carol and Rosalie had already entered the limousine. Rich came and stood beside Sarah as she was speaking to the captain.

"Captain, as it turns out, I have two sons, both fifty-four."

"Twins, ma'am?"

"It's a long story, Captain."

Sarah placed her arm around Rich's arm as they began walking to the limousine. "Rich, I need to go to the hospital. Would you like the driver to take you and Rosalie home, or would you prefer to go with me?"

"I couldn't sleep right now if I had to. Honestly, I'm as nervous as a cat."

"What about Rosalie?"

"Rosalie wouldn't go anywhere without me. We've never spent a night apart since we've been married…besides I'll need her with me tonight…I feel like a little boy."

"That makes two of us feeling over the edge. I've known you for only a few hours, but it's comforting to have you here."

Rich blushed from the comment. "It's very hard for me to picture the tycoon of the Bretherick Corporation needing comfort. I've always pictured someone of your stature as absolutely unshakeable."

"If we were dealing with a contract or losing money, I would probably live up to your perception, but tonight we're talking about losing my son, and I'm scared."

"I'll be with you, Sarah."

Carol was on the cell phone in the limousine, advising Memorial Hospital that Sarah was on her way. Gerald was still alive. Barely.

The hospital administrator met the limousine as it pulled up to the clinic. "Mrs. Bretherick, we are sorry that things have turned the way they have for Gerald. I personally asked Dr. Presley to oversee Dr. Game's management of your son's care while you were out of town."

Sarah cut him off in mid sentence. "Can you reach Dr. Game for me?"

"He is in the hospital now and so is Dr. Presley. They've been contacted to meet us upstairs."

The group walked together past the three-story waterfall in the lobby and down the marble hallway toward the elevators. Rosalie and Rich held hands. Sarah could see the apprehension on their faces. She suspected they would be uncomfortable in this setting, despite the circumstances of seeing Gerald. This morning, Rich was the big and strong confident farm boy. Tonight, he looked like a little boy being dragged to the principal's office.

In the fraction of a second it took for the elevator door to open, Sarah could see the pressure Dr. Game was experiencing. She also recognized a sacrificial lamb when she saw one. It was clear to her that the administrator and Dr. Presley were about to lay the responsibility of Gerald's quick demise on Game. She walked directly to Game and kissed him on the cheek.

Dr. Presley cleared his throat, "Sarah, I think we should prepare you for what you are about to see. Gerald has experienced a major setback. He is in a coma, connected to a lot of monitors, tubes, and IVs. His urinary output is minimal. We have the IVs as wide open as we dare. Again…I want you to remember that neither I nor the administration was in favor of this treatment plan. Dr. Game stood solely on his own in recommending stem cell treatment as a last resort."

There it was, stated plainly and clearly for everyone to hear. Dr. Game would not enjoy the aegis of the clinic in the event that she wanted to exercise her legal prowess and substantial wealth in punishing them. Sarah looked at them in disgust. She wondered how many lives and how many future advancements in medicine were shortchanged because of cowards like these. Determined, Sarah decided she would not explode in her anger against them. They would be surprised when they discovered how grateful she was for Dr. Game's willingness to help her.

"Gentlemen, it took at least ten years for me to appreciate the game of football. My husband thrived on watching football. After ten years of resisting, I too became an avid fan of the game. Some of our best days were spent watching the Browns. Now, you can't be a Browns fan and not appreciate the panic of a closely scored game. I became very familiar with the play called a Hail Mary. The play is called when the game clock has only a few seconds remaining and there is time for only one play. Every back and receiver is spread out across the field, and when the ball is snapped, they all run to the end zone. The quarterback throws the ball as far as he can, hopefully in the center of his receivers in the end zone. All the players, including the defense, know exactly what they are going to do, so they are standing in the end zone too, waiting to catch or knock the ball away. If the offense catches the ball, they win. If the defense knocks the ball away or catches it, the game is over and they win. Now, the difference is this: the offense has nothing to lose because if they catch the ball, they win. But if they drop it, they'd already lost the game anyway."

Sarah's eyes pierced Dr. Presley. "I remember meeting with everyone who is standing here. It was the consensus of this group that Gerald was inevitably going to die in the near future. It was my choice to ask if there was anything that could be done for Gerald. Dr. Presley, you told me explicitly that I had no hope for any other medical option. It is my full recollection that when I asked for a medical Hail Mary, the only one willing to step up and take on the effort was Dr. Game. He never promised me a cure. In fact, quite the opposite; but metaphorically speaking, he would be willing to put the ball in the air and try to snatch a victory out of the jaws of a sure defeat.

So you see—and be certain about this—I'm not talking about anything as trivial as a football game. I'm talking about the life of my son. Now, when the game clock of his life comes to an end, I'm satisfied that two of us in this group did everything that we were capable of doing to turn the end result. My gift to this hospital of ten million dollars remains in effect for stem cell research, in spite of the fact that it didn't work for Gerald. Hopefully, some other mothers will be spared the agony of losing a child so early in life.

I have only one condition for continued funds to stem cell research or capital building programs. Memorial Hospital must initiate a contract with Dr. Game, giving him explicit autonomy over the research. He should never again be subjected to the political correctness of a hospital administrator—or the lack of vision and courage of a fellow physician. Am I clear?"

Dr. Presley and the administrator shook their heads affirmatively. Sarah could see the relief on the administrator's face in spite of her castigation.

Sarah wrapped her arm around Dr. Game. "Thank you, gentlemen, for meeting me here tonight. It really wasn't necessary. Dr. Game will tell me what I need to know."

Rich stood wide-eyed, observing the strength of Sarah Bretherick as she set the record straight with the hospital staff. This certainly was what he expected of a corporate tycoon.

"Rich and Rosalie, this is Dr. Game, Gerald's primary physician. He is also the one that discovered through the DNA tests that Gerald was not my biological son."

Dr. Game extended his hand to Rich and Rosalie as he offered to guide them to Gerald's isolation room. They passed the main nursing station and walked to the end of the hall. Nurses sat at a circular desk with monitors stacked in a vertical column. "Bretherick" was written in black magic marker on a piece of white tape stuck to the top of a monitor. Standing across from the nursing station, Game pointed through a glass window to where Gerald was lying. He was alone in the room. Rich and Rosalie stood back, allowing Sarah and Dr. Game a moment alone.

"He's not going to live much longer, Sarah. His kidneys have stopped working. Therefore, his body is becoming toxic.

His blood pressure is not stable enough to perform dialysis. We have him on a ventilator because his respiration rate has dropped significantly. His heart is struggling to keep working, and we are medicating to maintain a reasonable blood pressure."

The sight of Gerald's chest heaving up and down to the rhythm of the ventilator shocked Sarah. His arms were bruised from the numerous IVs inserted through the flesh. She could see his head propped up on both sides. A mass of IV pumps, IV solutions, plastic lines, respiration monitors, oxygen and EKG attachments surrounded him on all sides. His skin was not the full ruddy color she had known during his lifetime. Now, he was a pasty pale white.

"Doctor, will you take us in?"

"Sarah, I can't take you into this room. It's a special room maintained to be as perfectly sterile as we can maintain it. Those fixtures at both ends of the room are laminar flow units, designed to clean the air of all contaminants. If you desire, I can have Gerald transferred to a private room so you may have some time with him alone."

"Can we cease the ventilator at the same time?"

"Yes, if you wish, but we should do it after he is moved."

"Will he linger long?"

"Normally, I don't like to guess on these matters. Given all the issues that Gerald is struggling with, I believe he will pass shortly."

Sarah's body began to quiver. Tears streamed down her face in torrents. She could not find the voice to speak. Looking into Dr. Game's eyes, she nodded her head affirmatively, hoping that the actual words of surrender would not have to be uttered.

Game understood. He guided Sarah back to Rich and Rosalie who rushed to surround her on both sides and locked arms around her. Game directed a nurse to take them to the room where Gerald would be assigned. They would come with Gerald momentarily.

The sound of a hospital bed could be heard moving down the hall toward their room. Game's voice could be heard calling for someone from respiratory to be sent to Gerald's room.

Sarah's mouth was dry, and she could feel the contents of her stomach churning within. She wanted to change her mind and stay the inevitable death as long as she could. She could find comfort in only one thought. Gerald would never have to experience the sense of grief and despair she now felt.

As the bed entered the room with Gerald, Rosalie looked at him and covered her mouth in shock. Her eye's immediately averted to Rich as he leaned over the bed and stared directly into Gerald's face. "Oh Lord!" Rich said in a booming voice. He began violently weeping.

Sarah went immediately to Rich, recognizing that something had impacted him powerfully. "Are you going to be all right?" she asked through her own tears.

Rich could not speak. Rosalie answered. "Remember when Rich asked if you were sure that Brett was your biological son, and you said 99 percent? I can assure you that you are 100 percent correct. Gerald is the perfect picture of his father. He is about the same age of his dad when he died. Looking at him tonight, he is a visual reminder of a very tragic event in our lives." Rosalie tucked her lower lip between her teeth before speaking. "Forgive us! We were totally unprepared for any of this."

Sarah understood. She had felt unprepared for everything that had happened in the past week. She wondered if anyone could have prepared for the devastating twists and turns they had experienced.

The IVs had been removed. Only the heart monitor, ventilator, and blood pressure cuff remained on Gerald. Dr. Game sat on the edge of the bed. "Do you have any questions?"

Carol knew that Sarah would have many questions later, but one question deserved answering this moment. She spoke for her. "Why didn't Gerald respond to the stem cell treatment?"

"I will give you my best estimate. These specialized stem cells attack cancer by destroying the stomal cells that provide the structural support for a tumor. Tumors and wounds have one thing in common, and they both require stomal cells to provide either support to the tumor or repair to the wound. In this case, I believe that Gerald's wounds from the surgery were so significant that when we introduced the stem cells into his body, they were distracted from the tumors and went directly to the wounds. Therefore, the tumor was not defused in time to halt the internal explosion of the cancer."

"What happens now?" Sarah questioned.

"A respiratory therapist will come in soon to disconnect the ventilator. The rest depends upon Gerald."

Sarah sat down on the bed and took Gerald's hand into her own. She stroked his face and massaged his hand. Sarah tried sweeping his disheveled hair with her fingers. His hand was that of a middle-aged man, but in her mind, the hand she held was that of the perpetual child, always in search of the next joy. Gerald was cold. She could feel it in his hand.

The respiratory therapist entered the room. She hesitated for a moment. "Would you like to step out while I take care of Gerald?"

Rosalie and Carol stepped outside. Rich put his hand on the top of his brother's head. "I would prefer to stay with him."

Sarah again could not speak. She cupped Gerald's hand between her own and lowered her head.

Game nodded his head for the therapist to begin.

The therapist stepped to the head of the bed and separated the tubing from the mouthpiece in Gerald's mouth. With the other hand, she turned off the ventilator. The silence in the room was instant and devastating. Game stood behind Sarah and motioned for the therapist to remove the tube still inserted in Gerald's throat. She smoothly removed the tube in one motion. Grabbing the tubing and unplugging the unit, she rolled the equipment out of the room. Gerald was now free. His breathing was slow, almost invisibly. Carol and Rosalie re-entered the room.

A nurse came into the room and placed her hands on Sarah's shoulders. Everyone in the room alternated glances from Gerald to the monitor. His heartbeat decreased by little increments and then would increase rapidly for a small time. The nurse went over and disabled the alarm on the monitor to keep it from alerting because of the diminishing heart rate. Sarah thought that perhaps his heart might fight back for a while. But then his heart rate would decrease even lower with each cycle of failed recovery. From time to time, a whimper came from one of them within the room. Tears flowed freely.

Sarah glanced out the window and saw the lights of an aircraft far off in the sky. She pictured stewardesses passing out cokes, cookies, and passengers reading dime-store novels, oblivious to everything. The world around them continued the normal activities of life. It seemed wrong. The universe should come to a halt in this reverent moment. The moment of the passing of her son. And then, the plane was gone.

Rich saw Gerald's muscles twitching. He motioned to the doctor, "Look, his arms and legs are moving a little."

Game could hear the hope in his voice. "I'm sorry. What you see is the reflexive activity of the muscles as they react to the lack of oxygen. That causes the arms and legs to move a little."

Sarah laid her head on Gerald's chest. The monitor read thirty beats per minute, increased for a few seconds to nearly forty, and then rapidly declined to the teens. Game reached over and turned off the monitor. They sat in silence for a few minutes. Game took the stethoscope from around his neck and placed it upon Gerald's chest. He looked at Sarah and closed Gerald's eyes. And, now, Gerald was gone.

Carol came forward, taking Sarah's and Rosalie's hands in each of her own. She bowed her head and Rosalie joined her, "Our Father, which art in heaven, hallowed be thy name…"

Chapter Ten

A bright light startled Sarah into opening her eyes. It had been years since the sun had caught her sleeping. The clock read 9:22 a.m. Oddly, in spite of sleeping so late in the morning, she still felt exhausted. Last evening seemed a nightmarish blur, but the morning sun made the whole experience seem like it was a year ago. The sun bathing her bedroom drove away the dreariness of the fears and unknowns of last night. She listened for the stirring of servants, Carol...someone. Then the wave of melancholy came over her. Gerald would never again come in the room to give her his daily greeting—never, ever, again. Sarah determined she would not give into this depression. Her heart would be damaged forever, but there was still room in her heart to love, and there existed a family that was part of her and Ben, a part that she was determined to know and love.

Rich and Rosalie were sitting in the enclosed porch area as Sarah entered the room. Sarah looked sheepish as she wondered if they thought she slept this late every day.

Rich stood up, "Good morning, Sarah. Your employees tell me this is the first time they have known you to sleep in. I'm glad. You obviously needed the rest."

Sarah hugged Rich and bent down and kissed Rosalie. "I can't tell you how much I appreciate the fact that you are here. We have much to discuss. Can I get you some breakfast, more coffee, anything at all?"

"No, thank you. Your staff has been gracious to us."

"Did you see Carol this morning? It is unusual that she is not here."

"Yes, we did. She said that she had some errands to run and she would return."

Sarah poured some coffee for herself. "I would like both of you to stay with me for a while. I know it is a tremendous imposition for me to ask you this, but bear with me." She smiled. "No, trust me, and I will do everything I can to alleviate any burden I can."

Sarah could see Rich and Rosalie were politely uncomfortable with the thought of staying much longer. She thought she could discern the reason without asking. Rich had already stated that farmers and preachers don't make much money. Therefore, absentee farmers don't make anything. She decided to deal with finances first.

"Rich, first of all, money will never be an issue that you should ever have to deal with again. On paper, Gerald had been an employee of the Bretherick Corporation from the first day. My husband made sure, regardless of whatever happened to our personal fortunes, Gerald's future would be secure. His estate includes stock incentives, a 401k, insurances, and private holdings, which should exceed ten million dollars easily. I'm making sure his entire estate will be yours. You're entitled to it."

Rich sat up straight in the couch. "Sarah, I'm entitled to nothing. I didn't earn it, and I was never able to be a brother to Gerald. Honestly, your offer is tempting. I don't have any money, but I have integrity and pride. I will have to say no. I will work for what I spend."

"Rich, I'm not talking business with you. I'm not trying to buy you or trap you. Can't you see that I'm trying to put together what Victoria tore apart fifty-four years ago? I want to put our families together. Money doesn't make a family, Rich. Love does. Your brother was born mentally handicapped. He had nothing to offer our corporation. He could never have worked for the wealth he attained. His value to Ben and me was based on one fact ... Gerald was our son. He was a vital part of a living and thriving family.

Today, I'm sitting in the room with his biological brother ... you! You are Gerald's real brother, like it or not. Only by Victoria's evil act were you separated from him. So even if you didn't know him in life, honor him in death. Take what was his and make it your own. Claim your birthright and, in doing so ... claim him! It is through our families that our existence is never forgotten."

Rosalie grasped Sarah's intentions. Years of desiring a child of her own had made her sensitive to the need of sharing her life with someone who would treasure her affection and those things that she cared about. Rich knew instinctively as he watched his wife change expression that Sarah had just connected with her heart. Money and greed had no room in her heart, but she would walk through hot flames for her family.

"Sarah, I can look at my wife right now and tell you that I better not say another word. However, I would appreciate it if you would split this estate between me and my brother. Brett is your son, and I still count him as my brother. I would never take what is rightfully his."

Sarah laughed out loud. "Rich, I'm only giving you Gerald's estate. Within a few days, your brother will be a joint owner of every asset and corporation I own. His income will be greater than the gross national product of most nations. You don't have to worry about Brett."

Rich shook his head in amazement. "You know, Sarah ... Brett and I have been frugal our whole lives. We've worked hard for every little thing we have. I can't imagine having the money for a real vacation or a vehicle that is brand new. My brother isn't much better. Neither one of us ever really cared about being rich or impressive, and here we are, both of us on the verge of having more money than a sane man could dream about."

Sarah enjoyed this moment. "Rosalie, I couldn't help overhearing that your brother was out of work. Is it possible I could hire him to run your farm while the two of you help me get through the next weeks? I will put him on the Bretherick payroll so that all employee benefits will take care of his family needs."

Rosalie's face glowed with joy. "What an answer to prayer. They were on the verge of putting their place up for sale and moving some place to find work. I dreaded to see them leave us. My brother loves farming."

"Sarah, Brett is about to become one of the richest men in America by receiving this wealth from a mother he doesn't know exists. Meanwhile, he's down there in Florida, completely unaware that his life is about to take a complete turn. Have you thought about how you're going to communicate all of this to him?" Rich wondered to himself when the incredulity of this whirlwind storm would begin to seem reasonable.

"Yesterday, when I pulled into your driveway, I didn't have the slightest idea what I was going to say to you. Somehow it all worked out!"

"No, this time it will go even better," Rosalie interjected. "Rich and I will go with you to Florida to help a mother and son get to know each other. Selfishly, I'm dying to see Aaron, the grandchildren, and spend time with Fay."

"Rich, did you mean it when you said that you wanted Brett to build a home on the meditation place?"

"Absolutely!" Rich couldn't believe that this dream of his brother spending more time on the farm might come true.

"Rosalie, is there a way you can get the cabin drawing Fay has stored away?" Sarah asked.

"You bet I can. Fay is the most trusting and naive person I know. That plan is as good as in the mail."

"I will supply the funds. Rosalie, get the plan. Rich, find us a builder…just one more question…"

Rich was beaming. "What is that?"

"Is there any way Rosalie's brother could locate the keys to the GTO? I want to have that car picked up and refurbished."

"Why sure, but what made you think to refurbish the GTO?" Rosalie quizzed.

"Yesterday, Rich told me how special that car was to Brett. It's normal for a new mother to bring a child home from the hospital to a room full of toys. Obviously, I didn't get to decorate his bedroom or buy a bunch of toys for Brett, so I would like to do something a little special. This new mom would like to give him back his first love ... that old GTO."

Rich stood up in the excitement of the thought. "Oh Sarah, you have no idea how special that will be to him."

"Oh ... I believe I do!"

⁓

"Mrs. Bretherick, security from the front gate states there is a pastor Mitch from a Baptist Church that would like to visit you. They want to know if you want him sent away?" Myra, a recently hired housekeeper, held the phone away from her mouth as she waited for Sarah's reply.

"No, let him in, please. I would like to see him." It occurred to her that she had never met with the pastor of the church Gerald had attended all these years. The driver always dropped Gerald off and brought him from church. While she doubted and challenged the existence of a loving God, she never once wanted to deny Gerald the joy and anticipation he experienced attending that church every week. This meeting was long overdue. She envisioned Brett making this type of grief call on other suffering families. She was thankful the pastor had come.

The pastor entered the house, wearing blue jeans, running shoes, and a regular work shirt. She had envisioned a dark suit, wing tips, and a pious, full-faced, middle-aged man. He came in the room with a warm smile and gave her a hug.

"Mrs. Bretherick, I just came from the hospital. The nurses confided to me that Gerald passed away last night. I wanted to come over and tell you how sorry I am that we had to let him go. Our church will miss him very much." The pastor remained smiling, but the tears in his eyes hinted of his inner feelings.

Sarah was a bit surprised. "You mean you've been visiting Gerald while he was in the hospital?"

"Normally, I like to visit the members in the hospital around seven a.m. in the morning, before anything else gets in the way of me going to the hospital. Unfortunately, going that early in the morning, I rarely get to meet with any of the family members. I apologize for not calling on you."

The pastor looked a bit sheepish when he said this. Sarah could not imagine why. She had never once attended his church, and he was certainly not obligated to her for anything.

Sarah felt obligated to make the pastor feel at ease. The church was a blessing to Gerald. It was one of the few places in his life that he claimed as his own and felt welcome. She had become so anti-religion and anti-God that it surprised her how thoughtless she had been in regard to Gerald and his church. Had he been a normal child, she would have gladly supported and attended his school or any sports activities. Since it was a church, she exercised tolerance, but never acceptance. She now felt the embarrassment over the years of cold indifference to the only thing her son was part of.

"Pastor, I must apologize to you for never attending with my son or supporting your church in any way. I suppose I will be regretting a lot of missed opportunities now that Gerald is gone."

"Mrs. Bretherick—"

Sarah cut him off. "Just Sarah, please!"

"Sarah, with all due respect, regrets are an extravagant waste of time. Regrets accomplish nothing for the past and cloud the future. Gerald was a happy man. He loved you very much. I suggest we dwell on the good and focus on making tomorrow better."

Sarah appreciated the pastor's blunt assessment. "I agree with you, but that doesn't stop me from wishing I'd done things differently."

"Sarah, if you feel that convicted about past regrets, I suggest you can deal with them today."

Sarah understood the point Mitch was alluding to, but she chose to change the subject. "You knew my son well, didn't you?"

"Yes ma'am."

Sarah had detected a bit of Southern accent before, but the "ma'am" reply was clearly Southern in dialect.

"Where's home, pastor? I detect from your accent. You're not a native of Cleveland. Where were you raised?"

"I was raised in Columbus, Georgia. After graduating from seminary, I felt compelled to come to the church I'm at today."

"Have you ever heard of a pastor by the name of Brett Walker?"

"Who hasn't? I've heard him preach two times, both times at our annual convention. He's one of my favorite preachers. Don't tell me that you know him!"

"Not yet, but in a few days I plan on spending a good deal of time with him."

The pastor's eyes lit up. "I would love to spend some time with that man. There is a lot I would like to ask him." The pastor looked at his watch. "Sarah, can I ask you for a large favor?"

"Of course."

"Ma'am, Gerald has been with our church for years. He has been part of my ministry from my first Sunday at the church. I know that church isn't something you desire, or are even comfortable with, but would you mind if we have a memorial service for Gerald? If you don't want to attend, I understand; but I would like your blessing to have a service for those of us at the church. I didn't want to interfere with any of your own personal plans. You wouldn't have to do a thing."

"Pastor, I'm feeling a little small right now. I wasn't really planning anything. I didn't know who would come to the service if I had one. His social circle consisted of our home and the church. Of course, you may schedule the service. I will be there sitting in the front seat. I only wish I had come before Gerald died." Sarah choked on her words and tried to look away. She truly meant what she had just said. She regretted never attending with him.

Sarah asked the pastor for his business card. "I will have the mortician call your office and arrange a time with you for the service. Would you be kind enough to call and let me know what time you have agreed to?" Sarah appreciated the thought of a memorial service for Gerald. It seemed more meaningful than interring his body without a word of memorial.

Carol walked into the room and immediately recognized the pastor. "Hey, Mitch." They gave each other a hug.

Sarah was surprised. "You two know each other?"

Mitch still had his arm around Carol. "Of course, she and Gerald have sat together in church for years."

"So that's how you knew of my intolerance for church."

Carol was blushing. "Sarah, I've always done my best not to create a barrier between us because of my faith. After my husband died, I couldn't stand sitting alone in church. So, one Sunday it occurred to me that Gerald might like someone to sit with him. I started meeting with Gerald, and we have worshipped together for these past six years. I will miss him every Sunday morning." Carol started to cry. One more time Sarah regretted that her coldness to religion had isolated her from sharing in what could have been very special moments.

"Carol, I'm sorry my judgmental attitude stifled our otherwise wonderful relationship. I just want you to know that I appreciate knowing today that my son had someone to share his church life." Sarah wanted to say, "I will go with you now." She didn't want to be rash in these moments of grief. She needed to be sure of the feelings and new thoughts that were filtering through her mind.

The pastor looked at his watch and grimaced. "Sarah, I really need to get going. There will be a bunch of teenagers at the church in a few minutes. I volunteered to be the adult supervision today."

Sarah grabbed his arm. "What can I do for your church? I would like to do something."

Mitch looked deeply into Sarah's eyes. "Ma'am, I know you have more money than I can imagine, but I really don't want a nickel of it. I would simply like you to come to the service."

She nodded her head.

Mitch opened the door and stopped. "Sarah, I spoke too soon. You said you were going to spend some time with Brett Walker. If there's any way you could talk him into making a trip to Cleveland, it would be a big boost to our church if he would come and speak to us…I don't hold out much hope you can get him…but wow…if you could!"

Carol laughed. "I think you better get ready for Brett Walker to come speak at your church. Sarah has more chance of getting him to come than any mortal in the universe."

⁓

Sitting in the limousine outside the large brick church made the reality of his absence burn again in her soul. She knew that the last three days she had been in denial of Gerald's death. Getting to know Rich and Rosalie and taking phone calls from friends giving their condolences had kept her busy. Emotionally, Gerald's death and informing Ben were major blows to her soul. She had busied herself to avoid thinking and dealing with this new reality. Ben's doctor advised that she tell Ben once and never mention it again. The doctor was sure that Ben could not process the concept of death. However, it wouldn't hurt to tell him one time.

Sarah was surprised by Ben's response. After telling him of Gerald's death, Ben looked mystified. He began crying, saying repeatedly, "My brother died, my brother died." Sarah concluded that Ben had made the connection that he had lost someone very close to him. His brain had made the connection to his brother rather than his son. On subsequent visits with Ben, he never mentioned the death of Gerald or his brother. Ben was now mentally separated from all reality. It had been a long time since he could remember Sarah's name. Most of the time during her visits with him he repeated over and over how hard he and his dad had worked today. Ben recalled memories of his childhood and relived them again in his mind. Sarah envied him in a way. Every day was a new adventure. He had no grudges to remember and nothing from yesterday to be angry about. He was able to resurrect loved ones and see them again. Ben was free of the present and the future because for him, they ceased to exist. The doctor informed Sarah that beyond the walls of his room, Ben would be frightened and unable to function, disoriented by all the activity and people involved in the funeral service. It was agreed that Ben should not attend.

Sarah looked around the interior of the limousine. She lived in such luxury, yet at this desperate moment of her life, she lacked the strength of a family member to lean against. Rich would be compassionate and was certainly trustworthy, but the intimacy could never be that of a mother and child. At this moment she wished she could simply die and be spared the agony of losing both her husband and child. She grasped her purse in her hands, looked upon her aged hands, and thought, "I've nothing left to live for, except one thing. I have a son that might still need me. He is the only remnant of my life that truly means anything to me." All their money could not buy Ben's sanity or redeem Gerald's life.

Sarah hadn't planned to have an elaborate funeral for Gerald. A few quiet moments with her and Carol at the interment was the plan. She couldn't think of anyone that would come to a service out of love and friendship for him. Politicians, business partners, and opportunists would flood the service in order that their faces and causes might gain favor with Sarah. This service hadn't been publicly advertised. She hoped Gerald's memorial service would be one of honoring him and not another subtle opportunity to stand next to Bretherick money.

Carol rolled down the window. Mitch poked his head in the limousine.

"Sarah, let me walk you in."

The pastor took her by the hand and together they walked through the front door of church. Mitch whispered in her ear. "I really appreciate you letting us have this service for Gerald. He was loved for many years in this church. You're a sport for coming!"

She smiled at him. "A sport!" Not once in her life had anyone ever called her a "sport." She liked Mitch. He didn't measure his words with her. No appeal was made for her influence or money. This pastor showed up at her house at her moment of grief in blue jeans. He called her a "sport." She trusted him. Her fears of this service being exploitative faded away. She was sure Mitch would not pander to her or anyone else.

Chapter Eleven

Carol came bounding in Sarah's bedroom with a hot cup of coffee in her hand. "Okay Sarah, it's nine thirty in the morning. Time to get up. I'm not about to let you sleep the rest of your life away in that bed. We've got things to do."

Sarah pulled her head out of the pillow and watched Carol flitting about her bedroom. "Do you know, Carol, that you're the only employee I have that would dare wake me up, especially when I have no inclination to get up?"

"Probably, but you already know that I'm one employee that doesn't need the money, so I'm not really afraid of you. Now get out of this bed before you find out just how reckless I am with my employment."

Sarah threw off the covers and sat on the edge of the bed with her feet dangling. "Carol, you're my best friend. You'll never have to worry about anything. You know that I hope."

"Yep, and I know I have plans for us today. First, we're going to take Rich and Rosalie to the most unique sandwich shop in downtown Cleveland. They serve the best corned beef sandwich in the world. Then we are going to take Rich and Rosalie to the airport for their flight home … and, by the way, I put some money in an envelope to tide them over until the estate paperwork is completed. I called the pilot and told him we will have them at the airport by two p.m. And then, we are going to make some visits concerning a gift that both of us will give in Gerald's memory. We will share the expense."

Sarah was intrigued and appreciative of her initiative. "Which sandwich shop?"

"You've never been there."

"What memorial? You know I can pay for whatever it is…what is it?" Sarah could never accept not knowing all there is to know.

Carol enjoyed watching Sarah trying to squirm the facts from her. She decided to tell her about the memorial. "Did you notice during the service yesterday that they did not play the pipe organ?"

Sarah had noticed and forgot to ask why. "Yes, I did."

"They haven't been able to use the pipe organ for several years. The cost of repairing the organ would cost the church in excess of $125,000. The church has had numerous major expenses, and the pipe organ repair was always set back. I thought, perhaps you and I could find someone and pay to have it refurbished in memory of Gerald."

"That is a great idea. Except, I will pay for it. You don't have to pay anything."

Carol looked hurt. "Sarah, it's not about who pays. I may not be a billionaire, but I am certainly wealthy enough. Thanks to you and Ben!" Carol threw a pillow at Sarah.

Sarah nodded her head in admiration of her friend.

"Today, there will be no limousines, drivers, or personal assistants." Carol insisted on driving her five-year old Honda Accord. Her frugality was well known to everyone familiar with her. The subject of her frugality brought much laughter to her friends. Carol wanted their day to be unobservable to the outside world. She made Sarah wear sunglasses and cover her head to avoid recognition as they traveled around the city. Long-legged Rich sat in the front passenger seat, while Rosalie and Sarah sat in the back.

Carol pulled into a small parking lot and handed the attendant five dollars to park her car. Rich exploded, "*Five dollars* to park a car for lunch!"

Carol was amused by Rich's naivete. She could still envision his large form walking out of the darkness of the barn as he approached their car. "It's the city, Rich. It's just a fact of living in the city."

Rich looked around in amazement. "Imagine that, Rosalie. You buy yourself a little half-acre plot of land. You grab a chair and sit down and charge five bucks for every car that pulls in, no matter how long they stay! I wish farming were that easy."

The line of people waiting to get into the sandwich shop extended forty feet down the sidewalk. Carol had warned them about the wait and the simplicity of the sandwich shop. Rich watched the number of people entering and exiting the shop. "They must serve some kind of sandwich in this place for all these people to be lined up."

Sarah responded, "I've never heard of this place before."

"I heard Rosalie talk about going someplace that was unique to Cleveland. I thought about taking them to the Twenty-Fifth Street Market Place to see all the ethnic foods and to eat bratwurst from one of the vendors, but due to the lack of time, I thought this to be a good choice. This was my husband's favorite place to eat lunch when he was alive. I could always tell when he had lunch here. Mysteriously, he never felt like eating supper. By the way, the only sandwich they serve here is corned beef. I know Sarah loves corned beef, and Rosalie said they were up for anything, so here we are."

In short order, they were in the shop. A line of customers passed quickly by a number of servers cutting mounds of steaming corned beef in slices. They heaped the corned beef generously on fresh baked rye bread, accompanied by a huge pickle on a paper plate. Sarah and Rosalie staked out a small circular table while Rich and Carol brought the sandwiches and drinks. After passing the food around the table, Sarah waited for Carol to bow her head for her usual pre-meal silent prayer. The moment she bowed her head, Rich and Rosalie bowed theirs in unison. Without thinking, Sarah blurted out, "Why don't you just pray out loud?" She surprised herself, but something within her felt left out. She wanted to be a part of them. Rich reached for Rosalie's and Carol's hands simultaneously, and they in turn held their hands out to Sarah to complete their circle of prayer. Rich led the prayer.

They reveled in the meal as they ate. "I cannot eat a bite more." Rich patted his stomach. "That is the biggest and best sandwich I've ever had."

Sarah chimed in, "I can't believe I haven't eaten here before. How could I have lived in Cleveland and never eaten here before?"

"It doesn't fit your persona, Sarah." Carol winked at her as she said it.

"Then there is something dreadfully wrong with my persona."

Carol reached into her purse as the waiter cleared the table, pulled out a squarely wrapped gift and gave it to Sarah. "I've always wanted to give you one of these, but always lacked the courage. I feel comfortable giving you this now." She handed Sarah the beautifully wrapped gift.

Removing the bow and ribbon and carefully removing the tape, Sarah could smell the aroma of leather. She loved the smell. She traced with her forefinger the gold lettering on the cover, Holy Bible. On the corner of the leather cover was embossed "Sarah Bretherick." Sarah turned the cover to read the inscription Carol had written.

Sarah, my dear friend,

In the weeks to come, you will be exposed to the wisdom of this book. Many of us call it the Book of Life. Your son is a teacher and messenger of the God of this book. He will have much to share with you concerning the revelations contained within the pages of this Holy Book. It is my prayer that one day you will know and trust in the Lord. I will continue to pray that one day you will be more than my employer and friend. I pray you will be my "sister in Christ" eternally. Read and have faith in him and he will answer.

All my love,

Carol

Sarah was moved by the inscription. She wanted to believe with the same faith as Carol and her son. However, she could not bring herself to confess to something she had neither felt, seen, touched, nor experienced. She thanked Carol again and embraced her. She verbally committed to read the whole book immediately. Coming from a normal person, the reality of reading a whole book the size of the Bible immediately was not realistic, nor would such a vow be truthful. If a commitment came out of the mouth of Sarah Bretherick, you could count on it. Carol considered her task as good as done. Once Sarah dug in for herself, God would take hold of her heart and soul.

Rich helped each of the ladies with their coats. They bumped and twisted themselves between the tables and chairs in order to make an exit. The shop was still crowded. Rich held the door for the ladies as they walked out.

The outdoor light caused Sarah a moment of blindness as she tried to adjust to the sunlight. Her eyes would not focus. In fact, as she gazed down the busy city street, everything became a massive blur. She dropped her purse and new Bible to the ground. She tried to move towards Rich, but everything went dark.

Sarah smashed face-first into the concrete. Blood splattered the sidewalk. Rich leaned down to pick her up, but a woman in the sandwich shop line yelled out, "I'm a nurse. Don't move her!"

The nurse reached for her wrist to check for a pulse. "Call an ambulance. Now!"

The nurse carefully lifted Sarah's face from the abrasive surface of the concrete. She had a large gash across her forehead and abrasions along her left cheek. The nurse checked her pulse rate.

The owner of the shop came out with a pad and paper. "Please, give me your name."

Carol informed him a name wasn't necessary. He insisted that he needed to contact his insurance company immediately. Carol didn't want the press involved. She wrote her name and phone number down for the store owner to quiet him down.

Sirens could be heard screaming down the street. Sarah

started talking, "What's going on? What happened to me?" She placed her bruised hand on her bloody face. "Oh, this isn't good." She said softly.

The emergency technicians jumped from the ambulance with a stretcher in their hands. Police were now on the scene, making everyone but Carol stand away.

"What's your name?" The technician leaned over her face.

Carol answered, "Sarah Bretherick."

The technician looked up at Carol, "Ma'am, I would like the patient to answer as many of these questions as possible. The questions help us determine what capacities might have been affected."

"Of course." Carol was determined to remain with her.

The technician continued to ask many questions as he hooked her up to an EKG machine and IVs. Sarah responded to each question with clarity and without hesitation.

The second technician spoke into a microphone. "Seventy-eight year old female. No prior health problems. BP is 50 systolic and 30 diastolic. EKG is normal. IV is established. Respiration is normal. Awaiting any further questions or orders before transport?"

The response was immediate, "No further orders or questions. Mercy is waiting. What is your ETA?"

The technician motioned for the other two emergency technicians to move her out. They moved her quickly into the ambulance. Speaking again into the microphone, "Mercy, ETA in twelve minutes."

Sarah spoke to Carol weakly, "Don't forget to bring my Bible." She managed to smile through the crusting blood.

Carol yelled out, "Can you take her to Memorial Hospital? Her primary doctor is there. We'll pay extra for taking her there."

"Sorry ma'am. By law we're required to take the patient to the nearest emergency facility and, in this case, it is Mercy." The technician slammed the back door shut. With siren wailing, the driver quickly accelerated into the busy street. Carol could see them working on Sarah through the back window of the vehicle. She prayed a silent prayer, "Please Lord, take care of her."

Carol looked at Rich and Rosalie, "Let's go to the hospital first. I will call a cab to take you to the airport from there."

Rich grabbed both ladies by the arms to hustle them across the busy street. "We're not going anywhere until we know she's going to be okay."

Carol grabbed for her cell phone and scrolled through the phone numbers in her speed dial, and locating Dr. Game, she pressed send.

~

It didn't take the medical staff at Mercy Hospital long to figure out that the lady arriving in the ambulance was the billionaire Sarah Bretherick. They surrounded her with a team of doctors from every medical discipline. When Sarah mentioned that her family was present, they were brought directly to Sarah, despite the sign warning, "Only one visitor per patient in the emergency room." After all the years she had worked for Sarah, Carol never failed to be amazed at the worship given to people that possessed money and power. When Sarah was taken for tests to another area of the hospital, a specially assigned liaison of the hospital, probably a public relations representative, took them to a private room to wait. Drinks and food were present with every movement. How unlike the treatment she received when her husband spent weeks dying in another hospital. She thought about sitting in her husband's room for hours on end, trying to catch a doctor who was not returning her phone calls. She tried not to resent the medical staff and the liaison for the injustice of their preferential care. To Carol, every life was precious and worthy of their best care, without preference to financial gain. She felt that way in spite of the fact that she loved Sarah. She hoped someone else's care was not being neglected because of this pandering.

The afternoon passed quickly for Carol as she listened to story after story about Brett, Fay, Aaron, and Adam. How unfair she thought, that Sarah and she possessed such extensive personal knowledge of this family, and yet they remained completely oblivious to the bombshell that was about to drop on them. A fifty-four year old mega-ton bomb, a grand deception that would in effect blow their personal lives to smithereens.

Rich started pacing the room. The farmer in him demanded more activity than eating, drinking, and sitting all day. The liaison entered the room. "Dr. Game is going to speak with Sarah now and wondered if you would like to join him."

Rich and Rosalie hesitated. Carol grabbed them by the arm. "You're the closest thing she has for family. I think you should come along."

Carol sat on the edge of Sarah's bed and took her hand. "This isn't how we planned our day, is it?"

Sarah looked washed out as she lay all covered in hospital blankets. "No…no it isn't."

Game came into the room and sat on the other side of the bed. "Sarah, we've discovered a couple of things today. First, the reason you passed out and hit the ground so hard, your blood pressure apparently bottomed out. You've been under some stress, I know. We can control your blood pressure with some medication and close follow-up until we get it stabilized. You look pretty beat up, but you didn't do anything to yourself that a few days of healing won't fix."

Her lawyer instincts were on full alert. "You said you found a couple of things. That didn't sound so bad, but I have this feeling that something bigger and more significant was found."

Game suspected she might know more than she was willing to admit. "Sarah, let me ask you something. Have you noticed yourself being short of breath over the past few months or coughing more than usual?"

"Not that I noticed specifically, but when I do get a little short of breath, I normally attribute it to being old."

"Well today, in the course of trying to figure out what caused you to pass out, we found this." Game held an x-ray up towards the light and pointed to a circular cloud appearance in the area of her left lung. "Sarah, this is a pretty significant tumor. It's not unusual for someone to have this medical condition and never know it. Obviously, you're one of them."

Sarah remained calm. "What now?"

"We need to find out if it is malignant, and if so, if it has metastasized. You have been through enough today. We'll begin testing in the morning. We will do a PET scan to see if there are any hot spots…spread of the cells…a biopsy…and a total body CT scan. By late tomorrow, we should be knowledgeable about what we are dealing with. In a way, you were lucky today. If your blood pressure hadn't bottomed out, this would have gone unnoticed."

Game turned to the nurse, "Dr. Fisherman has signed orders for Mrs. Bretherick to have sleeping medication. Additionally, she is to have only blood pressure medication until the tests are completed."

"Sarah, I don't have privileges at this hospital, but if you have any problems, call me. Dr. Fisherman has committed to sign any order I initiate. I trust him. Because of this agreement, we will not be transferring you to Memorial. They are surprisingly amenable here. I'll see you in the morning."

Carol placed the new Bible under Sarah's hand. "I've always found this book to be a good companion." She noticed for the first time as the Bible lay flat on the bed, Sarah's blood was splattered on the cover. Carol took a moistened towel and dabbed the blood away. Carol bent down and kissed Sarah on the forehead. "I'm gonna pray up a storm for you."

The nurse injected the sleeping medication into Sarah's IV port. Carol's words drifted in her brain. "I'm gonna pray…"

———

The room was dark, but even with the little light available, she could see the figure of a man standing over her. She noticed the blue jeans and denim shirt with a hospital badge clipped at an angle in the middle of his shirt. She looked at her watch. Six forty-five a.m. "You're early by fifteen minutes, Mitch. How are you?"

"Well, one thing's for sure, I'm doing a whole lot better than you. However, my memory is not as good as yours. You must remember my telling you about trying to visit at seven a.m. don't you?"

"Yes, I do."

"Why would you remember that?"

"The reason is so bizarre you wouldn't believe it."

"I'm a preacher, remember? I'm one of those bizarre people that are feared by those who don't go to church. Just by the nature of my calling people think me bizarre."

"Mitch, I don't think you're bizarre. I think you are a very loving and compassionate man. If you're bizarre, every man should be bizarre."

"Thanks for the compliment. Now tell me your bizarre story."

"Do you promise that you will keep what I tell you in confidence?"

"Sarah, preachers practice the Las Vegas Principle."

"And what in the world is the Principle of Vegas?"

"What happens in Vegas stays in Vegas."

Sarah saw the compassion in his eyes. She knew Carol had called him. He was doing his best to be positive and uplifting.

"Do you remember me telling you that I was going to spend some time with Brett Walker in the next few days?"

"I sure do. I've even selfishly prayed you could convince him to come to Cleveland to speak at our church. Realistically, I know there isn't much chance of that, but that's what Christians do. We pray that God will intervene supernaturally to bring about a result that is unnatural and unrealistic in the eyes of mere men."

"Well, your desire for him to come to Cleveland is not as unrealistic as you might think. I'm Brett's biological mother."

"What?" Clearly, Mitch was shocked by the news.

"Mitch, I didn't know that until the last few days of Gerald's life. A DNA test revealed the truth that Gerald could not be my biological son. After an extensive investigation, I discovered that Brett and Gerald had been switched at the hospital when they were born. Rich is Gerald's real blood brother. The reason I was going to see Brett was to tell him."

"I'm so sorry. I'm so sorry. But let me tell you something. You were a great mother to Gerald. And you are the mother of one of the most influential men in the Christian community today. You will be very proud of him! Sarah, you're facing a mountain right now. Carol told me about your tumor, and now I've learned about this. I don't want to pressure you in any way, but you need the Lord now. I hope you don't think the Lord is someone you meet by and by somewhere in the sky. He is Lord over the storms of our lives here and now."

Sarah remembered Carol's last words, "I'm gonna pray up a storm for you."

"Mitch, for the last few days, I've given it a lot of thought. Truthfully, I'm ignorant about Christianity and religion. I've spent a lifetime scoffing it, and pride keeps me from giving into that which I've scorned for a lifetime."

"Truthfully, I don't understand everything about Christianity. I don't understand a thing about how my car operates either, but that doesn't make me shun my car or make me leery to drive it. Christianity and religion are distinctly different. I don't want religion. Religion is man's arrogance teaching how man reaches a Holy God. Religion mandates how we must act, worship, and believe in order to be acceptable to God. Christianity isn't about how man reaches up to God, but how God reached down to man through Christ. In Christ, man was reconciled to a Holy God, something a mere mortal by his own actions could never accomplish."

"Mitch, I was raised a Jew."

Mitch's eyes brightened. "So was Jesus."

"Mitch, are you saying that in spite of my ignorance, my scorn of your faith all these years, and my Jewish heritage, I can be a Christian like Gerald, Carol, and Brett? This is important to me, Mitch! They are all I really care about in this world. The thought of losing them forever is unbearable. I've got a bad feeling about today, but I would never profess to be a Christian out of the fear of the unknown. I would profess Christ only if it is the truth."

Mitch looked her in the eye, "Sarah, Christ is the truth!"

Sarah believed in her heart that Mitch was right and could deny Christ no longer. "What must I do to become a Christian?"

"Sarah, do you believe you are a sinner in need of forgiveness?"

"Yes."

"Are you willing to trust that Christ is the Son of God and by his death, your sins have been reconciled with God, his Father?"

"Yes."

"Well, Sarah, based upon your faith in Christ and your willingness to trust him as Savior, you just became a Christian." He bent down and kissed her on the forehead, and then he whispered a prayer in her ear. When Mitch lifted his head, she grabbed his hand and with closed eyes whispered, "Amen."

As Mitch walked out, a nurse came in with another nurse pushing a hospital bed. "I'm sorry, Mrs. Bretherick. No matter how hard we try this morning, we can't seem to stay on schedule. We're going to take you to the operating room for your biopsy."

Sarah stared at the florescent lights in the ceiling scrolling by as her bed rolled down the corridor toward the operating room. She grinned all the way. "I'm sorry...we can't seem to stay on schedule this morning." The refrain repeated in the theater of her mind. Grinning still, she thought, "Of course not, God had other plans for me this morning." Sarah was at peace.

Dr. Game was gowned and ready in the operating room. He bent over and asked, "Did a nurse give you the sedative already? You look extremely calm." Game was looking at the monitor showing no increase in blood pressure or heart rate.

Sarah focused on the ceiling grid over the operating table. The metal grid surrounding the ceiling tiles was rusting. She wondered how rusting metal could be present directly over an operating table, an area that was supposed to be sterile and spotlessly clean.

She decided to say nothing about the rust on the ceiling and simply answer Game's question. "No, but I don't think I need any either. I'm not really concerned about these tests."

"Do you know what we are going to do to you this morning?"

"Yes and no."

"We are going to do two biopsies right now. The first biopsy is called a fine needle aspiration biopsy. We call it fine needle because a thin needle is used to remove the suspicious tissue we saw on the x-ray yesterday. When we retrieve that tissue, we'll give it to a pathologist to view under a microscope to determine if the tissue contains cancer cells. Also, while we're here and all set up, we'll do a bone marrow biopsy of your breastbone. We are doing this test simply as a matter of expediting the information we would need if cancer cells did show up in the first aspiration we perform. Normally, because of insurance, we would have waited until after the results of the first biopsy, but I assured them that you're not likely to worry about whether insurance pays or not. I hope you don't mind that we go ahead and do it now so we can gather what we're looking for faster and with less hassle to you."

"I agree. Let's get this over as quickly as possible. But what will the two tests will tell you?"

"The fine needle aspiration will tell us if there are cancer cells present in the tumor we saw on the x-ray. The bone marrow biopsy will tell us if there are any signs of cancer in the bone and bone marrow."

"Will there be more tests after this?"

"Last night, I told you that we would do a CT scan, which would take detailed pictures of various areas of your body. However, I'm not too worried about you suing me, so I'll order only one more test. We can do it later today, or I can have you stay over and we can do it tomorrow, depending on the results of these two biopsies."

Sarah didn't have to think about the answer. "I want it all wrapped up today."

"Okay, we will have a PET scan scheduled this afternoon."

"And what will that test tell us?"

"In the event that cancer cells show up on these tests, the PET scan would detect where other malignant tumor cells might be located in your body."

Sarah heard the certainty in Game's voice as he described what he wanted to do. "You already know it's cancer, don't you?"

"Now, Sarah, let's not get pessimistic. Wait until we get our homework done."

"Game, remember me? I'm the lady that likes to be told like it is."

"Sarah, I really can't be definitive until these tests are complete." As he looked into her eyes, he remembered her faithfulness to him the night Gerald died. "Sarah, I saw a pretty significant tumor on that x-ray."

Sarah knew without a doubt what the good doctor was telling her. He specifically noted it was a significant tumor. The tests would tell the story of how much more significant the cancer would be, but they both knew she had cancer.

—

Carol stood outside Sarah's hospital room. She was mesmerized by the sight of Sarah lying in bed reading her brand new Bible. She stood in the brightly lit hallway, listening to the blare of televisions in the surrounding rooms, cafeteria help gathering food trays onto carts, and medical personnel popping in and out of rooms. In the midst of the chaos, Sarah was lying in a darkened room with only a reading light on. She was completely absorbed in her reading. She was a picture of serenity in the midst of a blowing storm. Game had called Carol and requested for her to be at Sarah's room by seven p.m. He would have all the test results by then.

Carol remembered the long waits for test results when her own husband was diagnosed with cancer. She knew that Sarah was not waiting the same amount of time that a normal patient would. Carol was glad for her. She also remembered the moment the doctor told her, "Your husband has cancer." Panic, fear, desperation, and confusion flooded her total being, all in the same moment her mind registered the word "cancer." Carol would have preferred to miss this consultation with the doctor. She could not allow Sarah to be by herself in the event the tumor was malignant.

Carol walked in. "Hey, are you about finished reading the whole book?"

"I'll be surprised if I finish this whole book in a year," Sarah said as she sifted through the pages of her Bible.

"So, what are you reading?" Carol noted that Sarah had not started at the beginning.

"I thought I might start with the New Testament, so I'm reading the Gospel of Matthew."

Carol nodded her head half-heartedly. "Good book."

Sarah saw the absent look on Carol's face, "We're making small talk, aren't we? You're here to be with me while Dr. Game states the obvious."

Carol looked surprised, "No, I'm very interested in your venture of reading the Bible. I bought it for you, remember?" Carol remained standing at the far end of Sarah's bed, her arms folded.

"I know you're interested, but your mind is elsewhere. Remember, I've had a successful career, due in large part to a great ability to read the body language of others."

"So what is my body language telling you?" Carol challenged her.

"It tells me that you are dreading the news we are about to hear."

Carol glanced out the window and started fidgeting with the flowers on the window shelf. "Well, I'm not anticipating bad news."

"Carol, I'm anticipating bad news, and I want you to know I'm fully ready to accept it."

"You won't know that until Dr. Game tells you. First, you can't be absolutely sure you have cancer until they tell you. Second, people don't know how they will feel about being told they have cancer until they personally experience it."

"Do you remember yesterday in the emergency room when all the doctors were in the emergency room office? They were standing in front of my chest x-ray, conversing and pointing at the same thing Game showed us last night."

Carol nodded her head. "No, I never noticed them in there."

"I did. They pointed repeatedly at the x-ray. Then a nurse came out of that office and asked me if I had noticed a shortness of breath, loss of appetite, unusual tiredness, or any chest pain. I said no to all her questions, and she went back in the office and reported what I had just told her. I could see they had a hard time with the answer she reported. Then she came back and asked some more questions about whether I get hoarse or cough up any blood. I could tell by the line of questioning what they were trying to identify based on the seriousness of what they were seeing on my x-ray. They were trying to identify the symptoms of cancer. Remember last night Dr. Game asking some of the same questions again? I suppose he was asking me again to be sure."

"And so you have deduced from that exchange that you definitely have cancer?"

"Yes. And a lot of other things."

Now Carol probed Sarah's body language to determine her reaction to the thought of having cancer. "And are you frightened if Dr. Game confirms your suspicions?"

"Frightened? No! Apprehensive? Absolutely."

"What are you apprehensive about?"

"I suppose how much time I have left to accomplish everything that needs to be done."

Carol could imagine what some of the apprehensions were. She wanted Sarah to voice them. She remembered the relief she felt in those rare times when she shared her concerns with close friends during the months her husband was dying. "Tell me, what things need to be done that are concerning you?"

Sarah was usually closed to sharing her concerns with others. She would make an exception for Carol. "I'm concerned about Ben and what will happen to him. Who will watch over him? I'm concerned about what happens with Brett. I can't bear the thought of meeting him, and then his rejecting me. I'm really concerned about what will happen to Brett when the time comes, and a whole multi-national corporation becomes his responsibility. I'm concerned about how painfully I will die."

Sarah didn't want to minimize Sarah's concerns. "I'm hoping this conversation is all for nothing. In the event your intuition is right, it seems that most of your concerns involve your relationship with Brett. If he is the man I believe you will find, a godly man, he will want to take care of his father. He has a wonderful following among Christians. I refuse to believe he could preach and lead without a truly loving nature. I'm believing that your concerns are covered in God's plan. Speaking of God's plan, aren't you a little concerned about what happens once you die?"

Sarah's eyes gleamed. "Not since Mitch and I prayed this morning. I'm going to the same place as you and the rest of my family."

"Sarah Bretherick, I've prayed almost every day I've worked for you, that one day you would pray to receive Jesus. Please tell me that is what you and Mitch prayed about this morning?"

"It is."

Carol sat down on the bed, scooped Sarah into her arms, and began crying. Sarah started crying with her. Carol whispered in her ear, "Your pastor son would be so proud of his mom."

Dr. Game halted in the middle of the room when he grasped that both of the women were crying. He appeared unsure of how to proceed. "Would you like me to come back in a few minutes?"

Sarah laughed at the thought of this brilliant physician confounded by emotion. She wondered if he were as awkward with his wife. His lack of bedside manner was evident, though Sarah preferred his style to the condescension she received from others.

"Come on in, doctor. We've had enough drama for tonight. Let's get this out in the air. I know I have cancer, so let's fill in all the other details."

Game felt off balance. He didn't know how to affirm her assertion tenderly, so he launched into his presentation. "You're right, Sarah, we did find cancer."

He stopped and waited for her reaction. She was not emotional, but clearly her face took on a business-like expression.

Sarah patted the bed, indicating to Game that he should sit down. "Okay, now that we have put a name to the disease. Let's talk about ramifications. How bad is it? What is it? And all those kind of questions."

"Your cancer is called small cell carcinoma—a type of lung cancer. The tests indicated that your cancer is extensive … meaning the cancer has spread to other parts of your body."

Sarah sat up straighter. "Where, specifically, has the cancer spread in my body?"

"Besides your lung, you have it in your breast bone, indicating that it is in your bone marrow, and you have identifiable spots in your skull and hip."

"How aggressive is this cancer?"

He hesitated, "It is very aggressive."

She knew the answer already, but thought she would allow him to be the doctor. "Are there any worthwhile options I should consider?"

"Sarah, this is not like Gerald's situation. Your cancer has spread far and wide. There is no specific cure for small cell carcinoma. We could buy you more time perhaps, with radiation and chemotherapy."

"Doctor, your heart is not in this recommendation, is it? C'mon, shoot straight with me."

"Sarah, the radiation and chemo might gain you some time, but I'm not sure you would enjoy the time. Aside from a blood pressure problem, at present you're not experiencing any other difficulties. I think you have to make up your mind what you want the next few months to be like."

"You say 'few months.' Can you give me an idea?"

"I'm not God, Sarah. I don't get to fill in the dates when someone will cease living."

"I'm asking in your experience, your very educated experience, what kind of time frame are we talking about?"

"Given my experience with your type of cancer, I am guessing … around six months."

"What will I be feeling in the days to come? I suppose a lot of pain?"

"Actually, I'm surprised you haven't experienced anything by now. I would anticipate weight loss, a cough, hoarseness, maybe coughing up blood, but not the pain you are probably imagining … and let me add, we can manage the pain pretty easily."

"Will I be drugged very heavily?"

"We will medicate you according to the level of the pain you're experiencing when you begin to notice it; however, having said that, I believe you will be fully functional and coherent most of the period we are talking about."

Sarah looked at Carol. "Well, girl, we've got a lot to accomplish and not much time to do it."

Game grabbed Sarah's hand. "Is there anything else I can answer or anything I can do?"

Sarah looked at him slyly. "You wouldn't like to move to Florida to practice medicine for about six months would you?"

"Suppose you tell me what you're up to, and I'll look for a physician down there that I can refer you to."

"Start looking for a doctor in Fort Pierce, Florida, as soon as you can."

"Sarah, you can go home as soon as you want. You can go home now or in the morning. It's your choice."

"I'd like to go home now. Carol is here and I'm ready to sleep in my own bed."

"Okay." Game got up and left the room.

There was silence in the room. Neither one of them knew what to say to the other.

Carol spoke first, "Are you all right?"

"Oh, I know I will have my moments of regret, but it was just a week ago I was lamenting that it was Gerald dying and not me. I'm just trying to grasp the idea that in just a few months, I will be no more. My name and body will be nothing but a memory. My only hope is in the mercy of God to allow me to leave this life in peace."

Another grey day in Cleveland, but it didn't matter to Sarah. The wet logs cracked and hissed in the fireplace, and the flickers of the flame provided the only light in the massive room this midmorning. The newspaper lay on the end stand. She could care less what was going on outside her estate. She consciously listened to the classical music on the radio. As a child, she mocked her father for making her take the piano in order to play the works of the great masters. She regretted her ignorance of music and her intolerance of her father's love for the classics. What, she pondered, is the name of this beautiful composition? *The Fantasia?* She looked about the elegant room and tried not to think of her regrets.

She was not given to sitting idly. It was a habit she harshly condemned in others, yet this morning she had accomplished nothing but sitting, watching the fire, and listening to the splendid music. Thoughts came to her in random strikes. Some thoughts such as selling the estate. A fourteen-thousand-square-foot home for a dying seventy-eight year old woman seemed ludicrous. She no longer entertained or walked the gardens scattered around the hundred and thirty acres that stood walled and gated. She looked about the room and envisioned Ben and Gerald moving about. She knew she lacked the courage and fortitude to sell all that she held precious.

Sarah thought about the multinational corporation she now controlled. Why hadn't they ever thought about what would happen to these corporations, the massive wealth, and all the thousands of stockholders and employees who had trusted them? She considered divesting of everything, but that would take years, far beyond the time horizon of her life.

Mostly, Sarah thought about Brett. If she were like other mothers, she could simply engage him and tell him how much she would love to be part of his life. How much she would like him to share all that she was and had for him. Love was the greatest of all that she possessed.

Sarah knew otherwise. Once she engaged Brett, she knew

she would change his life forever. His birthright would include more than a loving mother. His birthright would include hiding behind closed walls and living in estates to protect those he loved from the sickness of those that would kidnap or hold hostage a billionaire. Her son would no longer have the privilege of being common. Eating in fast food restaurants on a whim or going to the movies in public would rarely be possible for a Bretherick. Brett would be pounced upon by power brokers, the press, and a host of would-be friends that would never love him as the man he was, but the wealth he represented. Sarah felt the weight of these thoughts driving her into a deep depression.

A desire to talk to someone overwhelmed her. Rich and Rosalie were gone. They promised they would keep the fifty-four-year-old crime a secret. She completely trusted them. She planned to visit Ben in the afternoon, but normally she left the hospital more depleted than when she came. Ben would never know and would never care if she ever came again, but Sarah would know and care.

Sarah looked at her watch and thought about the happy moments of her life. "Perhaps I should take a flight on the Gulfstream to New Orleans." She sighed. "This evening I could be sitting at the Caf» du Monde, drinking coffee and eating beignets." The thought of walking around Jackson Square, watching the mimes, viewing the art displayed on sidewalks, and listening to a lone musician playing a sax on a street corner seemed appealing. Eating dinner on a paddle wheeler while traveling up the Mississippi River past the battlefields had its intrigue. She checked her watch and calculated the hour difference between the time zones, and realized there was time to make this happen. It had been at least two years since she had shopped on the Riverwalk. Sparks popped out of the fireplace and were contained by the fire screen. Sarah knew her thought of leaving for New Orleans was no greater threat than one of those sparks. A moment of promise and fury, but a screen of depression would contain the idea until the glimmer was gone and the motivation cold.

The silence was broken as Myra entered the room. "Mrs.

Bretherick ... David Birmingham is on the phone. Do you want to speak with him?"

"Yes, I do!" Sarah took the portable phone from Myra.

"Good morning, David."

"Good morning. I'm calling to give you an update on some of the issues we last spoke about. First of all, the DNA tests were returned from our stealth medical tests of Brett. The results are undeniable. He is unquestionably your son. Also, we took a sample of Aaron's DNA as part of the whole operation. He too is undoubtedly your grandson. Congratulations, you've got boys!"

Sarah giggled. It was the first joy she had experienced since the memorial service. The thought of being a grandmother was exhilarating.

"Another bit of news. Willa Mae Summer's spoke with me. She said that she wanted to share something else with you. I couldn't convince her to tell me what she thought was so important. She will speak only to you."

Sarah could not bear the thought of delving into the dark matters of Willa Mae's evil today or anytime soon. "Tell Willa Mae I'll get back to her when I get the chance." Sarah intended to go to her grave without this conversation.

Birmingham decided to change the subject. "Sean called me a couple of days ago about the GTO at the Walker Farm. Let me say that this is the first time in my law practice I've ever been charged with the responsibility of having a car refurbished, but I have to admit it is the most enjoyable task. We found a well-known car restoration company just outside of New York City. The car is going to look fabulous when it's done. If you want someone to drive it to Florida for delivery, I'm volunteering. No charge!"

"You've got a deal. David, what about our other project, the one in Watkins Glen?" Sarah did not want to use words to describe it.

"Sarah, it is too cold yet for them to pour the concrete in the footers. It may be another month or so before the weather will allow them to set it."

"David, I need that project done as soon as possible. Please stay on it. You've done an excellent job for me. Stay in touch."

Laying the portable phone down on the end table, Sarah recognized the depression was gone. The beauty of the cherry crown molding, the antique furniture, and the valuable paintings took her by surprise. The afternoon sun was glimmering in rays through the windows, momentarily breaking the gloom of an otherwise grey day. "I am a grandmother!" She thought. I am absolutely, without question, a grandmother.

My son is a pastor. The thought stopped her. She remembered all the times she had heard Carol say, "God has a purpose and a plan." Certainly, her son, a pastor himself, would believe that God had a purpose and plan. The thought was comforting. Yes, I am a multinational industrialist. Yes, I am a billionaire. But I'm also a mother—Brett's mother—and if that is all part of God's purpose for my life and his, then I shouldn't have to fear it or control it. I have only to accept my destiny and his. She knew her newfound faith would guide her through the mysteries that lay ahead. Sarah determined to put into practice the principle of faith that was the cornerstone of what a Christian professes. She needed to go to Florida. Brett must know and complete God's purpose and plan for his life, regardless of the ramifications she anticipated. God does have a plan! Sarah didn't understand it, but she was going to trust it.

⁓

Over two weeks had passed since the last time Sarah had been to the Bretherick Tower in downtown Cleveland. Her routine for years included coming to the office by six thirty a.m. and holding a staff meeting at eight thirty a.m. every morning. Most of the staff consisted of attorneys, CPAs and MBAs, each reporting on specific opportunities and liabilities affecting the corporation. All of the staff reporting to her had a large contingent of professionals working for them. They digested reports received from corporate branches all around the world. The Bretherick Corporation possessed a department of political affairs, which engaged in distributing and collecting campaign funds for major politicians who were sympathetic to Brethericks' business plans. Sarah knew the decisions made by the group assembling in the conference room affected everything from nation building to the stock market. These conference meetings determined the policies and trade of world commerce. Today would test the size of the tremors that would eventually be heard around the world.

The staff was quiet this morning. Sarah had received numerous condolences from staff members over the loss of Gerald. Perhaps they were anticipating some shakeup in the status quo after such a devastating loss in her life. She continued to survey the view of the panorama of buildings in downtown Cleveland from the eleventh floor conference room. She knew without a doubt, she was leaving it.

Sean began the meeting while Sarah was still staring out the window. She was the only person allowed to be late or aloof during a staff meeting. Sean would start on time, and he expected everyone present to be there fully prepared.

Sean looked down at his agenda for the morning's meeting. "I'm going to suspend the agenda for a few minutes. Mrs. Bretherick has some directions and information that she wishes to discuss. Sarah?"

Sean looked stern. He never made a joke or smiled unless under duress. However, while discussing her plan for the future with him, he made known his desire to find a replacement for him. He gave her two years' notice. Actually, she was surprised by the two-year horizon. He had hinted previously for an earlier retirement date. Sarah knew the pressure to retire came from Sean's wife. Now he had a date to give her, but retiring was not his dream. He was prolonging. In her heart, she hoped his replacement would be Brett and the grandsons.

"Thank you, Sean. First, I would like to thank all of you for your gracious expressions of condolences. They have encouraged me. I also want to thank Sean and everyone in this room for continuing to run this company with such excellence. I read the last quarter financial statements for the whole Bretherick Corporation this morning, and because of your great management, we attained successes and new targets heretofore never accomplished. Good job!"

Sarah wanted to word the next statements carefully. "Over the next two years, there will be some significant changes in our company. The first of which will begin within the next month. Cleveland has always been the worldwide headquarters for the Bretherick Corporation. That will change temporarily. I want a representative from each of the different departments represented within this room to appoint a staffer, hopefully a willing volunteer, to relocate to Fort Pierce, Florida, for at least a minimum stay of twelve months. It may work out to be a permanent stay, but I want everyone to know, this is minimally a twelve-month stay.

Sarah folded her hands behind her back and walked around the conference table as she spoke. "I will be moving to Fort Pierce. I, or someone I appoint, will manage and coordinate from Florida with this headquarters, managed by Sean."

Sarah noted the expressions change on the faces of the young executives. She saw confusion. "I will need a real-estate attorney to leave immediately to the Fort Pierce area to locate temporary office facilities for thirty employees. We will decide whether to build new offices after a time. I want nothing leaked to the press or anyone outside this room. All negotiations and documents concerning this move will be on a need-to-know basis. Wording such as "relocation" will bring about repercussions that I will leave to your imagination.

I would love to tell you the reasons for these actions, but they are extremely personal and have nothing to do with the Cleveland area or politics. I love Cleveland very much, but I am compelled to leave it for reasons beyond anyone's control. Sean will be passing out assignments as to the budgeting, staffing, and technology required to accomplish this task. I know you can be trusted. Thanks to all of you."

Sean sat silent for a moment, digesting the body language of the staff. He was surprised. They unanimously looked happy.

Sean cleared his throat, "So, any questions?"

In unison they asked, "Where's Fort Pierce?" A voice in the

crowd could be heard, "Who cares, it's in Florida…you know, a place where they have sun and warm weather!" Hand raising and bids of "I'll go" could be heard throughout the room.

Sarah went to her office to call Rich and Rosalie to make travel arrangements for all of them to go to Florida. She would begin the search to find an Alzheimer's facility for Ben in the Fort Pierce area. Sarah hoped that Brett would help her in this transition. The time had come, and all that could be done was done. She wanted to see her son.

Chapter Twelve

Brett enjoyed Thursday afternoons. Friday and Saturday were his days off from the church, and today he had the river on his mind. Mentally he was thinking of all the things he had to get done before he could leave the office. All the weekly responsibilities were done. Now he was thinking of getting ice from the church kitchen to put on the boat, in case Fay wouldn't mind if he slipped out to the river after she had gone to bed. He loved to sit on his boat and fish the river late at night. He thought he might leave early and hook up the boat, just in case Fay didn't have any plans for the evening. It was also a strong hint to Fay what he really wanted to do whenever she came home and the boat was ready to go. "Perhaps," he thought, "I could talk her into buying something for dinner and entice her to eat with me on the boat." Afterward, she wouldn't mind if he fished for the next six hours after dinner. He stopped thinking about the whole idea when he remembered that Fay had been with the grandchildren all day. If she felt like she normally did after those days, she would be tired. But then again, if she was tired, she wouldn't mind if he left a little earlier for the river.

"Brett...Mrs. Popham is at the main desk inquiring if

you would have fifteen minutes to talk with her…what's your pleasure?" Anne smirked as she asked the question with phone in hand. She had been Brett's secretary from the first day he became the church's pastor, seventeen years ago. She knew he would say, "Okay, send her in," but she also knew how much energy Janice Popham could drain from a listener.

So much for leaving early and hooking up the boat. "All right, send her in."

Brett came to the Community Church directly out of seminary. He sent out over four hundred resumes, and Community was the only church that invited him for an interview. At the time, Brett was thirty-seven with a wife and two young children. Prior to going to seminary, he ran his own lucrative civil engineering firm. His background and lack of active church experience was not attractive to the pulpit committees to which he applied. Only one church invited him to interview: Community. Whenever speaking of his call to come to Community, he always attributed his calling and longevity to the fact that "Community was the only church whose standards were so low, I could be their pastor."

Everyone normally laughed when Brett repeated that same refrain. They knew it was his humorous way of maintaining humility. When Brett first arrived, Community was a forty-one year old church, located in the inner city of Fort Pierce, running slightly over a hundred in worship. Community had since relocated to eighty acres off the interstate with over three thousand in attendance. Larger churches from around the nation had tried to lure him away, but he loved the church, and he refused to move away from his grandchildren. Brett loved the life they had found at Community.

Nine full-time assistant pastors served with Brett at Community. It was a rare occasion when anyone could just drop by to see Brett. They were normally channeled to see one of the assistant pastors. Brett made sure there was an exception made for a few members. Those members that were with him during his first five years at Community were entitled to direct access to him. It was his way of thanking them for accepting him when others wouldn't think of calling him as pastor, and also a way of remembering their support as the church changed through the relocation and numerical growth. He knew that he was no longer the shepherd of the flock but the rancher of the herd. The list of the old members was quickly diminishing as each year went by, mostly by death. In some ways, the early years were the best years of his ministry. He knew each member well and felt a part of each family.

Janice Popham's name was on the list of those to be seen. Only three people were aware of the "to be seen list," but those were the three that controlled access to Brett.

Janice walked in, her grey hair puffed up over her head. Brett surmised that she had probably had a permanent this morning, a bad perm at that. She smelled like a perfume factory, and her clothes made just as strong of a statement. The office staff dreaded her coming into the office because it normally took two hours for the perfume odors to be removed by the air conditioning. The odor was so strong it would sting the nose. Andre, the sixty-five year old counselor on Brett's staff, said she was clinically "loony."

Brett had warm feelings for her. When he first arrived from seminary, he and Fay decided to buy a new home already under construction. The home wouldn't be ready for two more months after he arrived at the church, so Fay had taken the kids and spent the summer with Rich and Rosalie while it was being completed. During the time Fay was in New York, he had worked night and day at the church. Janice and her husband had Brett at their home for most of his meals that summer, and Janice insisted on doing his laundry and ironing. Yes, she was loony, but he loved her in spite of it. She had a magnificent heart and could cook a meal with the best of chefs. She would always have access to him.

Janice had an egg timer in her hand. She twisted it a quarter turn and set it on Brett's desk. "Brett, I'm only going to take fifteen minutes of your time. When that bell goes off, I'm going to be done. Harold told me not to come and bother you, but

I've got something on my mind that I just have to talk with you about."

Brent knew she would be there an hour. The egg timer would have no effect on her talking streak. "What's the matter, Janice?"

"I'm going to divorce Harold."

"Divorce Harold!" Brett struggled not to burst out laughing. Janice's face had the pout of a four-year-old whose favorite toy had just been taken away. Tick, tick, tick, tick … the absurd sound of the egg timer resounded in the office.

"Harold doesn't respect me the way he should."

Taking on a pastoral interest, Brett inquired, "Janice, how many years have you and Harold been married?"

"Going on fifty-eight years."

"Why after fifty-eight years are you now angry that he doesn't respect you?"

"Brett, I've known it from the first day we were married. The day we were married, Harold and I went to the motel. I went in and put on the prettiest nightie I had, and you know what Harold did? He invited his buddies over to our room for some beers. Now remember, his drinking days were before he became a Christian. Anyway, I put on my bathrobe and went to bed by myself on my wedding night. Now, I ask you, Brett, is that respect?"

Thankfully, Anne was knocking on the office door. Brett motioned for her to open the door. "Brett, your brother is on line one … said he really needed to talk with you."

Brett swept up the phone and pushed the button for line one, "Hey, big brother, shouldn't you be out in the barn right now? It's almost four forty-five. The cows will be staging a coup if you spend too long on the phone."

Rich hadn't been out in the barn much since returning from Cleveland. His brother-in-law was now running the farm. He didn't want to get into the subject on the phone, "Yeah, I'll get to it after we finish on the phone. I just wanted to catch you before you talked Fay into letting you go to the river tonight."

"When did you develop ESP?"

"Only you would believe it would take ESP to know that you want to go fishing tonight."

Brett looked up and noticed Janice was concentrating on his conversation. "So what's up?"

Rich blurted it out. "Rosalie and I will be down to see you on Sunday morning."

"Hey, big brother, if you had given a tad more notice, I would have taken this Sunday off, and we would have done something special." Brett hesitated. "Heck, soon as I get off the phone, I'll line up someone to preach for me. We'll meet you at the Orlando Airport. What time will you be getting in?"

Rich lacked the ability to be deceptive. "No, no, don't take Sunday off. We're coming in with a couple of ladies who want to hear you preach in person."

"Tell them I've read the sermon. They better come on another Sunday. It's not that good."

"C'mon, Brett, you've never preached a bad sermon in your life. However…if you could take some time off next week to spend with us, it would be appreciated."

"Who are the ladies that are coming with you?" Brett was curious. He couldn't picture any ladies close enough to Rich and Rosalie that they would vacation together.

"You wouldn't know them."

"Okay. I look forward to meeting them." Brett decided to leave the question of the ladies alone. He could sense a reticence in Rich's reply that indicated there was more to be told, but not now.

Brett decided he would change the subject. "I'll tell you what, I'll have Fay pick the four of you up Sunday morning, and I'll just see you guys at church when you get here."

Rich felt cornered again. How could he possibly explain to his brother that they would be arriving at the St. Lucie County airport on a corporate jet? "Brett, these ladies gave us this trip as a gift. It includes airfare, a car, and hotel rooms on the beach for three of us." He calculated that he had covered all the different hospitality options in that somewhat deceptive statement. A thought occurred to Rich. "Would you and Fay mind if one of the ladies stayed with you?"

"Rich, you know I wouldn't mind, but I'm really curious why the two of you would come all the way to Fort Pierce and not stay with us. That really is a mystery. In fact, I don't want to be the one to tell Fay that you guys are coming to town, but not staying with us. Please, either you or Rosalie needs to call her and explain this."

Rich knew his voice was about to give him away; he felt totally uncomfortable not being transparent with Brett. His integrity was on the line with Sarah, and his loyalty to Brett was stretched too far for his comfort. He decided to prevail upon Brett in the same manner Sarah had prevailed upon him. "Brett, we've got some things to talk about when we get down there. You've got to know that Rosalie and I love you and your family as much as is humanly possible. I would never hurt any of you for any reason if I could avoid it. I'm asking you to trust me. Trust me that I would always act in your best interests, and just leave it at that. Can you do that for me? Can you trust me?"

Brett knew this trip had some bad news attached to it. "Rich, if you're in some kind of trouble, Fay and I are leaving tonight to come to you." Janice shifted in her chair, reacting to the urgency in Brett's voice. She was caught up in the flow of the conversation.

"No, now don't start, Brett. You know you're a hundred times smarter than me, and if I stay on this phone much longer, you will work it out of me. I'm asking as a brother, please don't do that."

"All right, I'll quit probing, but I don't mind telling you, for the first time in our lives, you have me a little freaked out. Can I ask if everything is alright between you and Rosalie…and is everything ok with your health?"

"Yes, Brett, everything is great with us."

"I'll tell Fay that we'll have a house guest this next week. I'll try to skip over the fact that you guys will be staying in a hotel. By the way, what is this lady's name?"

Rich panicked. He was unsure if his brother would know

Sarah Bretherick. "Her name is Sarah. Hey, brother, I can hear those cows bellowing from inside the house. I've got to get going."

"Before you go, is there anything Fay can do to make her stay with us more pleasant? You know, any special cereal, coffee? C'mon, Rich, you know, the same things that Rosalie would ask if you had a guest coming to your house."

"I can't think of a thing," Rich paused. "Brett, I can think of one thing…treat her like she was your very own mother. Got to go. Bye."

Brett said, "Good-bye," to himself. A few minutes earlier, the weekend seemed clear with nothing on the horizon but a fishing pole and blue skies. Now, he felt uneasy. He wanted to call Rich back quickly, but hearing the plea in Rich's voice to accept what little was offered made Brett decide to leave him alone. Brett pondered his brother's reticence in being open with him, and he felt himself betrayed without even knowing why. He decided to do as Rich asked, simply trust him. Rich had always been one person in his life he had trusted, so there must be a good reason for all the secrecy. He decided to trust.

Janice stood up. Her egg timer had rung several minutes earlier, but she had remained to hear the whole telephone conversation. "I sure hope that brother of yours isn't planning to divorce his wife. Brett, you need to get on top of it. It's not good all these people getting divorces. I'm going to go home and bake you some pies for your company that's coming. Fay is way too busy with the church and those grandchildren to be doing all that cooking. Tell her I'll be dropping by your house on Saturday with those pies and maybe a couple of casseroles. Tell your brother if he respected his wife more, she probably wouldn't be thinking about divorce."

"Yes, Janice, that's for sure. Thanks for stopping in. I'll tell Fay you'll be stopping over." Brett couldn't help himself. He loved Janice Popham's cooking, and yes, he loved her too. She just needed to know that someone needed her. Perhaps that was her definition of respect, having someone in her life who needed her.

Chapter Thirteen

"We are approximately thirty minutes out from the St. Lucie County Airport," the pilot announced over the Gulfstream's cabin speakers. "It will be a very pleasant seventy-eight degrees upon our arrival."

Sarah took her eyes off Ben and noted the sun glistening off the numerous lakes and rivers scattered below on the Florida terrain. Sometimes the shadow of the Gulfstream would skim over the waters. As they skirted the shoreline, she stood and looked out the window facing east and watched the white-capped waves of the Atlantic. She felt sorry that Ben had to be medicated for the trip. He was sleeping and oblivious to everything that was changing in their lives. Sometimes, she hurt deeply over all the experiences Ben was missing with her, and then there were times she envied him. The Alzheimer's was a perfect Novocain to prevent emotional pain. She gripped her armchair, trying to dispel the stress of thinking about meeting Brett, admitting Ben to a new Alzheimer's unit, and simultaneously struggling with the foreknowledge of her own demise. Perhaps Ben had met a kinder fate, she wondered.

The familiar sound of the landing gear being lowered broke

her chain of thought. She focused with intense interest as the Gulfstream decreased altitude. The river and ocean were separated by a very narrow barrier island for many miles. She could see large boats approaching the inlet that must be the port of Fort Pierce. Rich had told her that Brett spent a lot of time on the water fishing. It was Saturday. She wondered if he might be in one of those boats.

The pilot broke the silence in the cabin. "Just out the window on the west side of the aircraft is I-95, and out the east side is US 1. We now have clearance to land, and we will be on the ground in ten minutes."

Sarah took a nervous breath. At seventy-eight years old, just months before leaving this earth, she was relocating to a town she had never been to in her life. She closed her eyes and prayed, "Lord, be with me. Give me the faith and courage to face the days ahead. Amen!"

As planned, the ambulance and attendants were waiting on the tarmac as the Gulfstream approached the new hanger assigned for the jet. The plane was now assigned to St. Lucie County.

The attendants came aboard, assisted Ben out of the aircraft, placed him on a stretcher, and were gone in moments to the seaside Brookview Facility for Alzheimer's patients. A brand new Lincoln Continental was also in the hanger, with the title made out to Sarah Bretherick lying conveniently on the seat. The keys were in the ignition. A Bretherick employee was also waiting to drive the Lincoln for Sarah. Sean, as usual, had her arrival orchestrated perfectly.

"Mrs. Bretherick, my name is Mabel Snyder. Mr. McCurdy assigned me as your personal assistant until your own arrives."

Carol had stayed behind to fly down to Florida with Rich and Rosalie. They were to arrive in Fort Pierce later in the evening on another one of the corporate jets. Sarah wanted to spend the day getting Ben situated, and she also wanted a few hours to herself to get an advance view of what she would experience tomorrow morning.

The day passed quickly, and Sarah was well pleased with the

Brookview facility. She felt very comfortable that Ben would receive excellent care in his new home.

She dismissed Mabel early. She wanted to be by herself. Remembering the inlet she saw from the plane, she chose that as her destination. Noting the signs pointing to the beach, she turned the Lincoln towards the east. She headed in the direction of a bridge that would take her over the Indian River to the Atlantic Ocean. The highway came to a stop with the choice of entering the inlet parking lot or turning right and driving south on A-1A along the ocean's edge. She chose the parking lot.

The smell of the ocean was immediate as she opened the door. Sarah breathed deeply. Diesel boat engines could be heard growling as they powered up to fight the currents of the tide change that pitted incoming ocean waves against the river water leaving the channel. Gulls flew low along the channel, watching and waiting for inbound boats to throw unused baitfish overboard. Wafting through the air was the occasional smell of fried seafood from nearby restaurants. The color of the water appeared divided directly across the channel from where she stood. She thought the darker side of the water was probably the tannin in the river water flowing out, in contrast to the bluish water of the ocean that was slowly darkening as the mineral-rich river water protruded into it. Fishing poles lined the jetty, stuck into rocks, with entranced fishermen standing by. Their huge coolers were filled with saltwater fish. Sarah surmised that the fishing was good. She wondered why she had never tried fishing. Perhaps her son would take her. The thought brought a return of the stress she desired to alleviate. She remembered then that her son had yet to meet her.

The horizon of the Western sky was bright orange as she turned the Lincoln back towards the mainland to locate her hotel. Rich had informed her that she would stay in this hotel only for tonight. He had made other arrangements for tomorrow night.

She hadn't noticed that she had passed the hotel on the way to the jetty. The hotel had a lovely view of the channel and ocean. She wondered why Rich had only reserved their rooms for one night. Another looming thought blasted through her brain. *I must purchase a permanent home this week,* she thought. Sarah spoke aloud to herself. "I'm too old to be a gypsy."

The view from the fourth floor was stunning. She ordered a seafood platter and carafe of white wine from room service and ate dinner by herself on the balcony. Sitting in the warm air, smelling the salt water, and watching the boats bob in the channel was peaceful.

Her appetite was not as great as she anticipated. The seafood was spectacular, but she was unable to eat more than a few bites. She put the plate back on the tray and placed it in the hall. Returning to the balcony, she saw herself in the mirror. "So, this is what he will see tomorrow," she thought with mixed feelings.

She examined herself closely in the mirror. Her grey hair was perfectly in place. She stood upright and touched the skin of her face. Sarah had never appreciated plastic surgery, but tonight she would have spent a million dollars if some surgeon could remove twenty years from her looks before morning. She continued her gaze. No, she was not young, but her brown eyes were as bright as ever, and she was still trim, even for her seventy-eight years. "Oh Lord, what will he see?"

She went to the closet and began rethinking what she would wear tomorrow. Sarah had already purchased three dresses for the occasion, but still she could not determine which was right. She started laying dresses out on the bed and setting shoes beside them.

A knock at the door halted her activity. She heard Carol's voice on the other side, and a glance through the security viewer confirmed her thought. She opened the door and Carol burst in and gave her a hug. "I love this place, Sarah. It is paradise!"

Rosalie gave Sarah a kiss and a hug while Rich awkwardly put his arm lightly around her shoulders. Sarah punched him in the rib. "C'mon, you big farm boy, you can do better than that!"

Rich scooped his massive arms around her and kissed her on the top of her head. He could feel the tension in her body. He put his head next to hers. "Everything is going to be just fine … trust me!"

Sarah did trust Rich, and the assurance made her feel better. Carol was examining the bed and knew immediately what Sarah was doing.

"So, which outfit did you pick?"

"I can't make up my mind."

"Well, is there any one outfit that you don't like?"

"No, I like all of them."

Coolly, Carol approached the bed, looked over all three outfits and shoes carefully, looked at Rosalie, and pointed to the rose-colored, two-piece suit with a white silk shell. Rosalie nodded her head in agreement. Without asking Sarah, Carol picked up the other two outfits and put them in the closet.

"Aren't you going to ask Rich and me what we think?"

"Sarah, I have chosen outfits for you for all these years and you have never said a word. We're not going to start tonight, are we?"

Rosalie chimed in, "I hope you don't want Rich's opinion on what to wear. If you let him choose, you'll look like a cow heading for the show ring at the county fair."

"Oh no, I'm not going to protest. I'm just a little stressed tonight. No, make that a lot stressed."

Rich spoke up. "Sarah, you're not going to meet a better man than the man you're meeting tomorrow. In fact, I'm ready to put all this worry and fuss to an end right now. Let's just get in the car and go see Brett right now. I'm telling you, everything's going to be fine…okay, maybe a little awkward…but my brother would do nothing to make you uncomfortable. I promise."

"No…as much as I would like to get this over tonight, let's consider Brett. He has to work in the morning, and I'm sure it would affect him in the same way it has affected us."

Rosalie grabbed Rich by the arm. "Sarah, you are right. Why don't we all just go to bed and we'll deal with it tomorrow when it gets here?"

As they were leaving the room, Carol stopped. "By the way, the GTO will be delivered to the hotel tomorrow at noon."

Sarah smiled weakly. She hoped her son would like what she had done to his first love.

Sarah returned to the balcony and covering herself with a blanket, sank deep into the cushions of the lounge chair. She knew she would spend the better part of the night watching the red and green lights of the fishing boats bobbing in the channel. She wished she could try fishing.

⁓

"Brett, it's time to get up. C'mon, Brett, I've let you sleep in too long already!" Fay pulled the covers off him. "You said you wanted to get to the office earlier today."

Brett hated Sunday mornings. Any other morning of the week, especially if he was heading out with the boat, he could be up and gone in fifteen minutes. Sundays were different. Sundays were marathons for Brett. Preaching for three consecutive worship services, the family gathering for lunch, returning to church at four p.m. to prepare, another preaching service at six, and then the meeting with trustees after the final service made him dread the day. Sundays required all the mental and physical energy he possessed. He could barely remember the last Sunday he woke up without a looming sense of dread. Brett was always amused by the younger pastors who envied his position as the pastor of this large church. Inwardly, he envied every pastor who would preach only one service on Sunday, and then enjoy a long lunch with those who attended church afterward. He couldn't place a name to 80 percent of the parishioners that would attend today at Community.

Fay was watching him shave as she stood at the other sink, putting on makeup. "You haven't said much about Rich and Rosalie coming. Normally by now, you would have called him twenty times to plan every moment of their stay. You didn't call once. What's up?" Fay knew Brett had been unsettled since receiving Rich's call.

"Rich wasn't himself on the phone. It seemed as if there was something he really wanted to tell me ... but couldn't." Brett took another stroke with the razor. "It really bothers me that they would come here but stay somewhere else. I mean, I always thought Rich and I were closer than any other brothers I've ever seen, and now he arrives on a Sunday morning, without us picking him up, and traveling with two ladies whom I've never heard of, pleading with me not to ask him any questions. Fay, none of this adds up. He's my brother, and I'm not understanding why he doesn't feel comfortable discussing whatever it is with me. I guess I'm just a little uneasy... though I can't give you a specific reason why."

After thirty-three years of marriage to Brett, Fay knew that when something was bothering him, that it was best to just let him talk it out. He wasn't looking for answers, just someone to share his frustrations with.

Fay smiled in the mirror. "You want something good to think about?"

"Definitely."

"Janice Popham dropped off a full pan of her macaroni and cheese, two blueberry pies, and a new mystery casserole she wanted you to try. Brett, if the woman was younger, I'd be jealous." Fay winked at him. Her trust in Brent was so explicit; jealousy would have been a wasted emotion.

"Now that is good news. You're a good cook, honey, but it never hurts when another good cook adds to the menu."

"Oh no, I'm not adding to the menu, whatever Janice brought is the menu. There's enough food out there to feed the whole church." Fay went over and hugged him, "I love you, and so does your brother. I don't know why your brother is acting so mysterious, but I'll bet everything we own that when he finally gets around to telling you whatever he's done it's because he thinks it is in our best interests. Honey, if we can't believe in Rich and Rosalie, we're in bad shape."

"I know you're right. I just wish, whatever it is, we get to it quickly."

⁓

"Oh Lord, this place looks like a college campus. I've never seen a church that was so huge." Carol sat straight up in the back seat of the Lincoln with the window down, gawking like a tourist going through Amish country.

"Can you believe this? A traffic jam getting into church." Rich was driving the Lincoln. He rolled the window down, allowing the parking attendant to ask if he wanted to "drop the ladies off before parking the car." The attendant held the flow of traffic, allowing Rich to pull the Lincoln into the eleven a.m. traffic lane for drop offs. At the drop off, attendants opened the doors to the Lincoln, allowing the ladies to exit the vehicle.

"Welcome to Community Church," they greeted. "Are you a first-time visitor with us?"

Carol beamed with joy and breezed around the welcome center, picking up every piece of introductory literature concerning every ministry of the church. She went into the bookstore and stood transfixed in the middle of the aisle.

Rosalie stood calmly with her arm around Sarah's arm. Sarah was visually taking in the sight of everything her son had dedicated himself to building. Nothing missed her visual inspection. The spectacular architecture of all the magnificent buildings, the landscaping of exotic trees and brilliant flowers, the entry fountain, and the elegance of the very high and wide entrance with the welcome station built of cherry wood. Brett and Fay's picture was prominently framed in the entryway. Sarah admired her son's features. Fay was truly a beauty.

"The picture doesn't do them justice. They are even more distinguished in person." Rosalie knew what Sarah was thinking.

As they were about to enter the sanctuary, an attendant stopped them. "Would you like to fill out a card for us so that we may have a record of your visit with us today?"

Before Rich could answer, Fay popped through a large group of people and answered, "These aren't visitors, Sue. These folks are our family from out of town." Fay gave Rich a tight hug. Rosalie stood in line to hug Fay. Fay had tears of joy in her eyes when she wrapped her arms around Rosalie. Not even the blindest of men could miss the love between these two women. Sarah wanted to hold Fay, but thought better of it. She would have to be content with just admiring the beauty of this blonde-haired, blue-eyed, fair-skinned lady. Her figure was that of a twenty-year-old's.

Fay caught Sarah staring at her. Fay thought she noticed a tear in her eye, but perhaps not. Putting her arm around Sarah's waist, "I'm Fay…I'm glad you came today."

Regaining her composure, Sarah purposely went beyond her normal comfort zone and placed her arm around Fay's waist, "My name is Sarah, and I can't tell you what a pleasure it is for me to be here this morning." Sarah fought to keep her voice from cracking.

Carol could see the strain Sarah was feeling, stepping forward with her hand extended, "I'm Carol, and I am totally in awe of your church."

The television monitors in the lobby switched from announcements to live viewings of the altar area. The orchestra began with a loud percussive roll of the kettledrum and a strong brassy declaration of trumpets. Fay pointed to the entry into the sanctuary. "Let's get a seat."

Fay led the way as they entered through two large doors that opened into a short tunnel, with two more large doors at the other end that opened into a sea of theater seats. Over three thousand seats arranged in a semicircle around a massive altar. Over two hundred people were seated in the choir loft. The panorama of all the hundreds of people and the power of the music were stunning. Sarah stood in the aisle, taking in every aspect of this wonderful worship center.

Rosalie took her by the arm, guiding her to sit between Fay and herself. Sarah couldn't feel her legs or feet. She was about to see her child in a manner few mothers ever see their child for the first time: in the middle of a group of three thousand people, sitting over a hundred feet away, her son standing center stage, framed in a spotlight, all the while focused in the lens of cameras directing the picture on huge screens at both ends of the stage. God could not have given her son a more pictur-esque entrance into her life than if a Hollywood producer had planned the event.

Sarah noticed the glow of a red light on the center camera. The camera projected the picture of a very distinguished, self-assured, grey-haired man. Sarah looked hard at the screen, as the camera projected his picture on the big screen. "My God, he has a lot of my father's features!" she thought. Her throat was sore from swallowing the flow of tears.

The camera followed the quick-paced pastor to the pul-pit as he looked out over the congregation. His face filled the whole frame of the screen. His brown eyes flashing bright and brilliant white teeth on display, grey hair luminous under the lighting, "Good morning, folks! My name is Brett Walker, and I would like to take this moment to welcome you to Community Church."

Carol choked down her own tears as she tried not to look at Sarah. If she were to look at Sarah this moment, she could not have held back her own emotions.

Fay could see the battle of emotions that Sarah and Carol were experiencing. She looked at Rosalie, but Rosalie was star-ing straight ahead, purposely avoiding looking at anything that was going on. Fay looked at Rich. He had his head bent down as if in prayer, but he wasn't praying. She saw tears.

Fay closed her own eyes and did pray, "Lord, you who know the hearts of men without ever having to hear our words. Please hear the need of their hearts and give them peace. Please!"

⁓

"Nana, Nana, do you know what we did this morning at church?" Seth, the six-year-old, spoke excitedly to Fay, his grandmother. Seth had the Bretherick brown eyes, and one of his front teeth was missing.

Fay played along with her excited grandson as she stroked his brown hair. "No, I couldn't guess."

"We played football." His dirty pants and disheveled shirt affirmed the truth of the statement.

Ava, his blonde-haired and blue-eyed sister came bounding in the house next. The four-year-old blasted into her grandmother and gave her a big hug. "Can I have grits for lunch?"

"No, dear, we have company today, so we're going to have something special for lunch."

Fay decided to have everyone come to the house for lunch. Janice Popham had prepared a king's feast, and Fay knew that it would be excellent.

Aaron and Lynne came through the front door. Rosalie could not contain herself. At the sight of Aaron, she ran to him and smothered him with a hug. Aaron was not shy about returning her affection with his own. He loved Aunt Rosalie and always wished they had lived closer to them.

Rich was not shy about hugging his blonde-haired, blue-eyed, six-foot nephew.

Rich squeezed Aaron harder so as not to appear mushy. "So, boy, are you still tough enough to do a day's worth of farm work?"

"I don't think so, Uncle Rich. I turned thirty last year, and I think I'm going downhill."

Sarah and Carol observed the family exchange embraces from the other side of the living room. Sarah felt terribly left out.

Fay broke into the moment, noticing Sarah and Carol sitting and watching with intense interest. "Aaron and Lynne, let me introduce you to Sarah Bretherick and Carol Thatcher. They are friends of Rich and Rosalie. They've come down with them for a vacation."

Aaron stepped forward and looked directly into Carol's eyes as he shook her hand with a firm grip. "Ms. Thatcher, it is real good to meet you." Carol admired his handsome looks, but she also admired his winning way. She noted a bit of southern drawl and the traditional southern charm. She knew instinctively how proud Sarah must be of Aaron's charisma.

Turning to Sarah and extending his hand. "Ms. Bretherick,

proud to meet you. I guess you know you have a pretty famous name, but I'm assuming you can't be the same person, or you wouldn't be here."

Sarah assessed her grandson as both charming and very bright. "I'm assuming you're talking about one of the founders of the Bretherick Corporation. Do you know anything about her?"

"Just the little I remember from college business classes. Ms. Bretherick was credited as being solely responsible for the booming economy of the nineties, advancing technology in the United States far beyond other nations, by creating whole new industries as well as new areas of employment."

Sarah beamed with delight at the description her grandson had just given concerning her life. "Perhaps one day we will spend some time on that subject. I have some insights that might be interesting to you." Sarah was dying within herself to begin the discussion, but first she had to discover how she would be received into this family.

"Aaron, where is your father? He should be home by now." Fay was putting the hot casseroles on the table.

"I'm sorry, Mom. Four of the infamous trustees cornered him after church. They are threatening and trying to intimidate him. Dad is still in his office, going toe to toe with them. Mr. Wilkes, the bank president, told Dad his bank would remove its offer of lending the church the six million dollars we had approved to build the Life Center. Mr. Hiles told Dad they were going to raise over one hundred thousand dollars in campaign contributions for his opponent. That's all I heard before Dad told them to meet him in his office."

Rich's face turned hard. "Aaron, what do you say you and I go over to that church and do a little intimidation of our own?"

"Don't worry, Uncle Rich. We both know the worst thing you can do is threaten Dad. The more they threaten, the more fixed he'll become."

Sarah felt her motherly instincts taking over. "Who is Mr. Wilkes? And what is your father running for that they are raising so much money to defeat him?"

Fay was surprised by the fire in Sarah's eyes. It was plain to see that those eyes that were tear filled all morning were now blazing with anger. "Mr. Wilkes is the president and one of the major stockholders in one of our local banks. He runs the Republican Party in this county with an iron fist. Brett has taken exception to the exploitation by him and his cronies of this county. So, Brett has decided to run for county commissioner. Brett could win, but the big money men in the county have vowed to defeat him, as Brett would challenge the moneymaking schemes they have gotten away with in our county. I'm afraid they will do their best to run him off from the church too."

Sarah couldn't help herself. The thought of her son being intimidated and threatened by a handful of small-town bullies was infuriating. She blurted out, "Their day of pushing on Brett has just come to an end."

Fay was startled by the firmness of Sarah's declaration. "Believe me, I'm praying day and night over all of this too. It would help if Brett weren't so headstrong. He won't give an inch. I'll be surprised if they don't figure a way to force him out of Community."

It really hadn't occurred to Sarah to pray about Brett's situation. She was thinking more about writing a check to the church for six million dollars; doing a hostile takeover of Mr. Wilkes' bank, and funding Brett's campaign three times more than whatever his opponent raised. She would teach these locals why it isn't smart to attack the lionesses' cub.

Fay decided to get on with the lunch. She wished the trustees had picked another time, other than challenging Brett after completing Sunday morning services, but that was the type of unspiritual monsters these men were. "Let's just complete setting everything out, and Brett will get here as soon as he can."

Rosalie, Lynne, and Carol gathered in the kitchen and took the food out to the porch area overlooking the pool. Sarah took the opportunity to look around Brett's home. The ceilings were ten feet tall, wood trim was used extensively throughout the rooms, and the art and decor were bright. Sarah noticed the hallway walls were covered with family pictures. Fay had carefully documented the growth of the family from its first days. Wedding pictures of Brett and Fay, Aaron and Lynne, and Adam and Michelle were hung in a row. All twelve school years were documented in a circle of pictures of Aaron's and Adam's progression through school, culminating with their graduation picture in the center. Graduation pictures of the boys graduating from high school and Florida State University were proudly displayed. A picture of a young soldier holding a rifle surrounded by other young soldiers hung at the edge. Another picture, this of a young Marine in dress uniform sat framed on the hallway table. A purple heart was draped over the top of the frame.

Each picture pierced Sarah's heart. She was absent from the family photos, the weddings, births, graduation photos. She pictured herself there, but she was not. The pain of the moment was more than she could withstand. She ran out the front door and continued running until she could hide herself behind a citrus tree in the backyard. She sobbed uncontrollably. All the things a mother could have desired in life, celebrating the victories of graduations, marriages, and grandchildren, had passed her by. Until this moment, she had blocked these thoughts out of her mind with the business of growing a multinational corporation. Now she would have traded everything she owned to be part of the picture collage that was hanging on that wall. She heard the sound of a car pulling into the driveway. Sarah wished she could run and hide. She was not ready to face Brett.

Fay had noticed Sarah caressing each of the photos as she inventoried each one on the wall. Sarah's emotions were also evident to Fay. Fay knew that Sarah had been under duress all morning. Rich and Rosalie were far from acting like themselves. She was ready to deal with whatever issue that was causing the underlying stress. She wanted to do it now.

"Hey, guys!" Brett exclaimed as Seth and Ava charged at their grandfather. Brett scooped both his grandchildren into his arms. Rosalie waited until the grandchildren let go of Brett, and then she hugged him with a long embrace. Fay noticed the tears running down her face.

Rich walked over and gave his brother an awkward hug, but there was a look of dread on his face that he was unable to hide.

Taking advantage of the fact that Brett was home, Fay took charge. "Rich, I'm 99 percent sure we should be sitting down and discussing whatever is happening here today. I'm totally in the dark as to anything we might have done, but all morning I couldn't help noticing the tears and melancholy of Rosalie, Carol, Sarah, and even you, Rich. Everything about your being here today feels unnatural. You two are important to us. We love you, and I'm feeling like something is terribly wrong, but I can't even imagine what it could be. Even now, Sarah is outside crying … I'm sure of it."

Brett knew Fay was right. This moment was too awkward for him. His desire was to make light of it, but the look on his brother's face told him that Fay was exactly right. "Okay Rich, whatever it is, let's have it. We'll deal with whatever it is that we have to deal with." Brett wrapped his arm around his brother's back.

Rich had tears coming down his face as he started to talk. "Give me a second." He took a tissue out of his pocket and blew his nose. "Let's sit down."

Carol saw the turmoil each of them was experiencing. "Would you like me to share what has happened?"

"No, Brett is my brother. He deserves to hear it from me." Rich cleared his throat and looked directly into Brett's face.

"I want you to know that after everything I tell you, nothing has changed for me and Rosalie. We're still family, right?"

Brett was more than mystified. He reached for Fay. She had been his rock from the first day he met her at the rehabilitation hospital after Vietnam.

"Brett, a few weeks ago, that lady, Sarah, who is outside crying, lost her fifty-four-year-old son to cancer. Now before her son died, the hospital did some experimental testing that involved DNA. The DNA testing documented the fact that this son she had raised was not her biological son."

Brett looked at the expression on Rosalie's and Carol's face.

He could not determine why they were looking so intensely at him.

"The son she raised had experienced some difficulties during childbirth. The umbilical cord had wrapped around the baby's neck and had deprived his brain of oxygen for a period long enough to cause permanent brain damage."

Fay could not bridge the gap between this unfortunate event and her husband. "So, Rich, why is this connected to you and Brett?"

Rich breathed in heavily. "Because this man was born in Watkins Glen, New York, on January 28, 1951. The head nurse who delivered both babies, our mother's and Sarah's, was the same person: Victoria Walker."

Brett felt no emotion. The name of Victoria Walker brought to mind a living demonstration of the reality of evil in the world.

"Are you saying to me that the lady who is crying outside is my real mother?"

Rich didn't want to admit that he and Brett were not biological brothers, but he found the strength to say it. "Yes."

Fay's face crumpled in agony as she held her husband. She envisioned briefly what would have been stolen from her if Aaron or Adam had been taken from her. "We must go to her Brett. We must go now."

She stood and held her hand out for her husband. She could see the cloud of confusion within Brett. Everything that he thought about himself was in question. What was true?

Together, they walked into the backyard. Sarah was staring into the oak hammock behind Brett's yard. She was trying to compose herself to go back into the house. The sound of movement behind her made her glance back. She could tell by looking into his face, he had been told. Sarah turned away, trying to hide the hurt in her face. She despised herself for the weakness she was demonstrating.

Fay let go of Brett's hand as he walked up behind Sarah. He wanted to say something comforting to her, but he could not process the thoughts to form a coherent sentence. He had comforted thousands of people during his seventeen years as pastor, but now in this critical moment with his own mother, he could not muster the words. He came up to her from behind, took her arms into his hands, and crossed them tightly under her rib cage. He kissed her on top of her head and whispered in her ear, "I hear we have a lot in common."

Sarah's fear flew away. In his arms, she felt safe and secure. She knew now that her son desired her as much as she desired him.

Fay came around front and looked into Sarah's eyes, "Welcome to our home, Mom."

Aaron came alongside and wrapped his father and mother into his arms, surrounding Sarah in the middle. "Then I must be your grandson. I'm the good-looking one."

Fay poked Aaron in the ribs. "Aaron, you're a mess."

Aaron's humor helped break the emotional stress of the moment. Brett let go of Sarah as she turned to look fully into his face. "You know, I must show you pictures of my father. You bear a strong resemblance to him."

Brett was engaged in looking into his mother's face. "Would you do me a favor? I'm no good with names. I know your first name is Sarah, but would you tell me what my last name is supposed to be?"

Sarah treasured the moment. "Bretherick...it's Bretherick."

―――

Rich, Rosalie, and Carol were sitting in the living room, silently considering what they should be doing. Carol thought it best to go outside to support Sarah. Rosalie and Rich then debated if they should return to the hotel to let Brett and Sarah work out the details of discovering each other. They could hear the family coming in the back porch.

Aaron walked in the living room. "C'mon, Uncle Rich, let's chow down. I'm about to starve to death if we don't start eating." Aaron surprised Rosalie, as he picked her up into his arms, "This doesn't change a thing, Auntie. I'm still going to spend vacations on the farm, send my kids up for you to help raise, and I'm still expecting presents for my birthday and Christmas. Got it?"

Rosalie wrapped her arms around her nephew's neck and kissed him on the cheek as she wept. "Oh yeah, I got it." This is the man she helped raise. She should have never doubted his loyalty to her or Rich.

Fay came in with a smile on her face. For the first time during the day, everyone else was smiling. Mostly, Sarah beamed.

Fay asked Carol if she would do a favor for her. "Of course, I will."

Fay handed her a camera, "Would you take a photo of our family? I need to update my wall." Fay placed Sarah between Brett and Aaron with all the rest of the family surrounding her. Everyone in the room was in the picture, from Ava, the youngest, to Sarah the oldest. Fay wrapped her arms around Rosalie and Rich as Carol yelled out to them all, "Cheese!"

As the dinner came to a conclusion, Brett looked over at Sarah. "I've taken the week off. I want to spend time with you. We've got a lot to catch up on. Is there anything in particular that you want to see or do?"

"Just being here with you and your family is quite enough. We have a tremendous amount of sharing to do, but our timing may not be right. I couldn't help hearing about the attack you experienced after church. I would like to help you with this campaign."

"Mom," Brett felt odd calling this strange lady Mom, but he was determined in his heart to honor her. "These men are sharks, and I wouldn't want you within a city block of them. As a matter of fact, they told me today they have lined up our popular senator to endorse my opponent. They have surrounded me for a feeding frenzy."

"Brett, we have a lot to discuss, but let me take a shortcut. I'm a grandmaster at dealing with sharks, and this grandmaster is going to show the world, these locals included, that Brett Bretherick-Walker has just experienced his last feeding frenzy."

Brett didn't know what to say. His mother sounded exactly like she was not only capable of dealing with these sharks, but she even relished the idea of it.

"These boys don't know it now; heck, Brett, you don't even realize it, but an atomic bomb is about to go off in their laps, and they don't have a foggy idea." Rich enjoyed the justice involved in leveling the playing field.

"In that case, I'm dying to know more about my mother. I do have one question I would like to find out now, whatever happened to my father?"

"Your father is at Brookview here in town. I admitted him there yesterday."

Brett took a deep breath. He had made many pastoral visits to Brookview over the years. He knew Brookview specialized in the care of Alzheimer's patients. He was taken aback that his father was checked in yesterday.

"I would like to go see him right now if we could."

"I would like that too, but I must warn you, he will not be able to understand a thing about you. His Alzheimer's is pretty far advanced."

"I understand, but I would still like to visit him."

"I would like to go with you." Fay was not about to let Brett experience anything that would disturb him without her being there. Fay remembered the nights of holding Brett, when in the midst of a nightmare he would wake up in a sweat screaming, "They're coming…they're coming…they're coming!" She was his constant reminder of home and love.

Rich remembered Brett's gift. "Sarah, how about I drive the three of you over to Brookview, so on the way back we can stop at the hotel for the other car?"

Sarah knew exactly what Rich was referring to. "Yes, I think that would be a good plan."

Chapter Fourteen

"Before we go in to see your father, I think there are some realities we must discuss."

Brett could see the serious expression on his mother's face. "I thought we had been dealing with realities from the minute Rich told me I was your son."

"Brett, I wish it were as simple as 'she's your mom' and that was all there was to say. For us, it is nowhere near that simple."

"Mom, what else do I need to know? You're my birth mother, and we are on the verge of meeting my real father, who has Alzheimer's, and I am fully aware of what Alzheimer's is about."

"Listen to her, Brett. I promise you, there are more realities to deal with." Rich glanced back in the mirror to make eye contact with his brother.

"Brett, you and Fay must think very carefully about acknowledging me as your mother in public. If you were to make this fact public, nothing in your life will ever be the same as it is today. Not only for the two of you, but all of your children and grandchildren. I simply want the best for our family. I'm prepared for the fact that no one may ever know you are my son. However, in the event that you wish to acknowledge me, I am also prepared to equip you and protect you to the fullest extent of my resources."

Fay jumped to a conclusion. "Oh my Lord, you're in a witness protection plan?"

Rich and Sarah laughed at the suggestion.

"No, dear. Nothing quite that clandestine, but the consequences aren't much different. Have the two of you ever heard of the Bretherick Corporation?" Sarah leaned over the front seat of the Lincoln to see their faces.

Brett and Fay looked from Sarah's face to each other and said in unison, "Yes."

"Brett, your dad and I own the majority of the Bretherick Corporation. In fact, we own numerous other major corporations all around the world."

Brett was stunned. Fay reached over to take his hand. She could not speak a word.

"Brett, you and your family are my sole living survivors. Everything that I possess will be yours one day. However, those possessions come at a cost. That kind of wealth will demand that you live and work in facilities with tight security. Your home is hardly equipped for the lunatics that would seek to kidnap one of your grandchildren or even one of you. Brett, when you are that wealthy, you must take precautions that are totally unnecessary for you to take today."

"I remember reading once that only Bill Gates is richer than you and Dad." Brett was stunned.

"Oh, I've read the same thing. But the people that publish this nonsense have no idea how much our foreign investments produce, and how many other corporations we own a percentage of; therefore, they never arrive at our precise worth. But I will share this with my family: we are worth a whole lot more than Bill Gates. But please keep that to yourself. I really like Bill and his wife, and they seem to enjoy the attention."

"So, you are offering us the choice not to acknowledge you, in order to maintain our lives just as they are?" Fay felt it necessary to summarize their choice.

"Yes." Sarah felt noble in her gesture of remaining the anonymous mother, but it was not the choice she desired in her heart.

"It's not honest." Fay found her voice. "It's not honest to pretend to be something you are not. God intended that you were to be Brett's mother, and only by an act of evil was that intention changed. Sarah, my whole life has been about raising my family. I have taught them that nothing is more important than trusting the Lord and following his plan for their lives. I have taught them that family is God's highest institution. I have taught them to honor their father and mother, and not to bear false witness. I'll have nothing to do with continuing any deception, regardless of how long it has gone on; nor will I be part of anything to do with Brett's denying his own mother and father. This is simply not the choice a Christian can make. God will make a way for us, and God has allowed you to come back into Brett's life. I choose to trust him, regardless of the changes we must make."

Sarah nodded. "Aaron already connected my last name to the Bretherick Corporation when I met him this afternoon. I didn't admit to being the same Bretherick for obvious reasons. I had more on my mind than admitting to that at the time. I would appreciate you letting me be there when you tell him. I want him to know that it was not his grandmother's choice to deceive him, but the timing was all wrong."

"Mom, don't worry about Aaron. He is one of the most loving and caring individuals you will ever meet." Brett loved his son deeply.

Rich pulled into the parking lot of Brookview. "I'll tell you what. I'm just going to stay in the car while the three of you visit with Ben."

Brett looked into the rearview mirror to look at Rich's face, "Rich, have you met my father?"

Rich sighed, "Yeah, I met him in Cleveland, when Rosalie and I went there ... when Gerald died."

"You mean Gerald, the boy Sarah raised?"

"Brett, we've got a lot to talk about. It was nothing secretive. We were just the first people Sarah discovered in her quest to find you. Trust me; the last three weeks have been as confusing to us as all this is to you now."

"Is there anything else of major consequence that I should be told?" Brett's voice gave way to his exasperation.

Sarah grabbed Brett's arm to lead him into the Brookview lobby. "Yes, a whole lot more, but emotionally I'm not able to deal with anymore today."

Brett could see the weariness on her face. She was doing the best she could. He knew it. "Yeah, me too. Let's try to spread fifty-four years of news over the next couple of days. But I must warn you, my life hasn't any the flair of yours."

"Brett, I've spent over four hundred thousand dollars to find you so quickly. I know more about you than I should, and what you just told me is not the truth. Your life is full of flair!"

Sarah negotiated Brett and Fay through the maze of hallways leading to the Alzheimer's unit. There, an attendant opened the door with a key to allow them to Ben's room.

Brett stood in the doorway, looking for the first time at his father. He looked distinguished, even with the advanced Alzheimer's. The television was on, but his father was not even watching it. Brett stood there several seconds before speaking. "Hey."

Ben turned his attention towards the door and seemed genuinely surprised when looking at Brett. "Hey, Irv. Why didn't you tell me you were coming over?"

Sarah gasped, "Oh my. He thinks you're my dad. When I saw you this morning, that was my first thought too."

"Ben, how you doing?" Brett swallowed hard, trying to mask his emotions.

"Oh, I've been working hard all day. My dad and I have been trying to rearrange the warehouse. My muscles hurt from all that work. How's Annette? I haven't seen her for a couple of weeks."

Brett looked at Sarah, confused. Sarah spoke up, "Annette's fine. She's just been visiting some friends in Cleveland."

Ben stared at Sarah, "Who are you?"

"I'm Sarah, your wife."

Ben turned to Brett. "Do you hear that, Irv? This lady thinks she's your daughter!"

Nobody said anything as Rich pulled the car out of Brookview's parking lot. Sarah was right. Emotionally they had all experienced more today than a mind should have to comprehend.

In a short time, they arrived at the hotel. Rich turned to Sarah. "I'm going to take your stuff over to Brett's house. Mabel packed it up and loaded it all in my rental car."

"I don't want to impose on Brett and Fay. I can stay here."

Immediately Brett and Fay understood why Rich and Rosalie were not staying with them, but the lady friend was. "No, Mom. You're staying with us. We need the time to get to know each other. Obviously, Rich had this planned a week ago when he called me, and knowing what I know now, it's a pretty good plan. Listen to me, you're coming home."

Sarah appreciated the voice of authority her son took with her. It was truly the voice of a son looking out for his mother. "I will, under one condition. I have a present for you that I want you to take with us tonight. Agreed?"

Brett smiled. "You have me at a tremendous disadvantage. I haven't a thing to give you."

Wrapping her arm around Fay, Sarah smiled. "You gave me the best gift I've ever been given, acceptance; and most of all, a beautiful daughter and grandchildren and even great-grandchildren. Brett, this has been a wonderful day. Please, I'm very excited about what you are about to get. Let's go find it. I haven't seen it yet myself."

Rich was already walking around the parking lot, looking for the GTO. Brett looked at Rich. "What in the world is wrong with my brother, running around this parking lot like a rabbit chased by a dog?"

With a mischievous look in her eye, Sarah challenged Brett, "Why don't you start running down the other end of this parking lot until you see something that might catch your eye? I have a feeling you might know what you're looking for once you see it."

Brett took her challenge and began darting through the

parking lot, looking for whatever it was that Sarah thought he would recognize. He couldn't imagine a thing, but he was willing to play along.

Brett stopped at the very end of the parking lot. He stood like a mannequin in a store window for a few seconds.

Fay grabbed Sarah's arm and tugged at it. "Sarah, he's stunned. What is he looking at?"

"He's looking at his GTO. I had it completely refurbished."

"Sarah, how did you know how much that car meant to him? You have hit the jackpot of all gifts. Oh, I know how much this will mean to him."

Fay started running towards Brett. Brett still looked confused. Fay yelled to him, "Well, what are you waiting for?"

Rich started running toward Brett too. The excitement on his face verified the possibility that Brett was processing in his mind. "This is my old GTO, isn't it?"

Rich couldn't contain himself. He was jumping up and down like a child on Christmas morning, waiting to open his big gift. "How does it look? How does it look?"

"It looks fantastic! It looks better than I remember it ever being!" He looked down the parking lot and saw his mother walking toward him under the lights of the parking lot. He started walking toward her. Her face was beaming with joy as he picked her up and kissed her. Sarah would have spent millions for this moment.

"What are you so excited about? You haven't even checked it out!"

"C'mon, that car looks brand new. Please tell me, how did you know how special that car is to me? What made you think to fix it up for me?"

"Rich gave us a tour of the farm where you grew up. I was attracted to this car like a magnet, even though it was covered by a canvas. Rich told me some of the special moments you had with this car, and I couldn't help myself. I was deprived of giving you baby gifts, little cars when you were a boy, and even your first car. I thought I'd try to make up some lost time by refurbishing your old GTO."

Brett opened the driver's door and sat behind the wheel. Sitting there, thoughts flooded his mind of his dad and him working late hours to keep it running, as well as memories of Ronnie spending wild nights with him before being shipped off to Vietnam and dying on the battlefield. He was filled with bittersweet thoughts as he laid his head on the steering wheel, attempting to fight back the tears.

Rich reached his big hand into the car and rubbed Brett's hair. "You're thinking about Dad and Ronnie, aren't you?"

"Yeah, I was."

"It's okay, Brett. Every one of them is rejoicing with you right now. Believe me. I know Dad and Ronnie are jumping up and down like I just did. You deserve this, brother. You really deserve this."

Sarah stood behind the GTO, allowing Brett his moment of discovery. Fay approached and stood with her. "You sure know how to give a gift, Mom. It will take Brett weeks to get over this one."

"Well, I hope it doesn't take weeks. I have a few more gifts that I have to get delivered in the next few weeks. I have your gift starting underway next week."

"Please tell me! I'm no good at waiting for a surprise."

Sarah examined Fay's face in the light of the parking lot. "Do you remember the place Brett proposed to you?"

"Of course, it was on Rich and Rosalie's farm. A secluded spot next to a stream. How in the world did you know that?"

"The same day that Rich gave us the tour of the farm; I saw the GTO and the meditation place. He told us that one day the two of you would like to build a cabin there. Rich said you had a house plan picked out and stored away."

Fay's expression changed. "Rosalie called over two weeks ago asking me for that plan."

Sarah nodded. "Being richer than Bill Gates has its benefits. I'm happy for the both of you. I hope it is everything you dreamed it would be."

Fay squeezed her mother-in-law. "You know…we would love you, if you didn't buy us a thing."

"I now know that's true, but I've had a lifetime of hoarding. I'm going to spend the last days of my life lavishing those I love with whatever strikes my fancy. So watch out!"

Fay rubbed the fender of the GTO with her fingers. "Brett, I think you and your mom ought to take this car for a drive."

"C'mon Fay, you can ride with me back to the house." Rich opened the door for Fay to get in.

Fay turned toward Brett, "Take your time, honey. You deserve a good drive." She gave him a kiss.

"Mom, would you mind if I put the roof down?"

"Brett, I would be disappointed if you didn't."

Brett hesitated before turning the key in the ignition. "Mom, I almost don't want to take you with me in this car. It seems that anyone who ever spent any amount of time with me in this car is dead. My dad, a guy you wouldn't know ..."

"You're talking about Ronnie, aren't you?"

"Is there anything you don't know?"

"I've spent hundreds of thousands of dollars and the last three weeks trying to find you, Brett. Everything I found was important to me. I want to know everything about you. But I do know this. I don't have that much longer to live, and when I go, don't associate my death with this car. My cancer was diagnosed before I got into this car."

"You're dying?" The joy in Brett's face disappeared.

"Yes, Brett, I am. I'm too mentally exhausted to talk about it tonight, but I also don't want to hide a thing from you. Time is too precious to me now. So how about a ride?"

His mother amazed him. He kissed her on the cheek and pulled her next to him. "Mom, we've got a lot to learn about each other, but you need to know that from now on, I'm going to be beside you and my father until the very end."

Brett turned the ignition. The GTO fired to life. Sarah pulled the passenger's visor down to look into the mirror to adjust her hair for the ride in the open air. She looked into her own eyes and thought, *Yes, and the lioness will protect her cub with everything she possesses.*

Chapter Fifteen

"Mom, wake up. It's nine-thirty in the morning, and we still have fifty-four years to make up." The thought of his newly revealed mother dying of cancer had kept Brett from sleeping much during the night. Driving the GTO until midnight had also stimulated his adrenaline significantly. He was ready to wake Sarah up at six thirty, but Fay made him be quiet.

Sarah appreciated her son's enthusiasm. She too wanted to spend as much time with him as she could. "I'll be right out! Is the coffee made?"

"I'm pouring your cup right now."

Sarah wasted no time. Looking in the mirror, she brushed her hair and put on her bathrobe. Fay was sitting at the table on the back porch, writing on a yellow pad. Brett was pouring coffee and preparing bagels in the toaster.

"What can I make you for breakfast? I'm a magician in the kitchen, as long as it is just breakfast stuff." Brett looked comfortable moving around the kitchen.

"It looks like you have already made anything that I would normally have for breakfast." Sarah gave him a kiss and walked out to the porch area with the coffee in her hand. Setting the coffee down, she gave Fay a kiss on the cheek. "It is a dream come true to wake up in this home and to be welcomed by the both of you."

Fay smiled warmly. "Mom, I'm glad you found us."

Sarah couldn't help notice the numbered items on Fay's yellow pad. "Fay, you have my curiosity aroused. What are you listing in such detail?"

"All the things that I want to be sure we accomplish together with you."

Making lists and checking every item had been a regular part of Sarah's life. Only lately, due to the craziness of all her circumstances, had she abandoned this practice. For over a month, she had learned to make decisions by improvising on a minute-by-minute basis. Fay's planning made Sarah feel secure again. Perhaps the chaos of the last few weeks would come to an end.

"It appears your first priority is to meet Adam and Michelle. I couldn't agree more." Sarah could tell by looking at the list, that family and their church was what Fay wanted most to share with her. "I'm ready to see Adam any time you're ready."

Fay removed her reading glasses. "Mom, is there any schedule you have that we have to keep in mind before I call the airlines? Adam and Michelle have already used their vacation time, so we'll have to go out to Seattle to see them. I don't want to make arrangements to go out there without first checking on what you have planned."

Sarah sipped her coffee. "Fay, I'm sure Brett told you that I've been diagnosed with terminal cancer. My plan for the last few months of my life is to be as much a part of your lives as the two of you can spare. I don't want to wear out my welcome, but you both are my priority now."

"Mom, all day yesterday I kept thinking how I would feel if I discovered that someone had kept me from raising Aaron or Adam. I would do anything to become part of their lives ..." Fay paused. "Then how about this. Let's see if Adam and Michelle can clear this next weekend for us, and I will call the airlines to get us reservations to leave this Thursday and return next Tuesday."

It had been years since Sarah had flown a commercial airline. She was beginning to see the adjustments this family would face in the days to come. "Fay, remember yesterday, when I was telling you all the changes you would experience simply by virtue of being a part of the Bretherick family?"

"Yes." Fay acknowledged the discussion, but seemed confused at the connection of being part of the Bretherick family and making plane reservations.

"We can go to Seattle, or anywhere else you want to go, anytime you want to leave or come home. We own our own jet, and that jet is sitting at the St. Lucie Airport, ready to go anywhere we desire."

Brett sat his coffee down on the table. "You have a jet here! How big is this jet?"

"Oh, big enough that I think we should ask Aaron to bring his family with us so all of us can be together at the same time."

The excitement of having the whole family together in Seattle overwhelmed Fay. "Oh Lord, that would be wonderful! Brett, can Aaron get the time off to go to Seattle with us?"

"Honey, I could give him the time off, but since he has used his vacation time too, well...it just wouldn't be paid time off, but I suppose we could help them out with lost pay. This is pretty extraordinary."

Fay didn't hesitate. "Then do it. Call Aaron. We need to tell him the rest of what is happening. Oh, the grandchildren are going to be so excited to see Uncle Adam and Aunt Michelle."

"Before you call Aaron, the both of you better hear the rest of what I have to tell you." Sarah was braced again to awaken Brett and Fay to a new reality. "Aaron and Adam will never have to worry about money ever again. I've established a brokerage account for both of them. The accounts will be fully activated when they fill out their portion of the forms. Each account has ten million dollars already. Further, both of the boys will each receive a sum of twenty-five thousand dollars a month, plus whatever benefits the Bretherick Corporation makes available to its executives. Therefore, if Aaron wants to work for the church for free, that is his option, but worrying about taking time off because he will not get paid for it is simply not my grandson's concern anymore. Brett, your situation is different. Your father, yourself, and I are majority owners of the Bretherick Corporation. As of today, you have one hundred million dollars in a brokerage account. I forged your name and used your social security number. You are compensated at the rate of seventy-thousand dollars a day, and you are already on the company benefit plan as of today. Therefore, if it is your desire, from now on you can work for your church totally for free or not. It is your business what you want to do. You do not have to work for Bretherick at all to receive what I have established for you."

Sarah evaluated Brett and Fay's faces. "Brett, upon my death, you will be the sole majority owner of Bretherick. I will make you guardian of your father; therefore, you will control his interests. Over the next few months, you have the option to sell all of our assets, both corporate or private, or you can maintain them as they are today. Again, the choice is totally yours."

Sarah hesitated. "Most kids get to grow into such circumstances, but you are being thrown into them. I'm sorry, but both of us know this wasn't a choice that either of us was given."

Words were difficult for all of them. Clearly, the realities of Sarah's world were not the realities of Brett and Fay's. She had never known financial hardship. They had always been comfortable but careful with their finances. Sarah's bequeath to them was more than they could fathom.

Brett broke the silence. "Mom, I don't know what to say. You have given all of us so much, and honestly, we are not deserving of what you're giving us. We haven't done anything for you that we would benefit so greatly." Brett's voice indicated the stress of the moment.

"Brett and Fay, let me ask you a question. Have you ever helped your kids financially? You know, college, buying a car, house payment, whatever? Have you?"

"Of course, we have." Brett saw the same intensity in his mother's eyes that he had witnessed in Fay's eyes when she was communicating with the boys.

"Can you tell me specifically what they did to deserve your

financial help? Did they turn in time cards, did they do piece work, or did you just pay them by the project?"

Brett was surprised by Sarah's rapid-fire questioning. "Mom, you sound like a lawyer."

"I am, Brett. I am…but you still haven't answered my question."

"Mom, you know the answer to what you're asking, and I'm getting the point. We didn't support them because we had a working agreement. We gave what we could because we loved them and wanted them to have what they needed." Her argument was now clear to Brett.

"This family is the only reason I can look forward to today and tomorrow. Our relationship lacks the years of development that other mothers have enjoyed, but that does not negate the fact that despite our years of separation. You are my son, and I am your children's grandmother. I am claiming only what is entitled to me, and I am giving to you only a portion of what I am capable of giving you. Son, money is a tool. It is not a substitute for living with someone and developing vital relationships with others. I believe that one day, in your hands, this great wealth will be used to bless many people. You are a godly man. I feel so blessed that God gave me a son who will honor his father's and mother's legacy."

Brett took a deep breath and exhaled. "It's hard to accept that you are paying me more money every two days than I will make at the church working the whole year."

Sarah winked at him. "Brett, I told you being a Bretherick would be difficult. Now, let me change the subject a little. Let me help you make these adjustments in your life. I don't want you to give up what you love. I want to give you options that most people never have available to them."

Fay was intrigued. "Such as?"

"Such as Brett running for county commissioner. I overheard the fact that Mr. Wilkes, one of your church trustees, was pressuring you not to run for office. He was reneging on a six-million dollar loan to the church and pressuring you by backing your opponent with significant financial support, and further, obtaining political endorsements from high-ranking politicians here in Florida. Brett, you now have the tools to deal with this tyrant."

"Mom, the real truth is this: I have no interest in running for this office. I'm only doing this because Aaron said he was going to run if I didn't. Mom, I would have had a hard time raising that much money to run against these guys. Wilkes and that bunch would have made his life miserable. Anyone that has ever challenged them has been buried in the press—politically and personally. These men are sharks, but Aaron wouldn't back down to them. So I told Aaron to sit it out, and I would take them on in this election. I was sure I could muster more votes than Aaron because of my work in the community. But in the end, I'm pretty sure I would have been beaten. I do agree with Aaron that these men have to be stopped. I just wish it wasn't me."

"So, what I think I'm hearing is that Aaron is the one that should be running for office."

"Honestly, yes." This was the first time Brett had admitted this to anyone other than Fay and Aaron.

Sarah could feel new energy coursing through her body. "Son, get Aaron on the phone. We need to get a lot of things lined up before we head out to Seattle on Thursday. I'm going to get him some high-ranking endorsements. We're going to raise a campaign fund that would sink the *Titanic*. Best of all, we're going to deal with Mr. Wilkes and company once and for all. Are you up for it?"

Brett was astounded. "Mom, you're one of a kind. I can see this campaign bringing out the fighter in you."

"Brett, this is the first battle I've ever had that involves my family directly. Those guys have no idea who they are messing with when it involves my son and grandson."

Fay frowned. "Are you two sure that these people won't hurt Aaron? They have destroyed peoples' lives in this town. They will assassinate his character in the newspaper and even cause him legal problems if they can. Sarah, I was afraid of these people when Brett was going to challenge them, but Brett could handle whatever they threw at him. I'm not so sure Aaron will be able to handle any of this nonsense."

Sarah hugged Fay. "Aaron is a good man. Nothing will happen to him, I promise. He will rise up like one of those prophets in the Old Testament and change this town. Don't worry Fay. I'm going to have Mr. Wilkes declawed by tomorrow afternoon."

"Mom, what are you going to do?" Brett was unsure of what "declawed" meant in his mother's vernacular. He was quickly learning to take her literally. She seemed capable of pulling off whatever she desired.

"Son, we are going to take over his bank and fire him! Now call Aaron and tell him to meet us at…" Sarah ran into the kitchen and pulled a notebook out of her purse and filed through it. "Meet us at 2550 Second Avenue at eleven a.m."

"What is 2550 Second Avenue? Why are we going there?" Brett was unfamiliar with this place.

"Oh, I haven't had the chance to tell you. That is the new local extension of the Bretherick Corporate offices."

"Mom, I don't recall ever hearing of that office being here before. When did it open?"

"Today!"

Fay gave Brett a bewildered look. "Is there ever going to be a moment with your mother that she doesn't confuse and amaze us?"

Sarah beamed at the statement. "I hope not, kids. I certainly hope not."

Chapter Sixteen

Fay crossed her arms around her purse as she stood in the lobby. The Bretherick office lacked any official sign on the outside; but clearly, there was no mistaking Bretherick ownership on the inside. The corporate logo was front and center, located directly over the main reception desk. The carpet surrounding the reception desk contained the corporate logo. The front doors to the main lobby were made of cherry wood and stood ten feet high. The main lobby floor was a highly polished marble. A directory in the lobby listed offices for the six-story building, most of which were void of names. "Corporate Officers" was written across the sixth floor identification.

Sarah traced her finger vertically up the marquee and stopped when she came to the sixth floor. "This would be where our offices are. Let me make someone aware that we are here." Sarah had started to enter the first floor hallway when a woman she didn't recognize halted in mid step. The stranger blurted out in surprise for all to hear, "Mrs. Bretherick!"

Brett and Fay noted an immediate change in the environment. Sarah looked at the shocked employee for a second. "Yes,

I am. Do you know who Sean put in charge of the office down here?"

"Yes. That would be Mr. Kelly. He has the office at the end of this hallway. May I announce that you are here?" The young executive clutched the papers she had been carrying in her hand.

"No, we can do that ourselves. Thank you." Sarah loved the element of surprise. She motioned for Brett and Fay to follow her.

Mark Kelly was an up and comer in the Cleveland office. Sean had shown much confidence in him. Frankly, Sarah was surprised he was here. In the past, he appeared a vital part of Sean's immediate management team. She felt comfortable with Sean's judgment in employees.

Sitting in the middle of a conference table, with blueprints laid out, Mark was surrounded by numerous people. Mark looked up and instantly recognized the intruders. "Mrs. Bretherick! I was wondering when we might hear from you. I'm just going over some details with these folks concerning this building, but I will take care of you immediately. Excuse me, gentlemen."

"Actually, why don't you finish your meeting with these folks? I'm assuming that the sixth floor is for me and my family." Sarah wasn't using a questioning tone of voice. She was stating fact in a polite questioning format. "Are the phones and office equipment in place right now?"

Mark seemed on top of everything. "The phones are hooked up; however, I'm going to make several changes. We need more dedicated lines and updated security. I think I can accomplish everything I need to with these folks in about fifteen minutes. I would really appreciate some time to go over things of concern to Sean as soon as you are available."

"I have issues to discuss also, so why don't you come up as soon as you finish here?"

"Would you like me to have someone take you up to the family complex—I mean the sixth floor?" Mark accidentally repeated the staff nickname for the sixth floor.

"That would be nice. Mark, I wouldn't want that description put on the marquee for security reasons, but I like the title of the sixth floor." She smiled as she turned to walk towards the private elevators. Mark's secretary came running up the hall to join them.

"Mrs. Bretherick, it's a real privilege to be here and to meet you personally. I have worked with your company as Mark's secretary for over fourteen years. It's good to meet you at last. My name is Edna Blackwell."

"Edna, it is good to meet you. This is exciting isn't it, opening a new office? I have had the same office for almost fifty years. It's about time for a change, don't you think?" Sarah turned to introduce Edna to her son but thought better of it. She knew the speed of office gossip and decided not to release the information in this manner.

The elevator opened to the sixth floor. The original oak flooring glistened under the beautiful lighting that hung from the fifteen-foot ceilings. All the office doors were opened, and new office furniture filled each room.

Sarah turned to Fay and Brett. "Pick out whatever office each of you would like. According to the blueprint I looked at, the three offices on that end overlook the river and ocean. The other offices offer a panoramic view of downtown Fort Pierce. I have made space for every member of our family, including," Sarah started walking down the hall, "ah, yes, here it is. A room for the great-grandchildren." The room contained a theater-sized television and numerous toys. "The room is soundproof, so they can make as much noise as they want."

Dazzled by the precise planning, Fay looked around, thinking that she heard Sarah talking like she had an office too. "You didn't make office space for me too, did you?"

"I certainly did. One of the great joys of my life was having Ben next door to me. Fay, you don't have to ever use this office, but if you just want to come up here and sleep, it is all yours."

Secretly, Fay had always desired to work with Brett, but church politics being what they were, she never mentioned it to anyone. "Thank you, Sarah. I haven't worked in years, but I have always wanted to work with Brett."

Brett walked to the end of the hall. "Mom, I'm not sure I

will need an office. I mean, I'm not sure what I want to do about the job I currently have."

"Brett, you can go right on preaching if you want. I'm very proud of you either way, but neither of your lives is simple any more. Your income and expenditures have just increased exponentially. I'm thinking that your kitchen table and your office at the church will not be the place where you will want to deal with millions of dollars and the people who will be approaching you. This office is a place to isolate the business away from your everyday lives, which will not be so everyday from now on."

Fay looked out the window of the front corner office. "I think you're right, Mom. I'm beginning to understand our lives will change in ways we cannot comprehend. Be patient with us. We probably appear pretty backward at this moment, but I think this: since we are the oldest in this family, why don't we take the front offices facing the ocean and river?"

Sarah nodded in agreement. "Why don't we put Brett in the middle office between us, so he is surrounded by the two women in his life?"

Fay took Brett by the arm and guided him into the center office. "Agreed. Brett, this is your new office."

Mark Kelly came into the office behind them. "I'm sorry Mr. and Mrs. Walker, for not introducing myself downstairs, but other than me, I am unaware of anyone else Sean has informed of your relationship to Mrs. Bretherick. I was just trying to be very cautious. I apologize for any appearance of rudeness."

"Please call me Brett. Trust me; it never occurred to me that you were being rude. In fact, we walked in on you while you were busy." Brett never appreciated those who just popped into his office when he was preoccupied with something.

"Mrs. Bretherick, can we go to the conference room so we can speak?" Mark motioned toward the conference room.

Mark and Sarah began walking down the hallway when Sarah stopped and turned around. "C'mon you two, we're in this together now. We've got a meeting. Let's go!"

Mark opened the door to the massive conference room. The smells of new paint and carpet pervaded the air. The new conference table gleamed under the light of the chandelier. "Mrs.

Bretherick, would you mind if I had Sean patched through on the intercom before I start discussing matters with you?"

"Please, get him on the intercom." Sarah answered, and then addressed Brett and Fay. "Sean is an old friend and partner of Ben and mine. He is the most detailed and exacting man I know. You can trust him."

"Sarah, how are you?" Sean's voice was as clear as if he were in the room with them.

"I'm better than fine, Sean, I'm great."

"How are you doing physically, lady? I'm concerned about you."

"Sean, I'm so old now, I can't tell if the ache and pain is from old age or the cancer."

"Well," Sean hesitated, "since you mentioned the cancer, if you can be free tomorrow at nine a.m., we will have your new local doctor scheduled to pay you a visit at your office."

Sarah's head dropped. She did not like discussing her health around Brett. "Sean, I have Brett and Fay with me here in the conference room."

"Oh, excuse me. I didn't know anyone else was in the room. Brett, I want you to know your mother is one of the best women in the world. You're a very fortunate man."

Brett could hear the sincerity in Sean's voice. "Yes sir, she is a surprise to me in more ways than you can imagine. I do feel very fortunate to have the opportunity to get to know her."

Sarah punched Brett in the arm, "Okay, you two, stop with the obligatory small talk. We've got some things to discuss with you, Sean."

"Sarah, let me go first. Some of what I'll share with you might affect what you're going to ask me."

"Okay, go ahead." Sarah was more than ready.

"Before I continue, what I'm about to share involves Bean Pole. Do you want me to continue?"

Sarah looked at Mark. "Besides Brett and Fay, Mark is in the room."

"I'll save my discussion concerning Bean Pole for last then. Sarah, I'm not sure how long we can keep a lid on your personal life in Fort Pierce. The preliminary paperwork moving joint ownership of the Bretherick Corporation to your son has stirred up a Wall Street analyst. He is calling everyone and is doing his best to track you down. He even checked our flight records. News of this transfer will shake Wall Street from one end to the other."

Sarah sighed. "Oh Lord, I thought we could have some days together in anonymity. I really need to meet my other grandson before this news is announced. I don't want his dad telling him over the phone or to hear all of this on the national news." Sarah saw the shock on Brett's face. Hearing the possibility of their lives being discussed on national news took him totally by surprise. "My son has a large congregation he should inform first."

Sarah's offer never to acknowledge her as his mother had seemed odd at the time. Now Fay understood why she was so concerned. The loss of their privacy would be tragic, but the priority of family above all else she would never surrender. She could never accept any circumstance in which a child of any age would denounce their mother.

"Sarah, we are using every stall technique we know, including offering the analyst some other juicy stories, but he doesn't seem interested in our tactics. I think you need to accept the fact that you have a few days, perhaps hours left, and the analyst will be all over this story."

Sarah was visibly shaken by the conversation. Brett took charge. "Sean, can we have a press conference at our church on Sunday afternoon? I'm not about to let someone get the best of us. We'll go on the offense. I'm going to tell the church at the last service. I just need to talk to my youngest son first."

"You're talking about your son in Seattle?"

"Sean, I see now why my mother trusts you so much. You're on top of everything."

"Mark, can you give me a few minutes alone with Mrs. Bretherick and her family? I have something very confidential to discuss with them. I'll call you later."

"Of course." Mark dismissed himself from the conference room and entered the elevator.

"Sarah, is it okay for me to discuss my conversation with Bean Pole now?"

"Absolutely. My son is about to be the majority owner in this corporation, and besides that, I trust them."

"Bean Pole called about a situation in Columbia concerning seven nuns who were kidnapped by the cartel. They are threatening to kill them if they don't receive a one-million-dollar ransom by Friday. Of course, our government cannot pay a ransom or negotiate with these kidnappers, but he was wondering what we could do to help him?"

"It's been a long time since Bean Pole has asked for our help. Tell him to make a connection for us. We will hire a consultant in Columbia for a million dollars. I'm fine with that; however, I have a request of him. My grandson is running for county commissioner down here, and I have heard rumors that a couple of state senators and a federal senator are considering endorsing his opponent. Tell him if that happens, he and everyone else in the party can lose our phone number."

"Okay, I'll tell him to take care of that situation, and I'll ask what endorsements he can line up for your grandson. Also, we need to get father and son together. Since your grandson works for the federal government, I'm going to ask that he give this young man a federal assignment in Fort Pierce immediately. We will have one of our corporate jets waiting to bring them to Florida tonight. That way everything will be tied up by Sunday."

"Good thinking, Sean. Make that happen. I still have something else to talk to you about. There is a bank down here I want taken over as soon as possible. The name of the bank is Mosaic Federal. I haven't had a chance to look over their financials, the board of directors, or any regulatory matters; but no matter what you see, short of the fact they are going bankrupt, I want them taken over. If it is not in the corporation's best interests to invest in this deal, take the cost out of my private funds. I'm about to set this town free!"

"I'll have our merger and acquisition group on this immediately. It's been years since we've done a hostile takeover. I don't want us to get rusty."

Sarah could feel Sean's energy increase by the moment. She could not imagine this superstar of business, sitting at home, retired with nothing to do. "Sean, one more thing, this political group down here raised seventy-five thousand dollars of campaign funds to run against my grandson. Tell the political group we will need a hundred and fifty thousand dollars. Also, send me down a public relations expert and some advertising people. We have a campaign to win."

Sean cleared his throat. "Sarah, before we hang up, I've got a couple of issues I want to bring up. First is security for you and your family. For the past two days, we have hired some security teams to cover all of you in Fort Pierce and your grandson in Seattle. It would make it easier on us if you would let us do some things for you."

Fay looked at Brett. "Did you hear that, honey? We've had security teams watching over us for the last two days. Good Lord. Adam and Michelle are being protected even as we speak, and they are unaware of anything that has transpired."

Sean responded immediately. "Brett, listen to me carefully. Those crazies down in Columbia kidnapped those nuns for one million dollars. We have crazies all around the world who know a million-dollar ransom for a Bretherick is pocket change. Please take me seriously." Sean continued, "We have a hundred-and-twenty-foot yacht sailing from Miami to Fort Pierce tonight. We would like the three of you to live on that yacht until things are settled. We also have a safe home on Hutchinson Island for your grandson to move in right now. The home is fully equipped. We can purchase the home if he likes it."

Fay jumped in, "Sean, this is Fay. You do whatever it takes to make my family safe. Mom and Brett will go along with whatever it will take. I will call my oldest son and inform him of his new residence."

"Sarah, I wish all of you could get out of town before that analyst shows up. I'll have the doctor come right now if you'll stay put."

"All right Sean, get the doctor over here and bring on the yacht. I've been thinking about eating beignets and shopping at the Riverwalk for over two weeks. If I can talk Aaron and his wife into going with us, we will be out of Fort Pierce later this afternoon. If you can get Bean Pole to take care of my other grandson's situation, redirect their jet to New Orleans to meet up with us. "

"Let me go to work, Sarah." Sean hung up the phone.

Sarah took charge. "Okay, Fay, you have an office. Go convince the kids to get ready to go to New Orleans. Tell them to take just what they would need to wear for today and tomorrow. We will go shopping on the Riverwalk tomorrow!"

Sarah turned to Brett. "Brett, go to your office and make an appointment with Mr. Wilkes for Sunday after church. That's when he will find out how much control he has lost over this community and your church."

"Mom, I just have one question. Who is Bean Pole?" Brett was confused.

"Oh, Bean Pole? That's a code word used between Sean and me for the President of the United States."

~

Rich, Rosalie, and Carol came out of the elevator on the sixth floor. Rich saw Brett sitting at his new desk, talking to someone on the phone. Rich gave the office a full-circle look and whistled, "Brett, this is impressive. That view of the river and ocean is to die for."

Brett looked up and acknowledged his brother with a wave of his hand, continuing his conversation on the phone. "Listen, Anne. Get the church staff together this afternoon and communicate this message to them exactly the way I give it to you. First, tell all the employees of the church, I mean *everyone* who works there to meet me in room 408 in the Administration Building at ten forty-five a.m. Sunday morning. Tell them I have an important announcement to share with them prior to my making a general announcement to the whole membership of the church. Please advertise in the weekly newsletter, e-mail list, and Sunday's bulletin that Pastor Brett will be sharing something important at the end of the eleven a.m. service. Tell those who come to the other services to return back to the church by 11:40 a.m. We will have every fellowship hall on the property properly equipped with screens and sound, so all those who cannot fit in the sanctuary can hear at the same time. In fact, Anne, tell the media guys to make sure we are piping this announcement over the outside speakers, just in case the over-flow capacity is inadequate. Do you understand what I have just told you, Anne?"

The silence on the phone was discomforting to Brett. He knew how emotional Anne could be. She possessed a compas-sionate heart, and he envisioned her sitting at her desk with tears rolling down her face as she wrote down the details con-cerning Sunday morning. During their seventeen years working together, they had shared a thousand conversations. He hated not telling her the whole story, but he also knew the pressure that would be put on her to tell the inside story. He didn't want to put her in that position. She had the highest of integrity and character and was incapable of deception. This week, she would be challenged without a doubt.

"Yeah, boss, I got it." She replied weakly. Anne wanted to say more, but this was one time she really didn't want to hear what Brett was going to announce. She thought this call was a prelude to a resignation, and she was sure everyone else would also.

"Anne, I need to speak to Andre. Can you switch me over to him?"

"Sure boss, it has been a real privilege to work with you all these years … I'm … I'm … I'm gonna switch you over to Andre. Bye."

Brett could hear Andre's phone ringing as Anne switched the call. "Hey boss! What's up?" Andre sounded in a very good mood.

"Well, what's up with you? You sound like you swallowed a happy pill."

"I've just had the best morning with your Carol Thatcher, Rosalie, and Rich. I took them on the nickel tour of our campus, and then a tour of our fair city. Brett, I asked Carol to accompany me to the outdoor concert in Vero Beach tonight. Of course, I asked Rosalie and Rich to come with us … so … for the first time since Betty died, I'm going out to dinner and a concert with a woman. I never thought I could do it, but tonight's the night. Thank the Lord, your brother and sister-in-law are coming with us, or my blood pressure would be off the chart."

Betty had died two years previously. Andre was Brett's confidant. He had always shared his heart with Andre. He was, by far, more of a friend than an employee. Fay had tried many ways to be a matchmaker for Andre, but nothing ever seemed to work out. He would distance himself from any relationship with another woman. His heart was buried with Betty the day of the funeral. Brett rejoiced over Andre's new adventure. "Listen, Buddy, I was given a car last night, an old classic GTO convertible. It's a real babe magnet. Why don't you take it tonight? You know, put the top down and go cruising?"

"Brett, I'm sixty-five years old. I'm more into orthopedic shoes and support hose than I am babe magnets, but I appreciate the offer."

"Andre, I'm about to head out of town for the rest of the week. I'm putting the keys to the GTO in the flowerpot on the front porch. I'm demanding that you take the GTO! Now, listen to me. I've just given Anne some instructions as to what is to take place on Sunday morning. I won't take time to go through the details because you can get them from Anne. Andre, I trust you as much as any member of my family. On Sunday, I'm going to announce that I will be taking a six-month sabbatical to determine what I'm going to do with the rest of my life. During the last twenty-four hours, my life has changed more than anyone could possibly imagine. I'm getting out of town so I can avoid the questions. Andre, I want you to take my place as Senior Pastor while I am gone. Wait just a minute, Andre. Let me do something here."

Brett heard his cell phone ringing. Looking at the caller identification, he could see that Adam was calling from Seattle. He punched the receive call button, "Just a minute, Adam. Wait just a second while I'm finishing talking to Andre on another line."

"Wait, Dad. I'm using Custom's cell phone. I don't want to run up their minutes. Is there a phone I can call you at in twenty minutes? Something crazy has just happened to me. Do you have a number? I know you're not at home or the office."

"Yeah, write this number down." Brett called out the numbers. "I'll be expecting a call in twenty minutes." Brett already knew what had happened to Adam. Old Bean Pole must have carried out Sean's request.

"Andre, are you still there?" Brett could hear nothing on the phone connection.

"Stunned, and a little disoriented, but yes, I'm still here. Would you mind if I asked why?"

"Andre, yesterday I met my biological mother. My biological mother is not like the average mom. Her name is Sarah Bretherick, as in Bretherick Corporation."

"Brett, you never mentioned that you were adopted. I had no idea."

"Andre, I wasn't adopted. It turns out that I was purposely switched with another child at birth. My biological mother discovered this deception only a few weeks ago by accident. The child she raised was going through experimental cancer treatments, and the DNA didn't match hers or my dad's. Andre, it is very complicated because of her extreme wealth. She is dying of cancer, and I need the time to get to know her."

Andre took a deep breath and exhaled it before speaking. "Brett, you and your family became my lifeline during Betty's illness, and even more after she died. You tell me anything, and it stays with me. You tell me what you want me to do, and if I can do it, it will be done. Take the time, buddy. Get to know your mother. You won't regret it."

Brett knew Andre would understand. "Then be prepared after Sunday services to take the helm of Community. Under your leadership, the church will prosper. I'm absolutely sure of it."

"Thanks for the vote of confidence, buddy. I'll do my best."

"Andre, I want you to enjoy tonight. Put all of this stuff out of your head. The best way to do that is to take the GTO, put the roof down, turn up the radio, and enjoy the ride. This is my last order for at least six months!"

"Okay, Brett. I'll take the babe machine. God bless you, friend. Bye."

Brett hung up the phone feeling a bit melancholy about the prospects of making this surprise announcement to the people of Community Church. They had loved him and his family for all of these years, and he wanted to treat them with that same kind of love. Seeing Fay and Sarah pass his door, he called them in to his office. "Hey, come in. Adam is going to call in a couple of minutes. I'll put him on the speakerphone so we can all talk to him."

Rosalie came running into the office. "Did I hear Adam will be calling?"

Brett could see the urgency in Rosalie's face. He had lived in great comfort when the boys were kids, knowing that if anything ever happened to Fay or him, the boys wouldn't miss an ounce of love. Rosalie and Rich loved the boys as their own. Carol came in to join the group.

Brett looked at Carol walking into the room, thinking of the joy she brought to Andre by accepting his invitation to the concert tonight. "So I hear the three of you are going to a concert in Vero tonight with Andre."

Carol blushed and looked to Sarah for her reaction. "This will be my first time out with a man since my husband died several years ago. Actually, after I agreed to go with him, I became filled with anxiety. Praise the Lord Rich and Rosalie are going with us, or I would be mortified."

Fay prayed daily that someone would come into Andre's life to help heal the suffering he felt after losing Betty. "Carol, you don't have to be mortified. Andre is a very godly man. You will be treated like royalty. I assure you, he will show you a good time."

Sarah wrapped her arm around Carol. "Girl, you're due some happiness. I was going to ask the three of you to come to New Orleans with us tonight and spend the week, but it sounds like I had better schedule another flight for tomorrow to pick up the three of you, if you want to come."

Rosalie spoke first. "I think Rich and I will stay here. We are going to extend our stay so we can spend more time with the family down here. I think it best that you guys have some time to come to terms with all that has transpired."

Carol interjected, "I agree with Rosalie. I'll meet up with all of you when you come back to Fort Pierce, if that is all right with you, Sarah."

"Oh, that's more than fine with me. Besides, you can't go out on any more dates if you're tripping around New Orleans with us." Inwardly, Sarah wanted Carol to find someone to love. Sarah was concerned what would happen with Carol in just a few short months after her death.

Fay took advantage of the silence. "I spoke with Aaron. Wow, he is really confused, but he is an obedient son. Lynne is packing for the trip to New Orleans even as we speak. He doesn't understand how we are all going to fly to New Orleans on a direct flight from the St. Lucie County Airport without ever ordering tickets beforehand. He's not sure how we can make up his lost wages because he has used up all his vacation time. Also, he doesn't understand why he must go to the elections office and pick up a packet of applications to run for county commissioner. He knows that you have already filled out the forms and plan to file them Monday. However, while he is questioning all of the above, he said he will do it and have it all done and ready for flight at four p.m. What a kid!"

Brett's phone rang. "Hey boy, I got you on a speakerphone."

"Dad, where are you? I've never seen this phone number before."

"I'll tell you when I see you and Michelle tonight."

"Hey! How in the world did you know I was coming home tonight? Dad, something is big time crazy here. I just found out in a closed-door session with some pretty high-ranking officials in Homeland Defense that Michelle and I are being flown out of Seattle tonight on somebody's private jet. Dad, I know I shouldn't have repeated this conversation, but you seem to know about it. You have no idea what has happened in the last two days. Honestly, I'm about freaked out, and I'm about to roust a group of guys who have been following me around. Dad, they are following Michelle. I've got her here in the conference room. I'm getting a few of my agent friends together, and we're going to take these guys down before I leave Seattle. Something really crazy is happening to me, and I'm going to get to the bottom of it."

"Adam, listen to me carefully. The guys who are following you and Michelle are to be left alone. I know who they are and why they are following you. They are there for your protection."

"Dad, how do you know these things? Your knowledge of what's going on out here goes way beyond the scope of a local pastor. Do you have a classified position, Dad? What's going on that you can't tell me about? Before I became a federal agent, you were the pastor of Community Church. Now I find out that you already know that the director of Homeland Defense called the highest ranking official in the Seattle office in a conference call with me and my immediate supervisor. They had me immediately reassigned to Fort Pierce, and incidentally, I'm leaving tonight! And then, there are teams of men casing my house around the clock and following Michelle and me around Seattle. You even know who they are? The director of Homeland Defense has never called our office before. Everyone here is in a dither, and the rumors are spreading fast that something is definitely wrong here to have a member of the president's cabinet call and have me reassigned within a few hours. I'm more than a little freaked out. Dad, all this is beyond the scope of a Community Church pastor. What's going on?"

Brett could hear the panic and frustration in Adam's voice. "First of all, there has been a change of plan. We are rerouting your flight to New Orleans. We will spend the rest of the week there. Don't worry about a thing. We will work it out with your superiors. Everything's fine! Don't worry about a thing! I've got a few revelations to tell you about. Oh, by the way, I've got you on the speakerphone. Your mom, Uncle Rich, Aunt Rosalie, and a relative you have never met before are here."

Silence. "Uncle Rich and Aunt Rosalie and a relative I've never met before! Dad, outside our immediate family, and my uncle and aunt, we don't have any other living relatives. I've heard you and Mom repeat that several times. Mom? Mom, are you there?"

Fay had never developed the art of using cell phones, and to a lesser degree, speakerphones. She believed the only way a listener could hear you was to talk extremely loud. "Yes, Adam. We really look forward to seeing you tonight, and your dad is right. Don't worry about a thing. Everything is perfectly normal. Well, as normal as they can be at the moment."

Adam tried another tactic. "Aunt Rosalie, you've never been able to pull off a practical joke in your life. Tell me the truth. What's going on? Did the doctor increase Mom's and Dad's medications? Are they now a threat to national security? Tell me the truth, Aunt Rosalie. What in the world is going on?"

Rosalie put her head next to the speakerphone. "It's good to hear your voice, Adam. You sound a little stressed right now, but I promise you, everything is really all right. A little hard to understand, but in a few hours, it will all be explained to you. Don't worry. What you're feeling right now, every member of our family has gone through in the last few days. Honey, please don't worry. Calm down. Everything will be just fine."

"Dad, is there anything you can tell me right now before we get hustled out of town? I'm worried we won't get to the airport with everything we need to last the next few days. How will I contact you or find you when we arrive in New Orleans? Dad, how do I go in and tell my boss this jet is taking me to New Orleans? By the way, Dad, can you tell me what provisions will be made for us, so we can sell our house and move our things?"

"Adam, do you like Seattle?"

"Dad, you know we have wanted to get back home; but yes, we like Seattle."

"Good. Then plan on leaving everything there, and stay at that house as you find time. Look, nothing I say now will make any sense until after we talk. We'll talk tonight."

"Dad, you didn't answer my question. How will we find each

other in New Orleans? I don't have any flight information to give you for arrival information."

Brett looked bewildered. He didn't know the answers to Adam's question.

Sarah stepped up to the phone. "Adam, my name is Sarah. I'm the relative you've never met. Don't worry about arrival information. I own both the jet we are coming in on and the jet you and Michelle are arriving on. The pilots work for me, and they will communicate arrival information to each other. We will know where you are from this moment on. Please dear, don't shoot the bodyguards I had assigned to you. They are there because of who I am, not because of anything that you have done. Our relationship will be explained tonight. I do business with some important officials in government, and they have released you from the Seattle office as a favor to me. Don't worry about missing the plane. If they left Seattle without you and Michelle, they would be summarily fired."

Adam sounded relieved. "Sarah, you're right. I don't know you, but you just made more sense than anyone I've talked to today. I'm dying to know more about you. I guess I'll see you tonight! Dad, is there anything else that will give me—or anyone else around me—a heart attack before this day is over?"

Brett smiled. "Can't think of a thing, son. We're bringing your brother and his family with us. I'm really looking forward to us all being together."

"I don't know, Dad. I'm looking forward to seeing you guys too, but I'm still wearing my gun!"

Brett pushed the speakerphone button to close the conversation. He sat back in his new chair. "You know, Mom, I'm learning everything in your world moves in nanoseconds. Within twenty-four hours, nothing about our lives is the same. Aaron is running around town, getting forms to run for office, thinking it is for me, and you have already set in motion endorsements from the highest ranking politicians in the state." Brett laughed heartily. "Poor kid doesn't even know he is the candidate. Adam is getting on a plane in Seattle with no more knowledge about his life than his brother, who's preparing to leave town and doesn't know why. And me, I'm preparing to step down from my position as pastor for the next six months, when just yesterday, I was thinking about what I would preach next week. I have to admit that I like the change of pace!"

Mark Kelly came down the hall, accompanied by a nurse and physician. "Mrs. Bretherick, this is Dr. Adona and his nurse. They came to see you."

The light-hearted spirit in the room became somber. Fay turned to her new mother-in-law, "Mom, I'm a nurse. Let me go with you."

"I know you are, dear. You nursed Brett to health when he came back from Vietnam, and you worked as a nurse to put him through college and seminary. Yes, you can come with me."

"Mom, how did you know all that?"

Rosalie sheepishly raised her hand. "I told her."

Chapter Seventeen

Sarah had flown the Gulfstream on business trips hundreds of times, but this trip was the most exciting of all. She was surrounded by every generation of her family, and her other grandson would be meeting them in New Orleans within an hour of their arrival. Entertaining thoughts of her own success in life occupied very little of Sarah's thinking. However, seeing her family in wide-eyed amazement gather around the Gulfstream gave her the greatest feeling of success she had ever experienced. Watching her family enjoy the fruit of her labor gave substance and meaning to her stressful life. They were the recipients of her work. She thought of Ben and wished that the Alzheimer's would recede just for enough time so he could understand what a beautiful family came from their union.

The flight crew was highly entertained with Seth and Ava, the great-grandchildren. The pilot took them up front to the cockpit. Aaron was as awed as the kids. He examined the whole plane and touched everything he looked at in the same manner someone would touch a fine work of art. Fay and Brett sat together in the back, holding hands like young lovers, enjoying the same things that Sarah was watching.

Aaron came back and sat next to Sarah. "So yesterday, when I teased you about your name being the same as the Bretherick Corporation, I was right without knowing it?"

Sarah looked directly into the eyes of her grandson. "You were dead on, Aaron! I didn't admit to it then because I had an even bigger hurdle to jump at the moment. My real goal was to be accepted by your dad as being his mother, and incidentally, by you as your grandmother."

"Well, everything is fine with me. In fact, even if you weren't the Bretherick of the corporation by the same name, everything would still be fine. So, I've got a heavy-duty question for you. What do me and my children call you? Is it Grandma, Grand-mother, or do you want us to call you Mrs. Bretherick?"

Sarah wrapped her arm through Aaron's arm. "When I was a child, I always called my grandmother Nana. I always had a thought that I would have liked to be called Nana. However, it was not until recently that the possibility of being a called Nana became probable. Aaron, you are a fine man. You're going places, I know that."

"Nana, you have set the bar pretty high for the rest of us to follow."

Brett could see the relationship forming between his mother and Aaron. "Mom, this might be a good time to fill Aaron in on our plan."

"Yeah, I agree. If we tell him now, it's not like he can get up and leave."

"Son, did you pick up the forms from the clerk's office to file as a candidate for county commissioner?"

Aaron looked puzzled. "Yes sir, but I don't know why. You already filled out yours. I know they are ready to file on Monday, just like we planned."

"Aaron, we both know I didn't want to run. The only reason I considered running was because you were determined to stop the exploitation of the people in the county. Son, the bottom line is this: I never wanted to run, so I'm not. The good news is…you are! When Monday comes, you're going to file as a candidate for a seat as a county commissioner."

"Dad, I'll get killed in this race. Wilkes and his cronies are having a fundraiser on Saturday for their boy. They're going to raise big money. They're going to have politicians from state and federal offices to give endorsements to their boy. Dad, they will sing the *Hallelujah Chorus* on Monday if they hear I'm running, rather than you. You are the only one in the county who could upset their applecart because the people all know who you are."

Sarah put on her business face. "Aaron, it's a whole new ball game now. There isn't a politician in the whole United States who could outspend you in a head-to-head campaign. Furthermore, you're going to find political endorsements lining up come Monday to support your candidacy. Right now, Aaron, you are David, and Goliath is coming down!"

"Nana, you don't understand. They have lined up advertising and signs. Everything we have is minimal, and all of it has Dad's name on it."

Sarah punched Aaron in the arm. "Aaron, give us some credit, will you? The advertising is being taken care of even as we speak. My corporate advertising department is contracting billboards, radio time, and television. We will have a public relations expert draft all your announcements. I'm telling you, Aaron, you're going to win! Trust me!"

"Dad, do you know what Wilkes will do when he hears I'm the one running for office? He is the chairman of the trustees. He will come after me."

"Son, after Sunday, I don't think Wilkes will be coming after anybody. His claws and fangs are about to be removed. I do think you should know that on Sunday, I will be announcing that I will be taking a six-month sabbatical from Community. You might want to consider asking the trustees for permission to take a six-month unpaid leave also."

"A six-month unpaid leave! Dad, I'm related to Sarah Bretherick, but that isn't going to keep my family housed and fed."

Sarah took exception to Aaron's proclamation. "Actually, it will. While we are in New Orleans, our corporate attorney will meet with all of us to activate your personal accounts. You now have an account with several million dollars in it, and you will receive an income of twenty-five thousand dollars a month. I would say being a Bretherick will house and feed your family, and that's exactly the way I want it. When we get to the hotel, a representative of the local Bretherick office will meet us there to give each of us an envelope with a debit card and twenty thousand dollars in cash. We will be shopping this week, and I thought everyone should have a little spending money."

Stunned, Aaron sank deep into his seat, trying to absorb the shock of his new evolving life. In a moment, he recognized the open-ended opportunities his Nana was giving him. The struggle within Aaron was not the enormity of the wealth just presented him, but the responsibility of it all. He had spent everyday of his working life since graduation from college as an assistant pastor to his father. Now, his dad was taking a long sabbatical, and the recommendation was that he should take a break to run for political office. Nothing about his tomorrows appeared to have anything in common with his yesterdays. He felt off balance.

"Folks, this is the captain speaking. This flight is just a quick hop straight across the Gulf, so we'll be landing in New Orleans in fifteen minutes. The conditions in New Orleans are fantastic, seventy-three degrees with winds coming out of the North at five miles per hour and clear skies. A good night for a buggy ride through the French Quarter. I have been notified by Captain Stewart that our Seattle flight left a little over an hour ago. They are currently over Colorado and due to arrive in New Orleans by six this evening. Mr. Walker, your son wanted me to convey to you that everything will be okay. He's packing heat. He said that you would know what that means."

Brett shook his head. "That is so much like Adam. Always seeking to be in control."

Fay despised handguns. "Tell me that he didn't get on that plane with his gun?"

"Mom, Adam is a federal agent. He is supposed to carry his gun, even on aircraft." Aaron was a true brother. He'd been his brother's defender since birth.

Sarah picked up the phone by her seat. "Captain, please

contact the pilot of the Seattle flight. Ask him to inform the kids that a limousine will be waiting for them at the airport to take them to the Windsor Court Hotel. Tell the kids they have room reservations there, and they can ring their dad's room when they arrive. Thank you."

Adam and Michelle walked hand in hand, unsure of themselves as they entered the lobby of the Windsor Hotel. The beauty of the Windsor overwhelmed their senses. They looked like teenagers on prom night, very much in love, and pretending every moment that every day was like this moment. Michelle pulled hard on Adam's arm, making him stop with her to appreciate the focal point of the lobby, a very large antique urn filled with a brilliant floral arrangement.

Brett and Fay were so excited about seeing the kids. As soon as they heard their limousine had left the airport, they had run to the lobby to wait for them. Both of them longed to see Adam and Michelle.

Fay spotted the kids first and took off running towards them, Brett following only a step behind. She grabbed Adam and squeezed him with all her strength, her face alight with undeniable joy. Brett hugged his daughter-in-law with no less delight than Fay's.

Adam embraced his father and then held him at arm's length. "Dad, we've got some talking to do. The limo driver just told me that the rooms here cost between two to four hundred dollars a night. Traveling in private jets and limousines and staying at the Windsor is not what the common folk do! Tell me, what's up? So far, I think I've figured this much out. The unknown relative said she owned the jets we both flew on. I asked the pilot who owned the plane when I got on, and he said it was a Bretherick Corporation aircraft. I asked him, 'What lady in the Bretherick Corporation could control the operations of these aircraft?' He said, 'Only Sarah Bretherick.' Now, are we talking about a family relationship to Sarah Bretherick?"

"You make a good agent, son. Yes, Sarah Bretherick is that family member. She is my biological mother, therefore making her your grandmother."

"Okay, I'm confused."

Fay pointed to a room with soft piano music coming from it. "Let's go in there and sit down and get the whole story told."

Brett ordered coffee for each of them and began to tell the story from the beginning. He shared the evil his grandmother Victoria had committed at his birth and the circumstances that led Sarah to seek him. Every detail he could remember from the last two days was repeated to the kids, including their new financial situation.

Michelle recovered first, turning to Adam. "I married you for your good looks and charming personality, and now I find out you have money too!"

A loud cheer arose from everyone in the room. The waiter turned the sound up on the television suspended above the bar. Every one in the room focused on the news report.

> This is breaking news from our correspondent in Columbia. Just moments ago, the seven nuns who were kidnapped by the Columbian Cartel boarded a United States military aircraft bound for the air force base in Charleston, South Carolina. Ambassador Greenburg denies reports that a ransom was paid. He also denies that covert military action was taken. Quite frankly, we down here have no clue as to why these nuns were released, when just this morning their deaths looked so imminent on Friday.

The waiter turned the television down as everyone applauded in celebration of the nuns' release.

Fay responded to the celebration without thinking. "Wow, Brett, I can't believe how quickly this deal went down. It was just a few short hours ago we had that conversation."

"All right, guys, you're freaking me out again. What do you know about this? Certainly you aren't involved in this too?" Adam sounded exasperated.

Brett leaned next to Adam's ear. "Can a federal agent keep a secret?"

"Of course."

"This morning, your grandmother made a deal with a high-ranking American official. She would take care of this situation in Columbia, if he would take care of a situation involving her grandson. Now remember, you're a federal employee, so he was in a position to make some things happen that are outside of normal processing. Do you get my point?"

"Loud and clear. So that is why someone from the president's cabinet roused my bosses to have me released today. Wow! That is power! I like it!"

Squealing could be heard as little Ava came running up to greet them. "Uncle Adam! Aunt Michelle! Uncle Adam!" She jumped into his lap.

Seth walked up to the table shyly, with a toothless grin. "Hi, Aunt Michelle." Michelle reached out and scooped him off the floor, doing exactly what he had hoped she would, kissing him repeatedly as he giggled.

Aaron and Lynne followed as Adam and Michelle stood to exchange embraces with them. Sarah stood with her hands folded a few steps away from the table, uncomfortable standing so close to so much familiarity and love, yet desperately wanting to be a part of it.

Adam noticed the short, grey-haired, brown-eyed, elegant woman standing solitarily a few feet away. Locking eyes with his father, he received the assuring nod. Indeed, this was his grandmother.

Adam stood and approached her. He towered over her. Cupping his hands around his grandmother's face, he said, "I'm Adam. I'm the good-looking grandson that is too unrighteous to have become a minister." He kissed her on the forehead and drew her into his arms.

Sarah held on to him, and the thought to check him for a gun came into her mind. On a whim, she patted his ribs. She whispered loudly, "You do have a gun."

"What? You were expecting a Bible? Wrong Walker."

Sarah embraced him again, confident nothing bad could happen to them in Adam's presence.

Sarah wanted to begin her life with her whole family present. "Is everybody able to party tonight?"

In unison, they all responded, "Yes!"

"Then I have taken our pilot's advice and arranged for two horse and carriages to be at our disposal. Let's take a ride around the French Quarter, eat at the Commanders' Palace, walk along the Mississippi River, have beignets at Caf» du Monde, and catch some jazz on Bourbon Street. The carriages are ready when we are."

Adam proposed that the family would meet for a nine thirty breakfast in order to give Seth and Ava some time to sleep in. Sarah and Adam were the first to make it to the breakfast buffet. Together they sat at a table drinking coffee, waiting for the rest of the family to come down.

"So, Adam, do you enjoy your job as a special agent for Customs?" Sarah wanted to get to know her grandson.

"I enjoy it immensely, but I can't picture myself moving around whenever the government has a need. When I first started, we thought we would fulfill our three years of required duty in Seattle and then transfer closer to home. I'm beginning to see the writing on the wall. We will never be allowed to come back to the East Coast unless the government has a need for us to move. As you can see, I'm close to my family. We're wanting to have kids, but we can't envision having kids so far from Dad and Mom and her parents. So, at this point, we're treading water."

"Financially, you're in a position to do whatever you want, even retire, if you desire."

"Oh boy! Retire? That's a word that wasn't on my radar screen for about another twenty-four years. Gosh, I'm not ready to sit in a cabana and play shuffleboard yet. My brother tells me he's going into politics. Dad says he's going to take six months off, and then go back to Community. Between you and me, I'm thinking this Sunday will probably be his last day as a pastor. Dad can be really idealistic. He has no idea how much his new identity will affect his ability to be the pastor he used to be. I'm not as idealistic as my dad and brother. I need a job that will challenge me and keep my adrenaline pumping."

Sarah felt sad at the thought that Brett's last day of being a pastor would be this Sunday. "Adam, there is a high-profile job at Bretherick you can start training for, but you would have to live in Cleveland, Ohio, for a couple of years. After that, it would be up to your father as to where the corporate headquarters would be located. But I'm sure the two of you could work that out."

Adam was interested. "What is the job?"

"You could start training to replace the chief operating officer of Bretherick when he retires in two years. During these two years, you could train under him and be prepared for the day he leaves the company. His name is Sean McCurdy. A great friend and partner of mine and your grandfather's for over fifty-five years. You would be learning from the best."

"What if I am interested? How would I proceed from here?"

"Just tell me if you want it, and that settles that. The job is yours. I own a large estate with a huge mansion in Cleveland. It would please me if you and Michelle moved into it." Sarah felt a bit selfish luring Adam into this job. He would be the safety net for all her dreams. The Bretherick Corporation would stay in family hands. The estate would be kept intact, and someone in the family would sustain her and Ben's legacy.

"Nana, let's keep this between us this morning. After yesterday, I don't see myself getting much enjoyment out of the job with everyone leery of who I am. Yesterday's phone call from the director of Homeland Defense pretty much made everyone suspect me of something. I'm going to say yes to your job offer, but let me talk to Michelle, so at least there is the appearance that she participated in the decision."

Sarah smiled. "I have DNA evidence that your father and brother belonged to me, but I won't need any from you. You're definitely Ben Bretherick's grandson. You sound and act just like him, and that's not bad. I love him dearly."

Brett and Fay came into the buffet area. "Mom, you must have left your cell phone in your room. Sean is trying to reach you. You can use mine, if you like."

Sarah dialed the familiar number. "Sean, good morning. What's the news today?"

"Good morning, Sarah. I called to tell you the report on Mosaic Bank is premium. I don't know how you do it, but this is a wonderful deal. The stock price is significantly under the current fair value of the share price. The board of directors are old men like me, and they have minimal regulatory issues. Taking over this bank is a great move for our company. We will run the acquisition through the parent company Bretherick Corporation, and we will begin filing SEC notices on Friday. It's a shame you want to fire the director, Wilkes. He actually has done a good job."

"Thanks for taking care of this matter, Sean. I'm glad it will make a good deal. Let me talk to my son about Wilkes. Perhaps with some new motivation, Wilkes can redirect his extracurricular activities away from local politics and church administration."

"Another thing, Sarah. Our attorneys will be at the Windsor Court Hotel at three thirty p.m. today. Will you and your family be free to meet with them concerning their personal accounts and company matters?"

"Yes, Sean. We will be here at three thirty to meet with the attorneys."

"One other thing. David Birmingham called, trying to reach you. He said to tell you that the project in Watkins Glen is complete. I gave him the Fort Pierce office mailing address to mail the paperwork. We will pay his fee from this office. He also mentioned that Willa Mae Summers called again. He's still not sure what she wants to talk to you about."

Sarah chose to ignore the information concerning Willa Mae. "You're a good man, Sean. I could never have made it without you. Bye."

Sarah looked up from the napkin she had been scribbling on as she spoke on the cell phone. The whole family was now assembled. "Well, how about we eat and then go shopping at the Riverwalk? We have to be back by three thirty this afternoon. So, ladies, how about I have the hotel find a sitter for the children? The boys and I need to conduct some business with some attorneys. I will schedule you at the same time for the works at the spa … a massage, facial, nails, makeover, you know, the works! I'll also arrange for dinner and dancing tonight on a paddle wheeler on the Mississippi."

Michelle snatched Seth off his feet. "The works! This will be the perfect day, shopping, the spa, dinner on the Mississippi, and dancing with these Walker boys. Seth, will you dance with Aunt Michelle?"

Seth puckered at the thought. "No, you're a girl."

Chapter Eighteen

The week spent in New Orleans passed by in a breath. Each member of the family dreaded the return to Fort Pierce, recognizing that after the public announcement in church and the media, their lives would never again be the same. Aaron and Lynne moved into the estate on Hutchinson Island. While they were in New Orleans, all of their belongings were moved into their new home. Sarah, Fay, and Brett moved onto the yacht to avoid nosy reporters or lunatics who might harm them. Rich, Rosalie, Carol, and Andre stopped by the yacht to check on Brett and to find out how the week had gone. Adam and Michelle checked into a hotel on North Beach. They had all agreed on meeting at the church in the morning at Brett's office.

Brett's cell phone rang. He spotted Rich standing by the marina gate at the same moment. "Hey, buddy. I can see you at the gate of the marina with the cell phone in your hand. Give me a second. I'll clear you guys to come down." Brett enjoyed the fact that he had caught them by surprise.

Rosalie came running down the ramp first. "Are the boys here?"

Fay was glad to see them. "No, they are trying to get settled for the night in their new places, but we're still here if you're interested in seeing us."

"Fay, I think this may be a major mistake living down here on the water. Brett will never take the fishing pole out of his hand now." Rich was speaking truth.

They each embraced each other, and then the steward on board asked everyone for beverage preferences.

Sarah took Carol off to the side. "So, how many nights did you go out with Andre this week?"

Carol blushed and giggled. "Every one of them. I had a great time."

Sarah grasped Carol's hands into hers. "Here are the new rules. Enjoy yourself. Bretherick business is now your last concern. Being happy is your first. We have a new motto: pleasure first. Business a distant last. I guess what I'm saying is just because I'm back, don't stop going on those dates. I'm all right now. I just want you to be happy. You're the best friend I have. I only want the best for you."

At the same time, Brett and Fay cornered Andre. "C'mon, tell us how the date went?"

"Great!"

"C'mon, buddy, did you take the GTO? Did you put the roof down?"

Andre grinned. "Yes, I took the babe magnet, and putting the roof down was exhilarating."

Fay bowed up. "Really Andre, 'babe magnet?' When did you start thinking like that?"

Brett winked. "Yeah, Andre, I'm surprised to hear a man of your age talking about babe magnets. So just how did you come up with the idea of equating the GTO to a babe magnet?"

Astutely, Fay surmised the irony in Brett's voice. "Never mind, Andre. I think I already know who influenced your thinking. I warned you about listening to that man. Sometimes his thinking can be so infantile. So, are you going to take her out again?"

Andre awkwardly grasped his hands together. "Yes, we have been out every chance we could. I think I should stop seeing her, though. This week has been the best week of my life in years. If I continue seeing her, I will not be able to keep my affections under control. I must remember in a short time she'll want to go home to Cleveland, and I don't want all the mental turmoil that will come with another separation. I'm just now starting to get into the flow of life after losing Betty."

Brett and Fay both took a step closer to Andre. Brett advised, "Take the risk, buddy. Let God guide your steps. Don't get in his way. Carol is a godly woman and you are a godly man. Both of you should keep your eyes on God and allow him to control your destiny. There is no guarantee this lady will ever want to return to Cleveland once she gets to know you."

Fay couldn't resist adding her opinion. "Andre, you owe yourself a chance at life. It may not work out, but if it doesn't, it doesn't. You're a preacher, remember? When is the last time you taught, 'Be careful of loving and being loved. Someone could get hurt?'"

"I know you're both right. I guess I'm a living example of preaching one thing and living another. All right, I'll take it day by day without prejudging the end." Andre knew he would keep the commitment to this couple and himself.

Sarah called everyone to gather and sat down. Andre pulled Carol's chair out for her to be seated. Brett started to sit down, but Fay grabbed his arm and pointed to Andre's example. Brett stood up straight and pulled Fay's chair out for her. Rich noticed Fay's insistence and decided Rosalie would be next to protest, so he went ahead and pulled Rosalie's chair out for her.

"Are you ready for tomorrow, Brett?" Andre could empathize with the anxiety Brett would have concerning his announcement to the church. He was feeling some tension himself, and he was not the one who would have to speak.

Brett gave his normal confident answer. "Sure, I can handle it." Inwardly, he wanted to stay on the yacht and fish. He would rather send an e-mail to the staff that they could post on the screen. He also had a meeting scheduled to deal with Wilkes and the media after the church announcement. Fishing definitely sounded better than all of that.

"Have you thought about what next week will look like?" Andre was wondering what changes Brett would make immediately in his life.

"Yes, I've got an office in downtown Fort Pierce. Mom has offered to introduce me to the inner workings of the Bretherick Corporation. I'm going to take advantage of that offer because, as of Monday, she has made me a joint owner of her company. I'm also thinking about accepting some speaking engagements around the country. I've always turned most of them down, but I'm thinking that next week I will contact those churches and conferences that I've turned down and offer to come at no cost. That way, the three of us can travel around the country a little bit, and I can still continue the one thing I love to do: preach and teach."

Sarah remembered her commitment to Mitch. "There is a pastor in Cleveland. He was Gerald and Carol's pastor. He was a very faithful guide to me. He asked if I would prevail upon you to come and speak at their church. Brett, it would mean a lot to me if you would go there. That pastor has heard you speak at conventions, and he believes your coming would greatly encourage his church. Mitch, the pastor I'm talking about helped me so much after Gerald died. He was faithful to come to the hospital when I was in for testing. Mitch guided me in accepting the Lord."

Brett smiled. "Well, there you go, Andre. I'm going to be speaking in Cleveland. Mom, if you have his number, I'll call him and schedule a date."

Carol excitedly reached for her cell phone. "I've got it on my call list." She scrolled down until she found it. "Have you got a piece of paper so I can write it down?"

Brett reached over and took her cell phone. "Is this a company cell phone?"

Carol looked confused. "Yes."

"Good! Then you won't mind." Brett pressed the send button to dial the pastor's number in Cleveland. "Hello, Pastor Mitch? This is Brett Walker from Community Church in Fort Pierce, Florida. Does my name ring a bell with you?"

"I'm in shock! Sarah pulled it off. Tell me you're coming up here to speak!"

"Pastor, I don't think there is anything my mother can't pull off. I owe you a big debt of gratitude for everything you have done ..." Brett hesitated, "for my brother Gerald and my mother. You tell me the best date for me to come, and I'll be there."

Sarah appreciated Brett calling Gerald his brother. She still loved him as a son—and missed him greatly.

"Brett, your mother and Carol gave us the funds to refurbish our pipe organ. We are planning to have a dedication service the third week in September. Could you be our speaker for that service?"

"Count on it, brother. You couldn't keep me away."

"Brett, can we go ahead and book your flight for you and your wife this week?"

"No, Mitch. Everything I do for the Lord from now on is a gift of thanks. In other words, no honorariums, no travel expenses, and not even meals. This is my gift to him. Are we clear?"

"Brett, your coming will be a morale booster for our church. Thank you."

"No, thank you!" Brett felt a sense of purpose looming before him in the wake of tomorrow's announcement at Community. He wondered as he closed the cell phone how many other small struggling churches out there could he help?

***

Brett arrived at Community at seven a.m., his normal time. He sat in his office, looking around more intensely than he could remember. Each picture on his wall had a meaning. A picture in the corner of the office depicted an angel carrying a dead soldier to heaven while a helicopter lay on its side, smoldering in a rice field. The surrounding forest was bright with flames. This picture was given to him by another Vietnam veteran who had been shot down twice during his tour. Then, he remembered the day a depressed woman came to his office and stated she had no reason to go on living. She thought she had no contribution left for mankind. Brett smiled as he remembered flippantly telling her to go take an art class at the college. She did. Her first attempted oil painting hung on his wall. It depicted a dynamic ocean scene with angry waves crashing in on the sands with palm trees bending, trying to stand in the fury of the wind. This was her first piece. In appreciation, she gave it to him. Now, her works were in studios all over the country.

The kids were major contributors to his walls. On the wall was a picture taken from outer space, showing the entire state of Florida from the heavens. He looked at this photo for weeks every time he accompanied the family to the discount store. The boys were in high school. For Christmas that year, they bought the picture and had it framed. After all these years, he still enjoyed searching the photo, looking for a stream or inlet visible from outer space. Adam and Michelle sent an evening photo of the City of Seattle horizon, so that he would have a constant reminder of them. Everything in the office had a story to tell. He couldn't shake the feeling that today he was saying "Good-bye," not "See you in a while." He locked his office door so no one could come in. He hadn't cried since Vietnam, but today he would, in private.

"Brett, are you in there? This is Andre."

Brett wiped his eyes and cleared his throat. "Yeah, just a second. Let me get the door." Brett checked his face in the mirror, but there would be no disguising the fact to Andre that he had been crying. He went ahead and opened the door. Brett turned his head away from Andre to mask his emotions.

Andre grabbed Brett like a professional wrestler and embraced him. "Okay, buddy! Take it from me. I'm a professional in emotional distress. We're not going to deny it, fight it, or play games with it. You're hurting right now. We're going to acknowledge it and work through it. I don't know a tougher guy than Brett Walker, but even your soul isn't made of stainless steel. It's okay, Brett, to feel what you're feeling. In fact, I would be worried about you if you felt any other way."

Brett could only nod his head in agreement. He wondered

how he would ever find the voice to get through the morning. He began to weep again.

"Do you remember the morning Betty died?"

"Yeah, how could I forget?" Brett felt small. His turmoil could never amount to the significance of the moment Andre lost Betty.

"If you remember, the moment I realized she was gone forever, I fell to my knees and began sobbing uncontrollably. Do you remember what you did?"

"No."

"You got down on your knees with me and held me like I was a child. Brett, did you think less of me as a man because I expressed so much emotion?"

"Of course not. You had just lost the love of your life. Everyone understood."

"Brett, you're not losing your wife today, but I suspect you're feeling as though you are losing your church. This place and these people have been your love for all these years. I don't know what God has in store for you, but I do know what has happened through you. Leaving this church, even for six months, is a really big deal."

Brett could feel a peace in what Andre was saying. He loved this church and the people. Brett knew that nothing happened in the universe that didn't first cross God's desk. "You know, Andre, God must have something pretty significant in store. I can't believe all this hurt would be caused for no purpose at all."

"Wait on him, Brett. I suspect he will reveal his purpose if you will be patient."

Brett glanced out the office door and the rest of the ministerial staff was waiting silently to come in for the morning staff prayer. "C'mon in, guys. I'm ready."

The staff filed in and stood around Brett. It was apparent that Aaron was feeling the same emotions as his father. Aaron winked at his dad to communicate solidarity with him. Stan, the minister of education spoke first. "We'd like to break this morning from our traditional prayer time of going around the room and praying for each staff member and the services. We know that at ten forty-five this morning we're scheduled to meet with you to hear your announcement. We agreed before we came in here that we want to spend time praying for you. We don't know what's coming, but whatever it is, it's obvious it involves our pastor. So today, we want to focus our prayer time around you."

"Yes, I would appreciate that."

The staff surrounded Brett and Aaron, placing their hands on their shoulders and offered prayers of protection, blessing, and guidance from the Lord upon them. After the prayer, Stan squeezed Brett's shoulders. "We'll be back at ten forty-five to meet with you, boss. Whatever it is you're facing this morning, please remember every one of us in this room will stand with you any time or any place."

The staff left the office in one movement, leaving Aaron, Andre, and Brett alone.

Hardly anyone came for the eight fifteen service. Aaron stood to announce the events that would take place over the next week. At the end of the announcements, the music began and Aaron came over to Brett. "Dad, this is the worst attendance for this service I've ever seen. We could shoot a shotgun straight down the middle and never hit anyone. I'll bet those people sitting out there are first-time visitors and haven't any idea that you're making a major announcement after the last service."

Andre came up to Brett. "Brett, there are only about a hundred and fifty people here. We are about eighteen hundred off in attendance right now. I'm sure the next service is going to look the same. This whole town is going to show up for the last service. Why don't you let me preach this service and the next? Save your emotional energy for the last one."

Brett hesitated to give less to these who were faithful to come. But Andre was right. His emotional energy was already at low tide, and preaching to an empty room would decrease what little energy that remained. It was discouraging to see a service at Community practically empty. Brett reluctantly agreed. He went into his office, locked the door, and left word with an usher to knock on his door at ten thirty. Brett lay down on the couch in his office and tried to rest, but his stomach felt like an acid pit. He wondered if his grandmother, Victoria, ever gave a thought to the evil she had committed.

Brett was wide awake when the usher knocked on the door. "Pastor, it's ten thirty."

"Thanks, John. I'm ready." Brett stood up and put on his coat. He slipped his wireless microphone over his belt and ran the microphone wire up through his shirt. He grabbed his Bible and opened his office door to begin the walk to room 408. Sitting in the office area in the guest chairs was his family, every one of them including Seth and Ava. Normally they would have been in Sunday school, but Lynne demanded that they would stay with the family today.

Adam stood and wrapped his arm around his father. "You didn't think we were going to let you do this alone, did you? We're all coming with you. Andre, you and Carol come with us too. We consider you a part of this Walker tribe."

Sarah held Carol's hand. "You have walked this far with me, lady. Don't leave me now."

Brett looked at the family that surrounded him. "I'm a blessed man. What a great family. Everyone in this room is special to me. Come walk with me. I'm not too proud. I need each one of you."

As Aaron opened the door to room 408, he was immediately surprised by the number of employees who had shown up for the promised announcement. There were in excess of a hundred employees: secretaries, maintenance, kitchen staff, technicians, and ministerial staff.

Brett walked to the podium. "I appreciate you coming this morning to hear what I'm about to announce to the whole world. The first part of what I have to say is this: I'm requesting a six-month leave of absence to take care of some things that are important to me. During this six months, I will seek what the Lord wants to do with the rest of my life. I just don't want to resign this day without having some time to pray and seek his will."

Brett took a nervous breath. "This week, my life changed

more than any other week in my life, and that includes the week I almost died in Vietnam." Brett paused a moment, then began with resolve. "I discovered this week that my life was randomly exchanged for another life over fifty-four years ago. A very evil woman took me away from my mother when I was born; and for reasons I don't care to discuss now, she intentionally switched me to another family, giving their child to my real mother to raise.

My mother raised and loved this child until the day he died. However, just before this man died, my mother discovered this child was not her biological son. She went in search of me and found me. I got to meet her for the first time last Sunday.

Now as dramatic as this whole episode appears at this moment, there are more complications that compel me to ask for this sabbatical. Mainly, I need to get a bearing on the rest of my life. My mother has terminal cancer. I've been cheated from knowing her all these years, and I want to spend the rest of the time she has remaining to get to know her. I really want her to know me too.

Finally, my other reason involves a complexity that I have to reconcile myself. My mother is here this morning." Indicating his mother, Brett waited for his mother to be recognized by the employees.

"Some of you may recognize her if you're current on American business leaders. Her name is Sarah Bretherick, the majority owner of the multinational corporation by that same name. Obviously, most of you recognize the unusual circumstances involved in our restored relationship. This week in the local newspapers and over the national news, you will see and hear that I will become a majority owner in the Bretherick Corporation. My life will involve a lot of changes, and I need the time to become familiar with my mother and my new situation. Please know I will be praying for all of you, and I ask that you would continue to pray for me.

I have no intention of belaboring the moment. I think you know how much I appreciate each of you. I'm proud to have served with you."

Brett started to walk out, but Stan asked him to wait. "Brett, we will keep this announcement to ourselves, but would you and your family remain here for just a moment?"

Brett didn't understand, but he agreed as the employees filed out in silence. When the last one left the room, Stan looked out into the hall and motioned Brett to proceed.

Brett held out his arms for Fay and Sarah to walk with him to the sanctuary. As they walked out the door, they were shocked to see all the employees had lined both sides of the hall for them to pass through. Each of them was clapping, and each calling out to Brett a word of encouragement, "We're with you, Pastor! I love you, Pastor! God bless you, Pastor."

The tears flowed freely among the family. Brett leaned over and whispered in Fay's ear, "This is gonna be hard."

Brett declined sitting at the altar today. He chose to sit by Fay and his mother on the first row. The rest of the family surrounded them. Andre came up to Brett while everyone was standing and singing. "It's crazy here this morning. Hardly anyone was here for the beginning of the nine fifteen service when we started, but people started pouring into the sanctuary while I was still preaching. They were coming early to get good seats for this service. Every overflow area is over capacity, and the parking lot is jammed with people sitting on the hoods of their cars, listening to the outdoor sound system. Brett, the Sheriffs' department called. They say the cars parked on the main street are causing some significant traffic and safety issues. I have an idea…"

"What can we do, Andre? You know these people aren't going anywhere until I talk with them." Brett looked around at the hundreds of members standing around the perimeter of the sanctuary because all the seating was taken. "This isn't safe or even comfortable for the people. What's your idea?"

"Get up and speak now. I know we've never intentionally reduced our worship for convenience purposes, but I think the Lord would understand."

Brett agreed. "Do it."

Andre walked up to the podium and stood next to the music director to get his attention. He leaned over and whispered in his ear, "Finish this hymn and give the pulpit to the pastor."

The music director understood without any further direction. He nodded his head in agreement and halted the music at the end of the verse they were singing. Silence. Not a sound could be heard in the expansive sanctuary. Everyone knew what was next.

Brett gripped his Bible and prepared to stand, but Fay gripped his upper arm, pulling him back into the seat. She kissed him and whispered to him, "I love you, Marine." Brett recalled that she started whispering that phrase to him while he was her patient in the hospital. Sarah continued to hold his hand and squeezed it hard, and then released it to let him stand.

Brett stood for a moment and looked over the sea of faces that he had served these past years. He looked to the heavens for a brief second and silently lifted a prayer, asking for strength.

He flipped his microphone on. "There is a little book in the Old Testament that seldom gets preached or discussed in church, but it is one that I have drawn much strength from over the years. The book is simply called Habakkuk. I'm fond of this book because it is the account of a godly man who had some serious issues with God. In fact, the book opens with a statement. 'The burden which Habakkuk the prophet did see.' That simply means Habakkuk saw some things that were so heavy on his soul that the only way he could deal with them was to lift them to God.

"However, when he lifted his burdens to God, he was not polite about it. The very next verse gets to the point. 'O Lord, how long shall I cry and thou wilt not hear! Even cry out unto thee of violence, and thou wilt not save!' I was a young man when I started lifting my burdens to God and I was not polite. Before I graduated from high school, my best friend was killed in Vietnam. Shortly after graduating, I found myself in Vietnam. There I witnessed atrocities that made me ask, 'God, where are you? Don't you even care?' Midway into my tour in Vietnam,

I was called home to attend my father's funeral. He was killed in a farming accident. I thought God had abandoned me. Within a month of returning to Vietnam, I was wounded in action. It was an event in my life that I have discussed with no one but God. I continually questioned the justice of God.

In my years of serving you at Community, I can look around the room and see the burdens some of you have lifted to God. A baby who dies. A job that was lost, an unfaithful spouse, an abusive parent, an abortion, you name it. Sooner or later, everyone in the reach of my voice has had a burden to lift to God, and you wonder, 'Does God even care? Does he even know?'

Last Sunday, I had the privilege of meeting my biological mother. Until last Sunday, I thought I knew my biological mother. It turns out that one evil person switched me at birth with another baby. I grew up in a wonderful home and so did the other child. Looking at the lives that were affected by this evil action, one might question God and ask, 'Even though mere mortals were fooled, you're the omniscient and omnipotent God. How could you let this happen?' And that is the same burden that Habakkuk speaks of. God, can't you see? Oh God, don't you even care?

That is the burden of Habakkuk in chapter one. He is thinking without trusting in the faithfulness of God. He is forgetting that God knows the beginning and end of every event. In chapter two, Habakkuk comes to his senses and remembers the goodness and faithfulness of God. He even makes the statement, 'But the just shall live by his faith.' I know exactly what he meant in that statement. It means my faith meter has expired. My strength is gone. Habakkuk is saying, 'My understanding is limited. Therefore, I'm trusting not in my own faith, but in you, God. I'm trusting in the worthiness of your name.'

Habakkuk had to do a couple of things to get to that point. He needed to get another perspective, so he told us, 'I will stand upon my watch, and set myself upon the tower, and will watch to see what he will say unto me, and what I shall answer when I am reproved.' Last Sunday, after meeting my mother for the first time, spiritually I had to get up on a tower. From a tower, you can see the landscape for miles around. It's a biblical way of saying, 'Look at your situation not from a mere puny human view, but look at it from God's perspective.'

After years of preaching and serving you, I've learned to climb the tower and get God's perspective. I purposely did not introduce my mother because many of you will know of her when I do. She is one of our country's most successful business persons. Her name is Sarah Bretherick. For those of you not familiar with her name, you will be familiar with her company. It is the Bretherick Corporation. She is fantastically wealthy, and I mention this only to give you a tower perspective of what God saw, something I couldn't see with my own mortal view.

I think of my life. It was a good life, but we struggled financially on our farm. My mother died when I was young, and my dad did the best he could. Today I could think, 'Wow, how much better my life could have been had my real mother raised me?' God, this is unfair! Had I been raised by Sarah Bretherick, I could have gone to college directly from high school. I never would have gone to Vietnam. Some of you soldiers out there, can you imagine a child of Sarah Bretherick's being assigned to a battlefront? I think of the months in rehabilitation and the years of working and going to college. My wife sacrificed so I could attend school and get ahead. None of this would have been necessary if God had protected me in my crib.

Folks, in his faith, I started climbing up the tower, and I began to get God's perspective. I reached the first rung and remembered my father, mother, and brother on that farm. How many stories have you folks heard about that glorious farm? My father and mother gave me love and a real home. They taught me love of country, family, and God. My brother, Rich." Brett looked down to address his brother in the audience. "Just because we discovered my genetics are different, doesn't change a thing. I am still your brother! I couldn't imagine life without my brother and the lady he brought into our lives: Rosalie.

Brett continued, returning to the congregation, "I climbed a few more rungs up the tower and could see the Vietnam experience. I could see the wholesale death and despair that would prepare me later in life to empathize with those of you whose lives have been destroyed. I believe we call those who have experienced such hurts 'wounded healers.' In Vietnam, I learned firsthand how to be a wounded healer.

"When I reached the top of the tower, I saw God's wisdom. The first face I saw below was that of my beloved wife, Fay. I recognized immediately that had I not been wounded in Vietnam, there would have been no Fay. She was my nurse in the Veterans' Hospital. I've loved her with all my heart these thirty-three years, and I could not imagine life without her. Without Fay in my life, there would be no pastor or associate pastor, because without her godly influence, I would never have pursued this life.

From the tower, I could see my sons, their wives, and my perfect grandchildren. As I stand here today, I promise you, if my going to Vietnam would assure me that God would give me this same family, I would be willing to go again, to be wounded again, and I would be willing to crawl across that country if I had to, to obtain the same family God has given me.

From the tower I see my mother, Sarah. She had the means to raise a child with many difficulties. His real parents could never have afforded the opportunities that Sarah could give him. She loved him, and I know he loved her.

My mother has changed the world. She has created jobs for literally thousands across the world. I know, personally, her wealth has preserved life.

We Christians often cite Romans 8:28, 'And we know that all things work together for good to them that love God, to them who are called according to his purpose.' I believe it.

In the last verse of chapter two, Habakkuk asserts, 'But the Lord is in his holy temple: let all the earth keep silence before him.' I find myself thinking the same thing this morning. In a few moments, my mother and I will be announcing to the national press that I am about to become a joint majority owner with my parents in the Bretherick Corporation. My mother tells me that this announcement will rock Wall Street and the world markets tomorrow. I'm not prepared mentally for the craziness that is about to break loose in my life. I will cling to the thought that God is in his temple. That means to me, he is still in control, even in the midst of the insanity around me.

Today, I'm asking the Community Church family to allow me to take six months off to finish my tower experience. My life has changed radically in the last week, and I need the time away to see what God is leading me to do. My desire is to stay here as your pastor, but there are obvious indications that I should wait until his direction is clearer. I'm removing myself from the payroll of this church. Fay and I will be donating the six million that formerly was required to begin the construction of the Life Center building. I guess this is my way of saying, 'Please keep striving.' Don't stop anything that we have been planning and dreaming. I've asked Andre to fill in as your Senior Pastor these next few months, until God's will for my life is clear.

I need the time to spend with my mother and to learn from her. Pray for my mother. She has been diagnosed with lung cancer, and the next few months will be difficult.

Habakkuk ended his little book with this verse, 'The Lord God is my strength, and he will make my feet like hinds feet, and he will make me to walk upon mine high places.' Habakkuk had completed the circle that a true believer often travels in his faith. In chapter one, he was angrily questioning God's justice and care. In chapter two, he questioned himself and sought God's perception, and in chapter three, he proclaimed God's faithfulness.

It is my prayer for all of us, despite wherever we are in this journey of faith, each of us will discover the strength and the faithfulness of God. God bless you all! Thank you for the love you have shown to me and my family."

Brett closed his Bible. The staff and choir members came to him immediately, embracing him and his family. The congregation rose and applauded continuously for ten minutes. Janice Popham stood in line for thirty minutes to hug him and to whisper, "Brett, I'm going to bake you some pies."

Chapter Nineteen

Sean's foresight to bring the yacht to Fort Pierce paid off. The press could not enter the gate at the marina, and private duty security surrounded the yacht to prevent interlopers from bothering Brett and his family. A table on the rear deck contained appetizers and numerous beverages. Seth and Ava sampled the fare directly from the platters to their mouths.

Lynne chased them away and made them each a plate. Brett replayed the day's events in his mind. "I'm sorry, Aaron. You never got the chance to say anything after I finished speaking today."

"Dad, it's just as well. I was amazed how quickly the people started coming out of their seats to speak with you. At that point, the service was over, and I wasn't about to get up and speak. Besides, it might turn out better. Now, when I make my announcement to run for county commissioner tomorrow, I can include those details then."

"Are you nervous about tomorrow?" Brett recalled the anxiety he experienced the past two days.

"Yes and no. Are you and the family going to be with me when I make the announcement?"

"Do you want us there?" Fay inquired.

"Absolutely. Nana, Uncle Rich, Aunt Rosalie, Andre, and Carol, if they don't mind being seen at a political announcement."

Brett looked at Andre carefully. "Son, I think it best Andre not be caught in any political endorsement. For years, I've worked hard to keep my ministry separate from politics. It was only recently my resolve weakened, mainly because a member of my family convinced me to step over that line."

Andre responded firmly. "Brett, I'm not you, and I'm not going to do things the way you did. I believe in Aaron. I have known him since he was a kid, and I have worked with him as a colleague at Community since he graduated from college. If you remember, I'm the one who convinced you in a heated debate to bring Aaron home to be an associate. You were afraid of the appearances of nepotism. Aaron was an obvious enhancement to our ministry. No, sir. I'm not hiding in any corners and pretending I'm not partial. He is a worthy candidate and a godly man. I'll stand beside you, Aaron, and I'll campaign for you. Not in the church, but I can go around town on my own time."

Carol cherished her inclusion in Sarah's family. Carol enthusiastically said, "I'm not a resident, so I can't vote. But as long as I'm here, I will do everything I can to help your campaign."

Sarah took charge. "All right, it is agreed. We'll all be present when Aaron makes his announcement to run."

"Mom," Brett winced, "if you're there, you know the press is going to ask you to say something. What would you say?"

"I'll say I'm very proud of my grandson and they better vote for him, or I'll buy up the town and send them packing!"

"No, Nana. You can't say anything like that," Aaron pleaded.

"I'm kidding, but maybe you could tell them that you're working with officials at Bretherick to bring some jobs to the county."

"That wouldn't be true, Nana. I haven't discussed anything with Bretherick officials about jobs coming to this area."

"Okay, ask Adam or me about bringing some jobs to the area and consider it done."

Brett responded to the answer first. "Ask Adam? When did Adam become an official of the Bretherick Corporation?"

Sarah, in her enthusiasm, had spoken in haste.

Adam jumped in. "Dad, I was going to tell you later, but now is just as good. Michelle and I have agreed to take a job with the company. We will be moving to Cleveland and staying at Nana's estate until we find a place of our own. I'm turning in my resignation to Customs tomorrow." Adam waited for his father's response.

"Does this mean that you two will start your family now?"

"Yes, sir. That's the plan."

"Then I'm in full agreement with this plan. Mom and I want to enjoy our grandchildren before we get any older."

Sarah snarled at Brett, "Be careful, mister, about that 'too old' business. You're talking about me."

Aaron provided a transition to relieve his brother of his parents' insistence to provide grandchildren. "Dad, I thought you and Nana were going to dismiss Mr. Wilkes from the bank today. I spoke to him after your meeting, and he was more cordial than I've ever seen him. Listen to this! He said he was going to endorse me. After all the things he said and did to discourage you and make you quit. He is endorsing me!"

"Son, Nana and I talked it over. Wilkes wants to be heard. He has manipulated our county and everyone knows it, but I just couldn't bring myself to be like him. In the end, if we fire him, we'd be like him. Truthfully, Sean says that Wilkes has done a great job building the bank. Therefore, Nana and I agreed to let him continue. We made some very strong suggestions about the image we desired from him in the community. He got the message loud and clear. Now he is yours to control in the political arena, but no longer can he use the bank to bully the community leadership."

Known for his compassion, Aaron agreed. "Dad, tomorrow's another intense day. We're going to head home." Everyone on the deck agreed it was time to call it a night. In one mass movement, the others were gone, leaving Brett and Sarah still sitting in their deck chairs. Fay declared total exhaustion and went to bed.

The city lights of Fort Pierce danced on the waters of the Indian River. Green and red lights on the bows of boats could be seen in the distance as they slowly made their approach into the harbor. Occasionally, a large yacht would turn into the inlet and begin its trek out to sea. Ripples of water slapped the yacht and the surrounding boats. The breeze moved softly over the deck as gulls passed overhead, quickly winging their way through the shimmers of light in the marina. Brett turned on the underwater lights that illuminated the water beneath the yacht. Huge jacks and barracudas were in a school, swimming randomly around each other under the docks and yacht.

Sarah watched her son as he stared intently at the waters. "A penny for your thoughts?"

Brett laughed. "Hadn't you heard? I'm Sarah Bretherick's kid. I don't deal in pennies anymore."

"Brett, you've become good at it." Sarah repositioned herself to face Brett directly.

"Okay, I'll bite. I've become good at what?"

"Deflection. Using your wit and charm to keep painful experiences at arm's length."

Surprised by his mother's observation, Brett challenged her. "Why would you say that?"

"For the past few weeks, I've focused on your life and what's happened to you. There are issues you touch on, but never discuss. Those nearest you know about facts in your life, but they don't know what you experienced or how you felt about them."

"Such as ...?"

"Oh, what happened to you in Vietnam. Why you stubbornly held onto your GTO but never got around to fixing it. The fact that I've come into your life, but you're content not to ask or require of me any details."

Brett sighed. "It's not that I'm deflecting those issues. They are personal and very painful, and I'm not comfortable discussing them."

"Brett, I really don't see the difference between deflecting hurtful experiences and not discussing them because they are personal. I have an idea they are not different at all. Ben and

I never discussed Gerald's retardation. Not once! Not even a small reference. If we were confronted with his condition by others, one of us would deflect the conversation so we would never have to deal with it. I carried within my heart and soul the guilt for Gerald's retardation. I considered the topic personal and painful; so I lived within my personal hell, continually feeling guilty and never thinking the condemnation could be lifted.

The last few days have been a respite from hell. My only regret is that I didn't have someone like you to talk with way back then. Everyone from my parents to my husband was content to deflect and hide the truth of Gerald's retardation, so I suffered in silence and wasted a lot of precious years. Brett, I can't give us back the years we've lost. I can give you my assets, but I want to give you something greater…peace! I'm your mother. Nothing you can say will change my feelings for you. My time with you is limited. I know that. Use this time well, son. I want it to be personal between us. Real. No deflection of anything."

Brett twisted a napkin in his hands. "What do you want to know?"

"This morning, I heard you state before the church that you never discussed with anyone but God what happened to you in Vietnam. Why? Don't you think you should have talked with Fay, Rich, or even your sons?"

"No. Telling them wouldn't change a thing. What happened is in the past."

Sarah touched Brett's hand. "No, Brett. You're wrong! What happened is still in the present. You think about it every day. It is just as real and daunting as the moment you experienced it. Share it with me, son. Let me take this experience to the grave for you. Let me help you with it!"

Sarah's eyes pleaded with him to let go of the memories. He could see his mother's desire to take away the torment in his soul. Brett could not look at her.

"Before I went into the Marine Corps, I was exercising my rights of teenage stupidity. I was drinking and racing that GTO every chance I could. My dad was invited on a regular basis to come visit the principal's office on my behalf. My father stood by me. No matter what ridiculous thing I had done. I was in rebellion against everything, but good man that he was, he never gave up on me.

When I signed up to go in the Marine Corps, my dad was proud of me, but I knew how responsible he felt that I didn't go to college. I never told him that I could have gone to college on a scholarship. I was tired of school, and I knew if he was aware of the scholarship, he would never let me go in the Marines. I've lived in regret that I deceived him. He saw so much promise in me, but I never lived up to that promise while he was alive.

The day before I left for boot camp, Dad, Rich, and I went out hunting. Way out in the woods, there was this small cemetery, a family plot of early settlers. The cemetery was not only remote, but well covered with weeds, limbs, and debris. I made the smart remark to Dad, 'Not even God knows where these people are.'

Dad jerked around. 'Brett, there's no place on this planet that God doesn't know where one of his children are.' I blew my dad off with a smart remark and moved on.

A few months later, I came home from Vietnam to bury Dad. I felt so unworthy of him when I came home. I had deceived him, and in our last year together, I had given him a hard time. He wasn't deserving of it … he was a simple farmer who did the best he could by his sons.

Later on, out of a sense of guilt, I gave Rich my share of the farm Dad left to me. I felt it was the only way I could balance the scale of justice with my dad. I felt entitled to nothing for which he had labored.

I became a sniper in the Marine Corps. I was sent out on missions to take out special objectives. Mom, I've put many human beings in the crosshairs of my scope and sent them to hell." Brett twisted the napkin so tightly that it started ripping in pieces. "Can't you imagine me telling this testimony on a Sunday morning?

Anyway, when I went back to Vietnam after the funeral, my attitude about everything had reached the bottom. I was sure I wasn't going to live to finish my tour, and life had become pretty cheap. The squeeze of a trigger and a thirty-five-cent government-issued bullet was my estimate.

Our strategic command discovered a North Vietnamese camp they believed was a temporary command and control center, so I was sent out with a small platoon to scout it and take out its ranking officers. I had been drinking hard for two days and was using marijuana regularly. I was in no condition to take on this assignment, but I did.

A sniper's rifle is a magnificent marvel. It requires continuous adjustment, and the sniper must be diligent to take into account all the random factors in a shoot, like distance, wind, and the way he breathes before he squeezes the trigger. I'd ceased doing all the right things. When we finally reached the location, I found a spot, located an officer, put him in the crosshairs, and fired. I missed!

All hell broke loose. An explosion sent shrapnel everywhere around us. I was hit…but I could still function. We began running, and the hillside was loaded with booby traps. I saw a soldier running beside me get skewered with a punji stick. It entered his buttock and exited his stomach. The woods were on fire. The air was thick with green tracers. I looked around and nearly all of us were dead or shot up. I ran over to pick up a soldier. He was burnt badly. When I grabbed his arm to pick him up, it came off in my hands.

I don't remember the moment I took the last hit. I remember it was dark. The North Vietnamese were walking among us, checking our bodies for information and personal belongings. When they came upon one of us still alive, they took a pistol and shot the wounded soldier in the head.

I remember praying when they came to me. I was lying on my belly, bathed in my own blood. A gaping hole in my shoulder and neck. I prayed God would spare my life. I'll never understand. The North Vietnamese soldier poked me with his gun butt and just walked away! He must have thought I was dead. Much too bloody to take anything off me.

I lay there all night. The next morning, one of our squads

came passing through. I heard a soldier tell his sergeant that we were all dead. Somehow, I managed to groan. The soldier grabbed me and called out that I was still living, but just barely.

He and another soldier debated whether to call in an airlift for me. The soldier who found me thought that I wouldn't be alive when the chopper got there.

The sergeant came over and bent over me. He asked me where I was from. I told him weakly, 'Horseheads, New York.' He commented that his home was Watkins Glen. I responded that I was born there. When Sergeant Summers heard where I was born, he ordered them to call in an airlift for me."

Sarah interrupted. "Did you say that sergeant's name was Summers from Watkins Glen?"

Brett knew from Sarah's expression that a spark ignited in her mind with this detail. "Sergeant Summers."

Tears welled in her eyes. "I met…Sergeant Summers'…mother, just a few weeks ago. He never made it back home." They were both content to sit for a while in silence.

When Sarah felt composed, she asked Brett to continue.

"I drifted in and out of consciousness for the next few minutes. I was trying to will myself to live. Finally, the airlift arrived and as they were carrying me to the 'copter, I heard one of them saying, 'There's not enough left of most of these guys to even pick up and ship home.'

In that moment, my dad's words came back to me, 'Brett, there's no place on this planet that God doesn't know where one of his children is.'"

Sarah motioned for Brett to come to her. Brett kneeled down beside his mother, and she pressed his head against her chest and kissed the top of his head. "I love you, son. I love you." Finally, Brett had told the story that haunted him.

Chapter Twenty

Brett and Sarah crammed fifty-four years of living into the summer months. They spent the morning hours at the Bretherick offices in downtown Fort Pierce. Sarah became the patient teacher, guiding her son through the intricacies of their corporation. Daily, Brett began assuming leadership of management meetings, supplemented with direction from Sean and Adam in the Cleveland headquarters.

Lunches were spent with Ben. His Alzheimer's had progressed to the point where he hardly recognized anyone, and his controlled manner was now eroding into hours of irritability. Sarah and Brett faithfully came to meet with him. They alternated a contest between them to discover the most delectable lunch they could bring, each day laying out a spread from some different restaurant or deli, forcing the other to guess what would be for lunch from the smell of the food or size of the container. Sarah cheated on more than one occasion, ordering food from out of town on a special delivery basis. The lunches made each day with Ben a celebration. The surprise menu gave them something to focus on and speak about in the dismal confines of both Ben's room and his mental condition.

In the evenings, they would sit on the rear deck of the yacht, fishing and talking about any subject that came into their minds, sometimes into the late hours of the night. Most often, the subject of the conversation was Aaron's campaign for county commissioner. Brett railed against the local newspaper when the editor would make comments concerning Aaron's youth and inexperience in business. Sarah would agree and threaten to buyout the local paper and fire the editor. They would phone Aaron in the midst of their conversations and give him advice on how to respond to issues in the letters to the editor or on radio talk programs. Brett and Sarah dedicated their hearts and minds to getting Aaron elected to office.

Fay encouraged Brett to spend as much time as he could with his mother. Fay administered Sarah's medications and monitored her physical condition. She was failing quickly, and Fay knew their days together were limited. Sarah's breathing was becoming more labored by the day. The patches and morphine she was taking for pain would ultimately retard her respiration as the doses increased. Fay admired her spirit. Sarah was in love with the moment and was doing everything possible to maintain a normal life. Sarah had succumbed to walking with a cane. The oxygen concentration produced by her lungs would soon be inadequate. Soon she would be more constricted with a portable oxygen machine to carry around with her. Sarah was tiring easily.

Aaron would stop by the office in the morning and occasionally visit with Brett and Sarah in the evenings. He used the GTO in two parades. He and Lynne sat on the top of the backseat, and Seth and Ava waved from the sides of the vehicle. Brett would gun the engine during halts in the parades to stir up the excitement of the grandchildren. Sarah would call out to the parade watchers intermittently, "Vote for Aaron." Fay walked behind the GTO with several volunteers, passing out folding fans to spectators, encouraging them to vote for Aaron Walker.

The summer was over. The time for the election had come. Months of hard work would come to a conclusion by evening.

Wilkes ran from office to office on the third floor of the Breth-erick offices, yelling, "Make sure our volunteers are at every poll a half hour before voting starts. Tell them not to get any closer than a hundred feet to the front door of the polling station. We don't want any condemnation for being too aggressive."

Sarah whispered in Brett's ear, "To think we almost fired him when we took over the bank. He's worked hard on our campaign."

Brett was concerned about his mother. She fatigued easily the past few days. "What do you want to do today, Mom?"

"What else? I want to help Aaron win. I'm going to stay in my office and coordinate phone calls to registered voters. I'm going to plead with them to go vote for Aaron."

Aaron came into the office with donuts, coffee, and orange juice to pass out to the volunteers. He yelled out, "Thanks to everyone that came today to help me get elected! Tonight, win or lose, we are having a celebration at the Beach Resort. I want everyone there, win or lose. I love you guys. Thank you! Mom has passes for everyone to get in! See her before you leave. She'll give you as many as you need." The bulk of the volunteers were members of the Community Church.

Aaron felt people wrapping their arms around him. "You're gonna win, brother. We've come down to do whatever you want us to do." Adam and Michelle came down from Cleveland to be with the family for the election. "What do you need me to do?"

Before Aaron could respond, Michelle embraced him. "I know what I want to do. Carol and Andre are putting together tonight's celebration at the Beach Resort. I want to help them."

Aaron was glad to see them. "Thanks for coming down. That would be great, Michelle. I was feeling a little guilty using all the volunteers for calling and standing at the polls. It would be great if you would go over and help them."

"Adam, spend the day with me. Dad's letting me use the GTO to drive to the polling stations around the county to encourage our volunteers. You can help me pass out the food and drinks to them."

Everyone started taking the packets of Aaron's campaign literature and the posters with his picture on it. The discussion among them was busy and excited as they headed out for their specific poll location. The calls began. "Hello, this is a call from the Aaron Walker campaign headquarters. We're asking you to vote for him today. Is there any question we can answer concerning Aaron?"

~

Brett, Fay, and Sarah were the first to arrive at the Beach Resort. Fay was concerned about Sarah's physical condition; she was relentless in calling the registered voters all day. Sarah sat at her desk the entire day, making calls without taking a break. She arrived at the resort with just enough strength to grab a seat at a corner table in the back of the room.

Fay pulled her seat up next to Sarah. "Mom, you've clearly overdone it today. Let's go home and watch the election returns on the television. We don't have to stay here. Aaron will call us with every little development."

"Oh, no we don't. I went unconscious once in my life and spent the rest of my life regretting it. I don't care if I die in this room. I'm not going home until my grandson has won."

Brett admonished Fay with a subtle shake of his head. He knew his mother wasn't going anywhere, come hell or high water.

Fay ignored him. "Then, Mom, I'm going to get you something to eat."

As Fay made her way to the kitchen, Andre and Carol approached the table. "Aaron's going to win, Sarah. I just know it." Carol was adamant in her proclamation.

Carol took the seat vacated by Fay and took Sarah's hand. Andre stood beside Carol and placed his hands on her shoulders. Andre cleared his throat. "There is something we want to tell both of you."

Brett could hear the engagement of Andre's pastoral voice whenever he was about to make a prolific announcement. Sarah and Brett looked at each other and communicated without words what they expected to hear.

"I know you might think this announcement a little hasty, in view of the fact we have only dated for a little over four months, but Carol has agreed to marry me."

Brett stood up to shake Andre's hand and give Carol a kiss. Sarah held Carol for several seconds before releasing her. This news delighted her. She was elated to see her best friend so happy. She felt comfort in the knowledge that Carol's life was now in good hands.

Brett poked Andre in the ribs. "Hasty? Hasty? At your age, boy, you'd better start thinking hasty. Mom and I have been wondering why it took so long. You're perfect for each other and you know it."

Andre took on the serious voice again. "I have wanted to propose before this, but Brett, you know what I went through with Betty. I'm over the emotional trauma now, but I'm far from over the financial trauma. The last treatments Betty received were experimental, so our insurance would not cover them. So I cashed in most of my retirement and mortgaged the house. I explained all this to Carol. I told her that I would probably have to work the rest of my life. I'm already sixty-five, but I'm in good health, so I've been honest and told her she will be a pastor's wife until the day I die or am unable to serve."

Sarah tried to search the truth in Carol's eyes, knowing that money was the least of Carol's worries. She was a millionaire several times over. Carol gave Sarah the look of "say nothing."

Carol didn't take a chance. "I told Andre that being a pastor's wife would be the fulfillment of my life's dreams. Standing alongside a preacher and teacher of the Word of God until the day he dies would more than satisfy me." Carol had learned from Sarah the value of a secret surprise. A few days after the wedding, she would share with Andre their abundant prosperity, but not until that time. These next few days she would spend praying that the money would not affect his desire to be a pastor.

Fay returned to the table with a platter for Sarah. She could see the rejoicing at the table from far across the room. "From the look on your faces, it looks like Aaron has already won the election."

"Oh, nothing quite that exciting, but close," Brett said. "Andre and Carol are going to get married, and I've decided I'm going to perform their wedding for free."

Andre held his hand up in the air. "Hold on, Brett. I'm not asking you to perform the wedding. You're not the only pastor in the Walker family I would ask to do my wedding."

The shock on Brett's face was discernible. "You're going to ask Aaron to do the wedding?" Brett regained his composure. "Then I hope Aaron charges you."

Andre laughed with his confidant. "He better not after today. No, Brett. I want you to stand with me and be my best man, and Carol wants your mother to be her maid of honor. This time, I'd like Aaron to take care of the nuptials while you take care of me. You stood with me through some tough times. Now I'd like you to stand with me in a great time."

Sarah turned to Carol. "I would be honored to be your maid of honor, but I'm not sure I can stand all that long." Recognizing the rapidity of her own decline, she asked, "So how long before the wedding?"

Sensing the urgency in the question, Carol's throat tightened. "After the last service this Sunday, Andre is going to step down from the pulpit. I'm going to walk up and meet him. We will take our vows right there and leave immediately for a week's honeymoon in St. Augustine."

Brett stepped in, "Oh no! Andre, you cheapskate! You're not going to save money by having it after church. I know, you want to save the cost of invitations, tuxes, and a reception afterward. Never mind, you don't have to think about it. I'm going to take care of everything. You guys deserve the best."

"No, no you're not, Brett. We both desire to do it this way. We don't want gifts, fine clothes, parties, or a big reception. We just want people to rejoice with us, no hassle, really!" Carole-kissed Brett on the cheek. "You're a good friend, Brett. Thank you for wanting the best for us, but we think we already have it."

"There must be over five hundred people here!" Andre yelled to Brett. "Senator Markum will be here in fifteen minutes, and Congressman Beckwith is already here. We have the big screens turned on, and the returns will be coming in soon."

Four computers sat on a conference room table where Sarah, Brett, and Aaron focused on every blip. Volunteers, Bretherick employees, and Community Church members passed by with encouraging words, affirming that Aaron would win. The supervisor of elections office opened the webpage, showing each of the seventy-two polling stations. A summary ran continuously on a ticker at the bottom of the screen, showing the total number of votes cast for each candidate and the percent of polls completed with the counting process.

Aaron took a deep breath and put his hands on the shoulders of Brett and Sarah. "I owe everything that is happening tonight to both of you. I hope tonight will be your reward for all that you have done."

Sarah grasped Aaron's hand. "Honey, I could care less about this county commissioner's office. All I care about is you. If this is what you want, everything that has been done is well worth it." Sarah spoke from the heart.

"Nana said it perfectly. Just be happy. Win or lose, we're just as proud. Son, if you have learned anything in the past four months, you must have learned that there are a lot of people that love you." Brett hugged his son.

A collective scream passed through the reception room as the first returns came in. Seven of seventy polls were counted. Aaron was leading by 2,732 votes. Eight minutes later, seventeen of seventy-two polls counted increased his lead to 8,345 votes. Fifteen minutes after the first polls began reporting, with only twenty-nine of seventy-two polls counted, Aaron led by a whopping 28,633 lead. A simultaneous cheer shook the hall when the announcers on the local affiliate and the public radio station called the election a sure win for Aaron Walker.

The announcer yelled into his microphone, "This is the

quickest decision in South Florida politics. A declared winner within fifteen minutes from the beginning moments of the first release. Aaron Walker delivered the knockout punch to a long-time political activist! Does tonight's election send a message to politicians across the state of Florida? There's a new voice to be heard and reckoned with. The voice of a young pastor. The voice of a handsome young man who can hold his own with any politician on any platform. The grandson of the multinational industrialist Sarah Bretherick has sent out a message today! And the message is, "I'm here! I'm here!"

Brett and Sarah leaned back in their chairs, releasing a day's worth of tension, while the people mobbed Aaron. Sarah leaned over and spoke to Brett. "Son, I think today marked my last battle on this earth. But what a glorious battle it was." Sarah hesitated. "While this is my last, I think this is just the beginning for you and this family. Mark my words, Brett. This boy is on his way to Washington. I would love to know which house he will occupy one day."

Senator Markum and Congressman Beckwith requested a private moment with Aaron. Aaron turned to Brett, "Dad, come with me."

Surprisingly, Aaron remained calm with the two high-ranking officials. "I want to thank both of you for your endorsements, and I especially appreciate that you came to celebrate with us tonight. Rest assured, I will remember this when you're both up for re-election."

Senator Markum shook Aaron's hand. "Aaron, people from our party have been watching this local election from all over the country. We think you might be the answer to a problem we are anticipating in four years."

Brett was first to ask. "I'm Aaron's father, Brett Walker … and if you don't mind my asking, what problem might my son be the answer to?"

"Mr. Walker, confidentially, in four years I'm retiring. Therefore, a seat in the Senate is at risk to be taken by the other party. We are pretty confident that Congressman Beckwith can fend off all challengers for my seat, but then that puts our party at risk for the Congressman's seat. As you know, we already have a slim margin in that house."

"So you're thinking Aaron could run for Congress in this district in four years?" Brett was thinking of his mother's comments only moments ago.

Congressman Beckwith wasted no time getting to the point. "He's an attractive candidate; he's handsome, well known for family values, an accomplished speaker, and wealthy enough to withstand the rigors of attaining and holding office. Above all else, he will be remembered for the vote he turned out today. I promise you, with these attributes and this great victory today, he will be a force to be reckoned with in a congressional race."

"Congressman and Senator, I'm going to think long and hard about your proposal. First of all, I'm still in awe of our win today. Secondly, I've got to give this job an honest try to see if I enjoy the political life. I propose we get together next year at this time, after I've had some time on the job, and we'll discuss it further. I'm not saying no tonight. I just need some time to consider everything."

The Congressman and Senator excused themselves gracefully and assured Aaron they would meet again in a year.

Brett returned to the table to sit with the family. He leaned over to Sarah, "Mom, earlier you were wondering which house in Washington Aaron would occupy? I've got an inside tip! Congress!"

~

Physically, Sarah was unable to sit through the whole church service, waiting until the end for Andre to announce his surprise wedding ceremony. Brett sat with her in his office as Aaron agreed to come to get them just prior to the end of the service. Sarah was uneasy, tentative. Brett knew something was on her mind.

"Mom, don't be nervous. All we have to do is stand there with them. All the attention will be on them, not us."

"Brett, I'm not concerned about the ceremony at all...I have something else on my mind."

"I'm here, Mom. What's bothering you?"

"Brett, I've been so happy here these past four months. I couldn't ask for better, but I think I would like to go home to Cleveland. I want to die in my own home." Sarah couldn't look at Brett. Her pain was more than physical.

Vietnam and years of dealing with terminal patients had taught Brett one thing. There comes a time when death must be discussed without denials or deflections.

"Mom, I can understand that. So what's the problem?"

"I cannot find the strength to leave this family behind; and even more, what to do about your father?"

"First of all, you're not leaving family behind. Fay and I will go home with you. We have one of our sons already living in your home up there. Fay was brought up around the Cleveland area, and I have my own history with that town. So the thought of all of us going to Cleveland is not earth shattering to me. Besides, in two weeks, I'm supposed to speak at Mitch's church."

"What about Dad? Brett, how do I leave him here?"

"Mom, Dad left several weeks ago. He hasn't said a word in weeks. I know it will be hard to leave him here, but I think we should. He is so disoriented now, Mom. Moving him would only make it worse. Mom, nothing about the next few weeks will be easy. Aaron will see to it that Dad is well taken care of until I get back. I'm absolutely confident of that."

"I can't think straight, Brett. The medications have slowed my mental processing almost to a halt. This I do know. I know what is happening to me. Brett, I know my time is very limited. I would like to go home."

"When would you like to leave?"

"I think late tomorrow afternoon, after our lunch with Ben, if that is all right with you and Fay. The mental turmoil of thinking about saying good-bye to this part of my life is more painful than the cancer."

Aaron opened the door and stood awkwardly for a moment, realizing he had interrupted his father and grandmother at an emotional moment. Attempting to instill a happier environment in the room, Aaron commented, "C'mon, you two! This is a wedding, not a funeral we're going to."

Realizing the irony of Aaron's statement, they both broke out in laughter.

~

The wedding was brief, and still held its sacredness. Those in the congregation who had shared in Betty's loss rejoiced to see their associate pastor happy again. The church gave them a standing ovation as they departed the sanctuary. Before departing, the wedding party ran into the office complex to put away their microphones and Bibles.

Sarah asked Andre if she could speak with Carol alone before they left. Sarah went into Brett's office and waited.

Carol came into the office. "Sarah, thank you for standing with me this morning. Your presence made it even more special. Sarah, who would have thought when we began looking for your son that I would discover my husband too? Our destinies were bound together. Isn't God good?"

"Yes, he is Carol. God is good."

"Andre said there was something you wanted to talk with me about."

Sarah's intention was only to say good-bye, knowing this would be their last time together, but the joy of the occasion was too special for any sad good-byes. "No, I just wanted to tell you how happy I am for you. Carol, be happy! I know this is a life you will treasure. You're going to make a great pastor's wife. I just wanted to thank you for all you've done for Ben and me. You've been through a lot with me these past few months, and I'm happy there is a silver lining for you too."

Sarah embraced Carol and kissed her on the cheek. "I have a present for you, but you cannot open it until you get into the car. Only then will it make sense."

Carol embraced Sarah in return. "I love you, Sarah Bretherick. I'll come see you when we get back."

Sarah fought back the emotion as she swallowed hard and motioned for Carol to leave.

Brett stood in front of the door, blocking their exit out of the office complex. "Mom, Fay and I bought a present for the both of you. I've broken the law twice today in order to give you this present, so I'm counting on both of you to be merciful."

Andre feared something dreadful, knowing Brett's ability to pull off a practical joke. "C'mon, Brett, we're too old for rice in our suitcases or tin cans on the car."

"Nothing that infantile." Brett held up keys to a car. "We bought you a convertible GTO, the same model as mine. We searched all over the country to find one. Luckily, on Wednesday we found it."

Andre loved driving Brett's GTO. After their first date, Andre would often ask Brett to borrow the Babe Magnet to take Carol out. Andre and Carol enjoyed driving with the top down in the cool of the South Florida evenings. "Just think of it, Carol! Our very own Babe Magnet!" Andre stopped, "So what did you do that was illegal?"

Brett grinned. "I had a locksmith that is a member of our church open your car so we could transfer your luggage, and then I had your car towed to Aaron's house for safe keeping until you get back home."

"You're forgiven, Brett. Totally forgiven."

They all walked out to the gleaming GTO and helped the newlyweds get in. Sarah told Carol she could open the gift.

Carol unwrapped the new scarf and wrapped it around her head. "This will keep me from looking like a windblown wreck when we arrive in St. Augustine."

Andre started the engine of his new GTO. "It sounds like a dream. We'll see you when we get back. We love you guys."

Sarah and Brett were the last to go into the offices. They watched Andre and Carol depart until they could see them no more. They locked eyes, and without words, both of them understood that another chapter of their lives was complete.

Fay and Brett spent the rest of Sunday, packing for the trip to Cleveland. Fay was excited to see Adam and Michelle, and to return back to her childhood home, but the purpose of the trip loomed heavily on their hearts. Underlying the unspoken plan, Sarah was returning home to Cleveland to die. Fay knew Sarah was weakening by the day. The time to go home was now.

Monday morning, Sarah announced over breakfast that she would be responsible for a surprise luncheon with Ben. She wanted the meal to be a little extra special. Brett teased her with inquiries about what she would have delivered to Ben's room, but Sarah maintained her secretive manner. This last meal would remain a secret to the last minute.

Brett asked, "Mom, do you want to go to the office today to say good-bye to everyone?" It had been over two weeks since Sarah had attended a staff meeting or visited her office.

Sarah sat expressionless as she gazed at the marina. "No, I need all the strength I have left to visit Ben and the trip home. Besides, I would start looking around and feel even worse than I already do. Please tell everyone for me that I'm sorry to have left without saying good-bye, but the whole experience would be too much. They'll understand."

Brett started to ask her what she wanted him to do with the contents of her office, but he could clearly see that his mother could care less about anything that had to do with the business. Sarah sipped her coffee, but showed no interest in eating.

Brett wanted to distract her from the misery of the painful good-bye she was anticipating. "Mom, can I ask you a really personal question? How did you and Dad get so rich?"

Sarah looked at her son with a gleam in her eyes. "I've wondered why you hadn't asked that question before."

"Mom, how much money someone has or how it's accumulated is really personal. I didn't want to offend you, but that doesn't mean I wasn't wondering."

"Brett, I told you one night that I wanted us to be personal. You can ask me anything you like, and I won't be offended. I would be happy to tell you. First of all, your dad and I became rich the old-fashioned way. We inherited it. We were both only children, and both of our parents were already extremely wealthy. So we began our marriage with a sizable fortune.

Your dad was an accomplished engineer. He designed a device that allowed automakers to build inexpensive automatic transmissions for automobiles. The patent and royalties from that device gave us millions of dollars to add to the already significant wealth we possessed. Your father increased the engineering firm and began developing many more devices for all modes of transportation, including aircraft. Your father's firm always held the patents and the royalties. That engineering firm today is worldwide and still turns out many breakthrough developments in all types of industries, including medical and other types of technology.

I took another path, but just as successful. I became a litigator, taking on large corporations in civil suits. One of the companies I sued was a young research firm that was on the verge of a new medical breakthrough. They had failed to take proper precautions in an experiment that included the patient I was representing. The patient was unaware of the experimental nature of the product that was being administered to him. Eventually, he had a bad reaction and experienced a major health setback. We won the case, and the settlement was extensive.

In the process of litigating against this company, I learned much about this developmental medical breakthrough. Honestly, I was impressed. Their failure was in consent and individual assessment, but I believed that aside from my client's reaction, this product was worth saving.

Because of the lawsuit, the company filed for bankruptcy. Ben and I bought the outstanding stock of this company for one cent per share, or $1,100,000. We put another million dollars into completing the research and development to complete the FDA approval process, and this solution revolutionized modern-day medical care. It is used every day, every hour in almost every medical facility around the world. Today, this medical product produces over six billion dollars in revenue worldwide annually.

I continued handling corporate litigation against automakers and other large industries. With our collective strengths, Dad and I began Bretherick Corporation with all the different divisions we have today. We continually looked for new targets to invest and develop." Sarah looked at her son for his reaction.

"Mom, how in the world can I continue what my grandparents, you, and Dad have accomplished?" Brett was overwhelmed by the precedent set before him.

"Son, you don't have to! Dad and I were in the right place at the right time. We did what we loved to do. You need to do what you love do. It appears Adam has a love for the business. Aaron seems more than content in the political arena. I want you to do the same."

Brett accepted what his mother intended, but in his heart, he wondered if it were possible for him to go back to Community Church with everything as it was. He doubted it.

Sarah, Fay, and Brett sat in Ben's room, waiting for lunch to arrive. Ben lay on the bed, smiling politely, but not engaging in conversation with his family. He could not recognize these people who were moving about his room.

Fay opened his closet, taking inventory of his clothes, the socks, the underwear. Often, his clothes were exchanged with other patients or lost in the cleaning process. Brett focused on his mother as he pushed her wheelchair under the table in the room. Immediately she laid her arm on the table to support her upper body. Fay had brought along a bottle of portable oxygen to give to Sarah. Her endurance was taxed by the slightest efforts.

Sarah looked at Ben and struggled to say the words. "Ben, I brought our special lunch for you today. It's a surprise. It will be here any moment."

On cue, the delivery appeared at the door. "Mrs. Bretherick, I have your order here. Would you like me to bring it in?"

"Just set it here on this table. Brett, would you pay this young man? Fay, would you mind putting it out on the table?" Sarah was too exhausted to move.

"Mom, aren't you going to make me guess what the lunch is today?" It was the game they had played all summer.

"No, not today. Let's just eat."

Fay removed the contents from the delivery box. Hot dogs with sauerkraut on top, large fried onion rings, and a large container of coffee.

"Mom, you said this was you and Dad's special meal. Frankly, as rich as you two are, I'm really surprised that hot dogs and fried onion rings would top the list."

Sarah spoke to Ben. "Honey, do you remember this meal? Can you remember the day we celebrated with this exact same meal, hot dogs with sauerkraut, fried onion rings, and coffee?"

Ben remained silent, not acknowledging Sarah's question. Fay guided him to the table to join them.

"Okay, Mom, why is this stuff so special? I was expecting something quite different. What's up with this?" Brett struggled to bite the hot dog without the sauerkraut falling off.

"It isn't the meal that is so special. It was the occasion when we had it. This is what Ben and I ate the day he asked me to marry him. Ben wanted to take me to a really nice restaurant to celebrate, but I was craving fried onion rings and coffee. I remember sitting at that table, sharing a large basket of onion rings and drinking coffee. At that table, we discussed our plans for the rest of our lives. We were going to build a house on the top of a hill overlooking Seneca Lake. I was going to practice law, preparing wills and real estate sales. Dad was going start an engineering firm. We dreamt of being big fish in that very small village of Watkins Glen. We enjoyed planning our wedding and our lives so much that we had three baskets of onion rings and nearly a gallon of coffee. We topped off the night with hot dogs with sauerkraut on them."

"Mom, why didn't you do any of the things you planned? You know, moving to Watkins Glen, building that house on the hill overlooking the lake, and starting your careers like you planned?" Fay wanted to know.

"After the accident and the shame and guilt that accompanied the accident, we never discussed our dream life again. We never went to Watkins Glen again. The first I had been there in years was in the early spring when I was searching for Brett. I can truly say the lives we lived were nothing like we planned."

Tears ran down Sarah's face. In distraction, she tried to eat a bite of an onion ring. Fay could not help herself as tears began running down her face.

Sarah set the onion ring down. "I can't eat. I'm just not hungry." She looked at Ben as he took small bites of the hot dog Fay had cut into pieces for him, alternating to an onion ring or a sip of coffee.

Sarah leaned forward in the direction of Ben. "I know you can't comprehend what's happening to me, Ben, but I have to go away. Like you, I'm sick, and I won't be able to come anymore. Don't worry, though. We have a son. Ben, we have a great son, and he will take care of you. Everything is going to be all right."

Ben looked at his wife, absently. He continued to eat his onion ring.

Sarah motioned for Brett to help her stand up. She walked around the table and tenderly kissed her husband of fifty-five years on his cheek. In a stream of tears, she whispered, "I love you, Ben Bretherick...I have always loved you. Good-bye."

Brett gripped the handles of his mother's wheelchair to distract himself from all the emotion that was in him. He swallowed hard to avoid letting out an audible cry. Sarah sat down and he started to push her out the room.

Ben spoke out loudly. "That bridge scared me. That bridge scared me." Ben stared at Sarah.

Sarah raised her left hand in the air, twisting her engagement ring with her right hand. "You don't have to be scared of the bridge, Ben. I've got the ring, Ben. I've got the ring." Sarah stared in amazement that Ben had spoken. She was grateful for his parting gift. He had remembered the day, standing on the rail of Suicide Bridge, waiting for her to accept his proposal. Sarah waved with her hand to him. "Thank you, Ben!"

Chapter Twenty-One

"Mrs. Bretherick, you must allow us to give you something for the pain. Your blood pressure is increasing, and we don't want the pain to get ahead of us," the hospice nurse insisted.

Sarah struggled for breath. The pain was intensifying, but she was determined to wait for the family to return before taking any medication. She wanted to talk with Brett before she went to sleep under the influence of the morphine. Brett and the rest of the family were at the Resurrection Baptist Church, participating in the pipe organ dedication. Brett wanted the rest of the family to stay with Sarah, but Sarah insisted that every member of her family should be present at the service. Andre and Carol flew up to Cleveland to be at the service and to visit with Sarah.

"No, nurse. No medication until after I talk with my son. I want to talk with my son."

The nurse could see the anxiety Sarah was feeling concerning the possibility of being medicated before talking to her son. "Mrs. Bretherick, we're not going to give you anything until you say so."

"Thank you. They should be coming any moment now."

Sarah concentrated on breathing. Earlier she had heard the doctor tell the nurse in the hallway that it wouldn't be long. She was determined not to die without talking with Brett one more time. Sarah focused on Ben's picture on the dresser. She tried to remember where the picture was taken, but she could not. She pictured Ben lying on his bed in Fort Pierce, oblivious to the world. She envied him. She rejoiced that Ben would not suffer the grief she had experienced in these last days.

"Hey, Mom, what's this I hear about you not taking the medication?" Brett came in and took his usual place in the recliner by her bed. He had slept the last three nights beside her in this chair.

"Did you preach well?" Sarah asked, ignoring his question.

"Probably not my best. I seem to have other things on my mind."

"Listen to you. I've only mothered you for a few months, and already you're blaming me for your mistakes." Sarah tried to lighten the moment. "Who's downstairs?"

"Everybody, including Andre, Sarah, and Mitch. Do you want me to have them come up?"

"I can't, son. I don't have the strength to talk to everyone. I want to use what little strength I have talking with you." Sarah's eyes clouded. "Son, I only want a graveside service, with only the family and the closest of friends. All the instructions are with Sean. He has everything that you will need when I'm gone."

"Mom, do we really need to talk about this?"

"Yes, because everybody and his brother is going to try to get you to have a major production. I'm sure every politician we contributed to would come; and so would every investment banker and everyone else who wants to get your ear by playing on their relationship to me. Son, I don't need it and you don't need it either. Resist them, please."

"Mom, I promise. I'll carry everything out just as you planned."

Sarah continued. "Brett, I really regret the years we missed, but I can't complain. Your father and I did some great things and accomplished what few people ever will. But when I look at you, I know you are our greatest accomplishment. I'm so proud of you and that family downstairs. We didn't get to raise you, but we had everything to do with your creation, and I'm satisfied with that. You've been a wonderful son to me these past months. These past few months have given meaning to a very weary life." Sarah was out of breath and rolled her head on the pillow to shake off the discomfort.

Brett sat on the side of the bed and stroked his mother's hair. "Mom, I remember the day I thought I was dying. My mind was the only thing that kept me alive. I willed myself to live. Mom, you're tired and in a lot of pain. I'm okay now. I'm okay! What I'm really trying to say, Mom, is if you want to go now, it's okay. You don't have to fight it anymore. I'm okay."

Sarah smiled at her son and shook her head in acknowledgment. Struggling for breath she whispered, "Tell me a funny story."

Brett stiffened. "What?"

"Brett, tell me a funny story. I've heard you tell thousands of people funny stories. Tell me a funny story. I want us to laugh."

Brett searched his mind for a funny story. His mind was clouded by grief. The context was all wrong, but for his mother, he would try. "The first time I preached I was in Seminary in New Orleans. A little church in the bayou had called the seminary and requested the school to send out a student to preach on Sunday, so they sent me.

I went to that church and preached up a storm. At the end of the service, a middle-aged man and an older woman came forward to accept the Lord. This church hadn't seen someone come forward in years, so they asked me to stay for their evening service to baptize them. I was so excited that I agreed to stay. They were my first baptisms.

This bayou church was so small that to conserve space they built the baptistry under the pulpit and strung a curtain behind the pulpit so the baptismal candidates could dress and undress.

The first one to come out from behind the curtain was the woman. As she came out, the middle-aged man went behind the curtain to take off his clothes and put on his gown. Now, this woman was all of three-hundred and fifty pounds, and the good old boys that filled the pool didn't take any time to clean the baptistry before they filled it with water.

I held out my hand to guide the woman down into the pool, but when she hit that first step, it was a little slimy, and she began to slide in. She pulled me into that pool head first, and with her other hand, she reached up and grabbed a hold of that curtain. Now, the guy behind the curtain didn't have a chance to put on his gown, and so there he stood, front and center, in the middle of that congregation with nothing on but his bikini underpants."

Sarah held up her hand for Brett to stop. They both were laughing. She coughed and rasped as she laughed. But she laughed. Sarah squeezed Brett's hand one last time and motioned for the nurse to give her the medication.

Sarah concentrated on Brett until his features were a blur. She departed from him with a smile on her face.

The hearses drove slowly to the top of the hill on the freshly paved drive winding around the huge maple trees. The hillside was dappled with bright orange and yellow leaves, lying lightly on top of the green grass, waiting for the gardener's rake or a breath of wind to take them away. Sarah had built a mausoleum in Watkins Glen on a hillside, overlooking Seneca Lake. She had taken everyone by surprise with this structure. Only David Birmingham and Carol were aware of this project. She and Gerald would be interred together at the mausoleum. Adam would read the Twenty-third Psalm. Aaron would pray, and Brett would read a letter Sarah had written to the family and close friends. The service would be simple and short.

The attendants placed the coffins in the mausoleum as the family waited in reverence. Andre and Carol walked the hillside. Aaron and Lynne played with the kids. Sean McCurdy and Adam watched every move the attendants made, while Brett, Fay, and Michelle sat on the bench, taking in the beauty of the fall scenery around the lake.

"Brett, this place is breathtaking. It's so peaceful." Fay seemed entranced by the setting.

Michelle was just as smitten. "The boats on the lake are out for the last ride of the fall. The sights from the water must be just as wonderful."

Adam came over and announced, "Dad, we're ready to begin."

Brett exhaled anxiously. "Okay, would you mind gathering up the others?" He took an envelope from his coat pocket. Sarah had written on the outside of the envelope, "Do not open until interment." Brett ripped the envelope open, but decided against reading it until the proper moment.

The group was assembled on the patio of the mausoleum, waiting for Brett to take over. Brett looked at Adam, noting he wasn't holding a Bible. "Son, I've got my Bible in the car. You can use that one."

"Don't need it, Dad. My pastor made me memorize the Twenty-third Psalm when I was a teenager."

Brett was surprised Adam could remember the Psalm. Adam had memorized the Twenty-third Psalm as punishment for misbehaving at church. Adam recited the Psalm without error, and Brett recited silently with him as he spoke. Aaron prayed one of the most tender prayers Brett could recall ever hearing him pray. Brett pulled the letter from his pocket, took a deep breath, and hesitated a moment to clear his tears.

Dear son,

We have now come full circle. Fifty-four years ago, I left this small village with my heart filled with pain, and you went on to an existence of which I would have no knowledge. Today we return to this same village, fully aware of each other, but today you leave with the pain, and I go to an existence of which you have no knowledge.

I have built this mausoleum with plenty of space for future generations of our family. It comforts me to know Gerald is with me. You will notice the name over the mausoleum is

Walker-Bretherick, as I feel our families are bound together forever. I look forward to meeting and thanking the Walkers for raising you to be the man you are. I also anticipate the delight of their getting to know their birth son, Gerald.

You will notice the phrase above the entry to the mausoleum, "In death we accomplished the desires of life." If one measures my accomplishments by monetary gain, one will have missed the true value in my life. In death, I have come to know peace with myself and others. Peace cannot be purchased with money. Peace can only come when we are content within ourselves and with others. I leave this world without malice toward anyone, and a heart full of love for the special gifts of life. To everyone gathered here at this moment, I consider you my highest treasures and greatest possessions.

Brett, you are the pinnacle of my life's experience. I would have spent my entire fortune to find you. Now that I have found you, I know that if it would have cost me my entire fortune, it would have been worth it. On earth, we were separated, but in heaven we will spend eternity together. I anticipate that in a little while, your dad will be with me. I rejoice that together, in this beautiful place, we will await the final dawn together. At last, our dream is accomplished.

I have one more surprise and one request to make of you before closing. First, the surprise. Rich has the keys to your new cabin on the farm ... enjoy! The request is as follows:

Please arrange with Cornell University to construct a building in your father's memory. I would like it located as close to the bridge as possible. Please build an elegant building and call it the Benjamin Bretherick School of Engineering.

That is it! I have dreamed what the future will bring for you and the grandchildren, but the one thing I have learned in life is that nothing is ever as we plan it.

There is a boat tour that departs Watkins Glen Marina every two hours. I'm told the boat captain stops in the middle of the lake and points out our mausoleum on the top of the hill as a point of interest. He tells the tourists, "That is the mausoleum belonging to the Brethericks, one of the richest families in America. Folks, you might want to invest in Watkins Glen because whatever the Brethericks touch, well, it prospers."

I certainly hope the boat captain is right. I have touched your lives and my greatest wish for every one of you is that you will prosper in every way possible.

I love you,
Mom

PS: Brett, when you arrive in heaven, I'll be there to greet you. I'm determined not to screw it up this time!

Brett folded the letter and put it back in his pocket. While wiping the tears from his eyes, he asked, "Can I take you all to lunch?"

Adam sighed. "Dad, Michelle and I need to get going. We have the Gulfstream waiting in Ithaca to take us back. Sean and I have a lot going on, and we need to get a jump on it. I'll call you tonight."

Carol kissed Brett. Andre embraced him and looked into Brett's eyes. "We flew over from Cleveland with Adam. We need to get back. Carol sold her home in Cleveland, and we are packing her stuff to be moved to Fort Pierce later this week."

Aaron hugged his father. "Dad, we will catch up with you later. We have a jet on hold at the Elmira Airport. I have a commissioners' meeting tomorrow, and the vote is going to be close. I need to get back."

Rich wrapped his massive arm around Brett's shoulders. "We're taking Aaron's family to the airport. We'll catch you later."

Fay and Brett sat on the bench, watching their families depart down the hill. They sat a long while on the bench, absorbing the majesty of the lake, and the brilliant colors of fall. Startled from reflection, they noticed an older Buick approaching. The car came to a stop at Sarah's mausoleum. A middle-aged woman got out of the car and assisted a legless old woman into a wheel chair. The shiny metal sides of the wheel chair reflected brightly in the afternoon sun as it rolled down the hill toward the tomb.

Brett stood and walked to greet the two ladies. "May I help you?"

The legless old woman spoke softly, "We just came to pay our respects."

Brett was mystified as to the identity of the two women. "I'm sorry, but we concluded the service for my mother just a few minutes ago. By the way, my name is Brett Walker."

The legless woman stared awkwardly for several seconds at Brett. "My name is Willa Mae Summers and this here is my daughter." She stared at Brent for a little longer. "Can we speak alone?" Her daughter retreated before Brett could respond.

She began, "Did your mother ever mention my name to you?"

Brett tried to recall a moment when his mother mentioned this woman, but he had no immediate recall. "No."

"I was the nurse's aide the night you were born," she stopped and stared again.

This time Brett made the connection. "Yes! I know who you are now." He was apprehensive and confused by this woman's presence at Sarah's tomb. He was glad that Fay remained on the bench and the kids were gone. This conversation would test his kindness.

Willa Mae turned her head toward the lake and began speaking. "I've followed you as best as I could since the night you were born. I watched you the day the Walkers took you home from the hospital. I read about your playing sports in school. I even went to a few of your football games. I want you to know that I'm real sorry about everything. I wish it was all different."

Although Brett didn't feel hospitable, he found the strength to reply. "There's not much we can change now."

Willa Mae looked directly into Brett's eyes. "You're a preacher. If I tell you something, are you bound to keep my secret?"

Startled by her request, Brett fired back, "I'm not your pastor."

Willa Mae was determined to have this exchange. "Are you a pastor or not? Can I share what I need to share in confidence?"

Impatience more than pastoral obligation led Brett to reply, "Yes, I will hear what you say in confidence." He felt sure that she would exude more guilt and seek forgiveness from him.

Willa Mae blurted out, "I killed your grandmother, Victoria. She had it coming and I killed her." The legless woman paused and looked into the distance, "and I have no regrets."

Brett was ambushed by this admission. "She died in a house fire. Did you start it?"

"Yes, I did. One evening while Victoria was working at the hospital, I went over to her house just before she got home. I went up to her attic and wrapped the attic lights in towels. I knew she would never see the lights turned on in the attic once I closed the door. During the night while she was sleeping, the heat from the lights caught the towels on fire. I knew they would, and I knew nobody would ever know the difference."

Brett took a long while to process this incredible story told by this aged, legless woman. Seeking to understand, he asked her, "I know she was evil, but why would you kill her?"

"She was evil. Her evil cursed me and my whole family. I told Sarah how Victoria brought me and those I loved so much harm, but I never did get to tell her that I'd killed that evil old woman. When I got word that my boy Wallace was killed in Vietnam, right then I made up my mind Victoria was never gonna harm anyone else."

Brett stopped breathing. "Was your son a sergeant in the Marine Corps?" He distinctly remembered the Marine, Sergeant Wallace Summers, pulling his shattered body from the battlefield after his own fire-fight. The sergeant went the extra mile to save him because he was from his hometown area. It couldn't be possible.

"Yes, my son, Wallace, was a sergeant in the Marine Corps." She looked again at Brent. "I remember you served with the Marines about the same time. Did you know him?"

Brett lost the will to speak anymore. He looked at her and made a decision. He had his own demons to conquer. "Yes, but we met very briefly." Leaning over he bent close to her face and kissed her on the cheek. "I'm so sorry for both of us."

Willa Mae never answered. She nodded to her daughter who then rolled the wheel chair back to the car.

Brett stared intently as Willa Mae disappeared over the crest of the hill. Brent knew that Willa Mae's purpose was to let him know that justice had been done; however, he did not share her sense of justice.

It would take him years to sort out the oddity of this meeting with this old woman. She was present at the moment of his birth. Her son would save his life nineteen-years later in a jungle in Vietnam. This woman would be the murderer of a grandmother that he never knew, and the day they meet would be on the day of his mother's funeral—A mother that he almost never came to know.

He turned his attention back to the lake and in his periphery, he saw his elegant and loving wife still sitting on the bench. She sat patiently waiting. Fay was deep in her own thoughts. He sat down on the bench next to her.

"Brett, what was that all about?" Fay asked.

He wrapped his arm around her and gently pulled her close. "Just an inquisitive old lady." Fay was not protected by pastoral privilege, and she was much too pure to be tainted with the knowledge of an admitted cold-blooded murder. He was comfortable protecting her from the knowledge of this evil.

Feeling the finality of all the great changes in their lives, Fay pulled from Brett's grasp in order to face him squarely, "Brett, what are we going to do now?"

Brett turned to look at Sarah's tomb. "I don't know, Fay. I honestly don't know—but I do know that the just live by his faith."